"Jake Diamond is back and it feels like the return of an old friend. One of my all-time favorite PI series—*Circling the Runway* is the best yet."
—Steve Hamilton, Edgar Award-winning
author *The Lock Artist*

"Think it is impossible to find a new take on the wise-cracking San Francisco PI? Meet Jake Diamond and think again. Jake and his crew—both the good guys and the bad guys—are sharp and smart, convincing and complex."
—SJ Rozan, Edgar Award-winning
author (as Sam Cabot) of *Skin of the Wolf*

"J.L. Abramo's *Circling the Runway* offers the swagger and strut of Raymond Chandler, the skintight plotting of James M. Cain and smart-ass one-line humor smacking of Mickey Spillane. "
—Jack Getze, author of
Big Money and *Big Mojo*

"In *Circling the Runway*, J.L. Abramo is shooting at us again— and he's doing it from every shadow and hidden doorway, from every window and passing car. And damned if every bullet doesn't hit its mark perfectly. "
—Trey Barker, author of
Death is Not Forever and *Exit Blood*

"J.L. Abramo's *Circling the Runway* takes up where Black Mask boys like Hammett, Gardner, and Carroll John Daly left off. It's loaded with tough guys and hard-boiled action— emphasis on the *hard*."
—David Housewright, Edgar Award-winning
author of *Unidentified Woman #15*

CIRCLING THE RUNWAY

ALSO BY J. L. ABRAMO

Jake Diamond Mystery
Catching Water in a Net
Clutching at Straws
Counting to Infinity

Jimmy Pigeon Mystery
Chasing Charlie Chan

Stand Alone Novels
Gravesend

J. L. ABRAMO

CIRCLING THE RUNWAY

A Jake Diamond Mystery

Down & Out Books
3959 Van Dyke Rd, Ste. 265
Lutz, FL 33558
www.DownAndOutBooks.com

The characters and events in this book are fictitious. Any similarity to real persons, living or dead, is coincidental and not intended by the author.

Cover design by JT Lindroos

ISBN: 1-937495-87-6
ISBN-13: 978-1-937495-87-9

For everyone who ever told me
I should do what I need to do.

CAST OF CHARACTERS

James Bingham. . . . . .a dead doorman

Ethan Lloyd. . . . . .a dog walker

Blake Sanchez. . . . . .a kid with a bad idea

Jake Diamond. . . . . .a private investigator

Benny Carlucci. . . . .a young man in the wrong place at the wrong time

Darlene Roman. . . . . .Jake's associate

Joe "Joey Clams" Vongoli. . . . . .an Italian American businessman

Tony Carlucci. . . . . .trouble

Kenny Gerard. . . . . .another doorman

Tug McGraw. . . . . .a loyal companion

Norman Hall. . . . . .a stalker

Sergeant Roxton "Rocky" Johnson. . . . . .an SFPD police detective

Amy Singleton Johnson. . . . . .a Philadelphia Singleton

Davey Cutler. . . . . .a police officer

Lieutenant Laura Lopez. .a homicide detective

Roberto Sandoval. . . . . .a deceased Assistant District Attorney

Manny Sandoval. . . . . a low-life, no relation

Dr. Steven Altman. . . . . .a medical examiner

Angelo Verdi. . . . . .a talkative specialty grocer

Vinnie "Strings" Stradivarius. . . . . .a friend who tries

Sergeant Yardley. . . . . .a surly desk sergeant

Hank Strode. . . . . .a back door man

Lionel Katz. . . . . a mouthpiece

Liam Duffey. . . . . .a District Attorney

Marco Weido. . . . . .a man with no allegiances

Megan Nicolace. . . . . .a vice detective

Nicolai Roman. . . . . .Darlene's father

Don Folgueras. .an Oakland police lieutenant

Sal DiMarco. . . . . .a double-crossed hit man

Bruce Perry. . . . . .an Oakland police officer

Travis Duncan. . . . . .a scary friend

Ralph Morrison. . . . . .a police wannabe

Ray Boyle. . . . . .a Los Angeles homicide detective

Bobo Bigelow. . . . . .a multi-talented felon

Carmine Cicero. . . . . .a thug

Justin Walker. . . . . .a person of interest

Juliana Lani. . . . . .a sharp cookie

Daniel Gibson. . . . . .an immigration man

Derek London. . . . . .a businessman

Part One

SLEEPLESS NIGHTS

There are people who observe the rules of honor as we observe the stars—from a distance.

—Victor Hugo

ONE

James Bingham stood at the curb in front of the high-rise residence, talking with the taxi driver who had dropped off the occupant of apartment 3501 a few minutes earlier. Bingham was inquiring into the availability of deeply discounted cartons of cigarettes. The cab driver assured Bingham he would hook him up that weekend.

Bingham walked back into the lobby as the cab pulled away.

As James Bingham approached the security desk he heard footsteps approaching from behind. Before Bingham could turn to the sound, his head was clamped between two large hands and with the twist of two powerful wrists Bingham was dead.

The woman opened the door leading from the stairwell to the thirty-fifth floor apartments only wide enough to see the hallway in both directions. Finding the hallway deserted, she pushed the door open just enough to slip through. She moved down the hall to the right and stopped in front of the door marked 3501. She pulled a plain white letter-sized envelope from the pocket of her coat and slipped it under the door. She returned to the stairwell doorway, passed through it and started down the stairs. She looked at her wristwatch—it was twenty-six minutes after midnight. She walked down to the thirty-second floor and took the elevator to the lobby. She glanced out of the elevator door. The security guard station was still unoccupied. She quickly exited, nearly colliding with a man walking a dog in front of the building.

The dog walker, Ethan Lloyd, would later say he saw a woman wearing a long blue coat at nearly half-past twelve, alone, sporting sunglasses. A blue scarf wrapped around her head. Ethan considered the coat unnecessarily heavy for such

3

a mild evening, thought the dark glasses were oddly inappropriate for the time of night, and added that the scarf did a very good job of hiding her face and hair. He watched the woman as she moved away from the building along Third Street. Lloyd lost sight of her heading north toward Market Street.

Ethan Lloyd entered the building wondering, as he had wondered going out less than twenty minutes earlier, why James Bingham, the lobby doorman, was not at his post.

Bingham was actually there, but Ethan Lloyd could not see him. James was on the floor, hidden behind the large desk with a broken neck.

The man who had unceremoniously snapped James Bingham's neck moved to the door of apartment 3501 and he used a key to enter. Less than three minutes later he was about to open the apartment door to leave when he saw a white envelope slide under the door. He stood perfectly still. He heard footsteps moving away from the door and he heard the stairwell door close. He waited a full fifteen minutes before leaving and, as instructed, used a shoe found in a hall closet to keep the door from shutting completely.

The man left the building through the parking garage and he walked calmly down Third Street to Howard Street. Before reaching the intersection of Third and Hawthorne, just beyond the Thirsty Bear Brewing Company, the passenger door of a parked Cadillac opened to the sidewalk and he was invited by the driver to get in.

"Well?" the driver asked.

"Done deal," Sal DiMarco answered.

"Did you ditch the key?"

"I did."

Fuck me, Sal thought—remembering he had forgotten to ditch the key.

He carefully slipped the apartment key from his pocket and dropped it under the seat of the Cadillac while the driver was occupied watching for an opening in the busy street traffic.

"Any problems?"

"A bit of collateral damage, no worries."

"Tell me about it," the driver said as he pulled away from the curb.

The woman in blue continued walking up Third Street to Market Street, crossed Market to O'Farrell Street, went west to Powell Street and circled back down to Market.

The woman disappeared down into the Powell Street BART Station.

At half-past midnight the raucous crowd at Johnny Foley's Irish Pub and Restaurant was so deafening that Tom Romano, Ira Fennessy and Jake Diamond had to escape. They clawed their way out onto O'Farrell Street heading for the Powell Street BART Station one block away to grab a taxi.

"Did you see that woman?" asked Ira, as they crawled into a cab.

"What woman?" Tom asked.

"Going down into the station. Did *you* see her, Jake?"

"I can't see anything, Ira. What about her?"

"She was all in blue."

"And..."

"Should have been green, don't you think."

"I can't think," Diamond said.

"Where to?" asked the cabbie.

"O'Reilly's Bar, Green Street, North Beach," Ira answered.

"Jesus, Ira, have a heart," Jake pleaded. "Let's end this nightmare."

"Not until the fat lady sings *Danny Boy.*"

"God forgive us," said Diamond. "We should have played pinochle."

"Anyone in the market for cheap cigarettes?" the taxi driver asked as he pointed the cab toward Broadway.

. . .

5

Benny Carlucci stumbled out of The Chieftain Irish Pub on Third and Howard Streets. Carlucci was asked to leave—not very politely. He found himself out on the street alone. He tried to remember if he had arrived with anyone, but soon gave up trying.

He walked west on Howard Street toward Fourth, passing the Moscone Center on his left and the Metreon to his right. Benny walked down Fourth toward the train station at King Street. He spotted a black Cadillac parked halfway up on the sidewalk between Harrison and Bryant under the Highway 80 overpass.

There was definitely something not right about *that* car in *that* place at *that* time.

Benny was a curious kid. The vehicle stimulated his interest.

Carlucci casually approached the Cadillac, looking up and down Fourth Street as he moved. Other than what appeared to be three teenage boys horsing around a few streets down toward the train station, the area was deserted.

Benny expected to find another drunk, like so many others running and falling all over town—this one most likely passed out cold behind the wheel of the big car. Carlucci peered into the passenger door window. The vehicle was unoccupied and the keys dangled from the ignition. He quickly surveyed the street once again and tried the door. It was unlocked. Carlucci pulled it open and slipped into the driver's seat. He was thinking a ride home in a Coupe de Ville would beat the hell out of a long drunken trip on the train and then a bus ride from the train station to his place on Cole Street off Fulton. The car started with the first turn of the key.

Carlucci turned left onto Bryant Street, turned up Third one block to Harrison, then Harrison onto Ninth Street heading toward Market. Market onto Hayes onto Franklin to Fulton Street and Benny Carlucci was on his way home in style.

The police cruiser, siren blaring, pulled Carlucci over at Masonic Avenue, across from the University of San Francisco, just three short blocks from Benny's apartment.

. . .

The attractive woman who came out of the Civic Center BART station had little resemblance to the woman who had walked down into the Powell Street station twenty minutes earlier. Gone were the dark glasses. Also gone were the heavy blue coat and the blue scarf, replaced by an emerald green two-piece jogging suit and a mane of strawberry blond hair tied back with a green elastic terrycloth band. The .38 caliber Smith and Wesson was now strapped around her ankle.

Once above ground, on Hyde across from the plaza, she jogged in place for a minute before starting up McAllister to the Civic Center Parking Garage. She picked up her car and drove out Geary Boulevard to 25th and then up Lincoln Boulevard to Baker Beach for a solitary run in the sand.

Just before one in the morning, Blake Sanchez stood at a dark street corner in Oakland and watched as one of his least favorite neighbors moved the doormat on his porch and lifted a loose board. Sanchez saw the man place something through the opening and under the porch and then replace the board and the mat before entering the house.

Sanchez took another deep pull off his dope pipe and made a mental note.

What I don't know would fill a book. What I didn't know about her could fill a library. It felt as if I was getting closer to her, but it was like looking into a fun-house mirror. She had constructed so many layers of self-deception, she could deflect a jackhammer. I had no idea what she wanted and I convinced myself I didn't care. It was not an attraction based on the intellectual or the spiritual. It was nothing logical, just biological. The sex wasn't all that great, come to think of it— and I was thinking about it too often. I thought I was in love with her long after I was sure I didn't like her. If she had any idea about what she wanted, she kept it a deep dark secret from herself. At first I saw something in her, honesty, selflessness—something she couldn't see, because it was never really there.

"What do you think?"

"About what?" asked Ira Fennessy.

"I wrote that," Tom Romano said, sitting between Jake and Ira in the back seat of the taxicab, holding a tattered sheet of paper in his hand.

"Why would you write something like that?" Ira asked.

Jake decided to stay out of it. His head felt the size of the Trans America Pyramid, point and all.

"I don't know," Tom said. "For fun I guess."

The taxi pulled up in front of O'Reilly's to let them out. The insane crowd was spilling out onto Green Street.

"You have no idea what fun is," Ira said, "but you are about to find out."

Jake wanted to protest. He desperately wanted to say something, anything that might rescue them.

But he couldn't get his tongue to work.

"I liked what you wrote," said the cab driver as they piled out of the taxi to join the mob.

It was well past midnight, a new day—but it was still St. Patrick's Day in San Francisco.

TWO

Thursday, March 18, 2004.

Trouble is like rain.

It arrives when you least need it.

And when you are least prepared for it.

I opened my eyes and looked up.

6:04 A.M.

The time was projected on the ceiling in large bright green numbers and letters from the clock radio beside the bed—a birthday gift I thought was cute for about two days. It was like an advertisement for unfulfilled wishes. I had hoped it would be much later. I wanted to close my eyes again. Not move. But my bladder was a merciless bully.

I tossed off the bed covers and the cold hit me like an ice cream truck. I discovered I was dressed for going out, or at least dressed the way I had dressed to go out the night before.

I felt infinitely worse than I had when I fell into the bed only three hours earlier, which seemed incredible though not surprising. I tried remembering how I had made it home, but gave up on it quickly. Not a clue.

It had been nearly a year since I had moved back into the house near the Presidio, but I often woke up forgetting where I was. At that particular moment I was having a lot of trouble remembering *who* I was.

I slipped on my baby blue Crocs and staggered to the bathroom to urinate, intending to be back in the sack in record time. Instead, I finished my business and stumbled down the stairs, found my jacket on the steps halfway down, tried keeping my balance as I put it on and made it out to the front porch for more self-abuse.

I lit a Camel non-filtered cigarette.

It was colder outside than in, but wouldn't be for long. The porch faced east and once the morning haze burned off it would be drenched in sunlight. The house had been marketed

9

as being cool in summer. The pitch neglected to publicize the *frigid in all other seasons* feature. On a balmy day in late winter, which this day promised to be, when you entered the house was when you battled the elements.

Both cars were safe in the driveway, which led me to believe I had not driven either one the night before. If I had, one or both would have been twisted knots of tortured rubber, glass, vinyl and steel. Most of the automobiles in the neighborhood were less than two years old and had names that were German or Swedish. My vehicles were a brown 1978 Toyota Corona four-door sedan and a red 1963 Chevy Impala convertible. I loved them both for different reasons and used them accordingly. I was relieved to find them both intact after a stupidly excessive night of green beer and Jameson's Irish whiskey. I am not a big drinker—but give me a good excuse like St. Patrick's Day, a pal's birthday, a Friday or Saturday night, or the joyful sounds of birds singing and I can usually keep up with the Jones'.

I dropped my unfinished cigarette to the ground, to be picked up and discarded at some later time, and returned to the chill inside. I removed the jacket, grabbed a bottle of water from the refrigerator, and I carefully negotiated the stairway. Up. I washed down a couple of Excedrin to ease my aching body—understanding it was like using a Band-Aid to treat a severed limb.

I struggled free of my party clothes and into sweat pants and shirt. There are many good things to say about down comforters which you forget completely when you are not under one. I covered myself to my chin in an urgent attempt to recall the wonders of goose feathers. I used the remote control to start up a Five For Fighting CD and prayed against all odds that the gentle piano would quiet the drum beating in my head. The projection on the ceiling insisted it was twenty-three minutes after six. I promised myself I would figure out how to disable the slideshow as soon as humanly possible. I closed my eyes and begged for sleep.

My prayers were answered for precisely six minutes.

My eyes popped open. I looked up. The lit numbers on the ceiling screamed six twenty-nine. Judging by the sound that woke me I expected to find myself sitting beside Quasimodo atop the cathedral tower, him pulling the rope with one hand and punching me in the side of my head with the other. Another peel of the deafening bell and another sock in the ear and then another. When it happened the fifth time, I realized at last it was the telephone. I struggled to grab the receiver and hit the talk button. It reduced the buzzing in my head by fifty per cent.

"Jake."

"Darlene?"

"Since when does my name have five syllables?"

"Give me a break, Darlene. I'm not doing very well."

"I'll say. I've heard myna birds with better diction."

"Did you call this early to torture me?"

"I called this early because Joey tried calling you and when he couldn't reach you he called me."

"I was outside smoking and must have missed the call."

"Well, I was having a very pleasant dream featuring Hugh Jackman."

"What's so special about Hugh Jackman?"

"You'll never know until you see the X-Men movies."

"And what is it with grown women dreaming about movie stars?"

"It's probably a bit like a World War Two G.I. keeping a photo of Betty Grable in his locker or like the picture of Rachel Weisz you keep in your wallet. Are you going to ask why Joey called, or do you want to continue trying to beat the subject of idol worship to death?"

"Why did Joey call?" I asked.

"Tony Carlucci called Joey so Joey called you."

"I'm having some difficulty putting the two actions together."

"The way you're slurring your words makes me wonder if you could manage to put your two hands together," Darlene said, without a hint of sarcasm. "Call Joey."

"Are you going back to sleep?"

"Too late for that, Hugh's gone. I may as well go for my morning run and get ready to go to the office. Pay some bills, stare at a silent telephone, and calculate the odds that you will show up there before noon. Call Joey."

The line went dead.

Joey was Joseph Vongoli a.k.a. Joey Russo a.k.a. Joey Clams.

From the day I met him, and for the next five years, he was Joey Russo. Nearly a year ago he took a trip to Chicago to save my neck, and while he was at it he avenged the death of his sister and reinstated the family name.

Joey's father, Louis Vongoli, a.k.a. Louie Clams, was forced out of the Chicago suburb of Cicero, Illinois by the Giancana family in the thirties. Vongoli relocated to San Francisco with his wife and son and he changed his name to Russo for protection against reprisal. When Joey reclaimed the name Vongoli he went from being known as Joey Russo to being known as Joey Clams, *vongoli* being the Italian word for clams and clams being easier to pronounce for Anglos.

Tony Carlucci was generally a world of trouble.

I called Joey to find out exactly what sort this time.

He picked up the phone after half a ring.

"Joey, what's up?"

"Jake, you sound like crap."

I'd managed three words and he already had me pegged.

"Too much Jameson's last night."

"Don't tell me you went Irish pub hopping."

"It was Ira Fennessy's idea."

"You call that an idea?"

"We got together to play cards with Tom Romano and Ira talked us into checking out Celtic landmarks instead."

"Sorry to hear it. Tony Carlucci woke me up earlier this morning."

"I heard."

"Tony needs to speak with you as soon as possible."

"What did I do this time, leave food on my plate?"

Carlucci ran a restaurant in North Beach where I ate occasionally because his mother was on some kind of mission to fatten me up. Not unlike my own mother's crusade. If I didn't clean my plate it caused undue grief. If Tony's mom was not happy, Tony was not happy.

And when Tony Carlucci was not happy with you, he was a nightmare.

"It's no joke, Jake. Tony sounded very upset. Don't ask me what about, he wouldn't say—but he insisted he had to talk with you right away. He will call at your office at nine and expects you to be there. Be there, Jake."

Great.

"I certainly will be, Joey."

"Give me a call as soon as Tony's done with you."

Interesting choice of words I thought.

I promised Joey I would call immediately after Tony was done with me and then I painfully negotiated my way across the hall toward the shower.

THREE

Kenny Gerard was nothing if not punctual.

Kenny was never late for work or, for that matter, early.

His work was that of a doorman slash security guard in a high-rise apartment building at Mission and Third. Kenny worked the day shift, seven in the morning until three in the afternoon, five days a week. His work area was limited to the building lobby, the street-front just outside the building entrance, and occasionally the elevator bank if a tenant needed help with shopping packages. Radios, iPods, portable televisions, chats with friends and book reading were all prohibited while on duty. Fraternizing with the tenants was frowned upon—though there were a good number of young woman residents who Kenny would have loved to do some fraternizing with.

Gerard bounced into the lobby at exactly seven on that Thursday morning. The first thing he noticed was that Jim Bingham was absent from his post.

The large duty desk was an L-shaped affair, fronted by a tall counter which hid the desktop and all but the top of the head of a seated person. Kenny often used the cover of the counter to take in a few pages of a graphic novel or to struggle with the *Examiner* crossword puzzle.

The days were long and boring.

Kenny sometimes thought he might prefer the three to eleven shift, when there was more activity—tenants coming in from their jobs and going out on the town. Women were friendlier in the evenings than they were rushing away in the morning to their workplaces. But Gerard would rather have the day shift than the graveyard. Kenny pitied James Bingham. The poor bastard was stuck with nothing to do and not much to see from eleven at night until he was replaced at seven. And at seven, Bingham was usually standing right at the doorway itching to get away, waiting on Kenny Gerard like a member of a tag team race.

But not this morning.

And Kenny Gerard continued to wonder where Bingham was until he discovered James hidden behind the security desk.

Bingham didn't look good.

First at the scene were two San Francisco patrol car officers who were closest when the call came in. Murdoch, a rookie, and Winger, a three-year veteran. The pair were affectionately known at the station as the tall skinny kid and whatshisname.

Kenny Gerard thought they appeared to be very young, and he was correct.

The two officers looked down at the body, which was stuffed under the desk between the counter and the chair. Only Winger had touched the body, and only long enough to check for pulse. James Bingham's head sat at an angle to his torso that brought Linda Blair to Kenny Gerard's mind, though he didn't mention it.

"Do you think he slipped way underneath the desk and snapped his neck?" Murdoch asked.

"I suppose it's possible," Winger answered.

"Who do we call now—the forensic guys, the M.E., or homicide?"

"Call it in as a D.O.A., cause of death unknown," said Winger. "Let them figure out who the hell to send."

Darlene Roman did her laps around Buena Vista Park alone.

She missed having Tug McGraw running beside her.

Her best friend Rose and Rose's husband were taking the kids up to Stinson Beach for a four-day weekend and the two little girls pleaded with 'Aunt' Darlene to let Tug go along.

Darlene couldn't say no because the girls were just too cute and the dog loved the beach. Darlene had joined them for dinner the night before and she left Tug there with them when she left for home, so they could get an early start north in the morning. At the dinner table with Rose, Daniel, and the two girls, Darlene wondered how she would like a family of her own.

She often speculated, but never for very long. There was a lot about being free to be herself she was not willing to give up. Sometimes Darlene felt it could be a selfish reluctance. Most of the time she understood she definitely had it in her to love and comfort and be loyal and be compassionate *and* passionate, but she was far from ready to have anyone be wholly dependent on her and would never let herself be totally dependent on another.

Meantime, she did have her trusty pooch.

And she did have her fun.

Darlene jogged in place for a minute before skipping up the front stairs and entering her small house opposite Buena Vista Park.

Norman Hall stood across Roosevelt Way in the park and watched as Darlene Roman closed the front door. Norman had been watching her jog around the park nearly every morning for more than a week. Hall sat down on a park bench and he stared at the house. He lit another cigarette and wondered where the dog was.

Sergeant Johnson was having one of his worst days in recent memory and it was not yet eight in the morning.

Things had actually been going downhill since the previous day. His wife had flown to Philadelphia in the afternoon. She was attending a big bash to celebrate her parents' fortieth wedding anniversary on Saturday. Johnson politely declined the invitation to join her. He didn't get along particularly well with his father-in-law. If he had to describe the man in two words they would be *pompous ass*. The man never missed the opportunity to insult Johnson, never blew a chance to remind his daughter she could have done a lot better choosing a husband. Johnson's wife, Amy, came from Pennsylvania aristocracy—and marrying a police officer, the son of a San

Francisco welder, was something her father and other members of her self-important dynasty could never understand. Even after the old man's stroke, nearly eighteen months earlier, when for two months he could hardly speak, he managed somehow to articulate his lack of respect for his son-in-law and his disappointment in Amy for bringing someone so *common* into the family.

Rocky could only imagine what they all would think if they had known Johnson in his late teens and early twenties, when he ran with the *Polk Street Pirates,* a gang that plagued the neighborhood with an extended rash of vandalism and petty burglary. But, then again, to these people, being a cop was not all that different from being a thug.

Johnson had seen plenty of ugly things in his sixteen years on the job and sometimes had difficulty seeing the distinction himself, but he always saw a bad cop as the exception and not the rule and did not abide with anyone who preached police corruption was a given. He never saw himself as a knight in shining armor, but he knew when citizens needed protection or sought justice a good cop was their best bet.

And he was a good cop.

Every time Johnson was forced to deal with Amy's dad he was given grief and the only thing that kept him from tearing the old goat's head off after another barrage of unveiled insults was the thought of his own father and the pride in his dad's eyes when Johnson graduated from the police academy after all of the troubled years when Bert Johnson feared his only son might end up on the wrong side of the jail cell bars.

The only ally he had in his wife's family was Amy's mother, who apparently cared enough about her daughter to wish her well. But to have to put up with an arrogant jerk-off like her husband for forty years made Amy's mother a saint or a masochist or both. Johnson felt sorry for the woman, but not sorry enough to join the festivities in the Quaker State.

Amy, of course, was on his side.

She recognized his dilemma. She was very familiar with her father's rudeness and understood Johnson's reluctance to subject himself to verbal abuse. Amy Johnson could not insist her husband accompany her to Philadelphia, nor could she ignore her mother's pleas that Amy be there.

So Johnson stayed at home alone.

And he tried preparing his own dinner after Amy left but he burnt the crap out of it.

He was cajoled into a drink fest with one of the old gang from his Polk Street days and was sick as a dog and couldn't sleep, especially without Amy there to scold him and then hold him.

After lying in a very hot bath for more than an hour and drinking more than a gallon of water he finally achieved some semblance of sleep.

And less than two hours later the telephone rudely woke him.

Now, before eight in the morning, the sergeant was crowded behind a desk in the lobby of a high-rise apartment house looking down at a dead doorman.

The lobby was a menagerie by now. Police officers escorting tenants from the elevators out to the street, keeping them away from the security desk and the victim, more officers outside interviewing tenants and trying to keep rubber-necking pedestrians moving along the street, crime scene investigators collecting evidence, ambulance personnel waiting for the body.

Dr. Steven Altman, the Medical Examiner, rose from the corpse to stand beside Johnson.

"How did he break his neck?" Johnson asked.

"Someone broke it for him," Altman said.

"Great."

"Where is the lovely Lieutenant Lopez?"

"She has the day off."

"Lucky girl."

Johnson tried to imagine anything less appealing than attempting to create order out of this chaos.

For an instant, he thought that being in Philadelphia wishing a pretentious old fuck a happy anniversary might be worse. But maybe not.

FOUR

I walked into the office at ten minutes before nine. I looked like a million bucks. Green and wrinkled.

Darlene was sitting at her desk with her head in the morning *Examiner*. She looked up at me long enough to say, "I'm amazed to see you so soon you look terrible."

Darlene's brutal honesty is one of her strong points.

"I'm expecting an important phone call and I'd be foolish to miss it."

"Are you going to tell me about it," she asked, giving me another quick glance, "or should I just ignore you?"

"Ignore me. Check back me with me after the call if you're still interested, and if I haven't jumped out of the window. Where's the wonder dog?"

"Obedience school. He wouldn't finish his spinach."

I let it go.

"Is there anything worth learning about in the newspaper," I tried.

"The government doubled the reward on Osama bin Laden to fifty million dollars."

"What does that tell you?" I asked.

"We should consider moving the office to Kabul."

Darlene was on a roll.

"Alright," I said, knowing it was the only way to slow her down. "Tony Carlucci is going to phone and he insisted I be here to take the call. I have no idea what it's about but Joey said it sounded urgent and he strongly recommended I be accessible. So, where's the dog?"

"At Stinson Beach with my friend Rose and her kids. I'm leaving early today, probably before three. I want to get my run in this afternoon so I can be ready for tonight."

"Heavy date?"

"Not your concern."

"I like you better when the dog is around."

19

"He's gone until Sunday, live with it. What time is Carlucci supposed to call?"

"Nine. Sharp."

Darlene looked up at the wall clock.

"Five, four, three, two, one," she said.

The telephone rang.

For nearly two years I had been trying to talk Darlene into putting her name up on the door with mine. Time after time she had shown she was as good at this business as I am. She claimed it would overcrowd the opaque windowpane and be a tongue twister when the occasional telephone call came along. I don't know. I have a sneaking suspicion she kind of likes the quaint role of unsung hero.

Darlene answers phone calls according to her mood. It is a cheery *Diamond Investigations, how can we help you?* when she's having a good day.

Otherwise, the list of possibilities is endless.

Diamond Investigations, I hope we can help you.

Diamond Investigations, please let us help you.

Diamond Investigations, no assignment too mundane.

Or one of my favorites in Darlene Roman's arsenal of endearing salutations: *I'm sorry you've reached the wrong number.*

Knowing as well as I did who was calling at the moment I half hoped she would say just that. Instead she picked up the receiver and handed it to me without a word.

"Diamond Investigations, Jake Diamond speaking."

I lack Darlene's imagination.

"Diamond."

"Tony, what a pleasant surprise."

"It's Benny."

"Benny? Benny who?"

"Benny Carlucci."

"Astonishing," I said. "You sound exactly like Anthony Carlucci, are you related?"

"Don't fuck with me, Diamond."

I thought I was being serious.

"Benny is my cousin Guido's kid," Tony Carlucci said.

Cousin Guido. Okay.

"What about your cousin Guido's son Benny, Tony?"

Darlene was biting on the wooden handle of the letter opener, trying to avoid interrupting the conversation with maniacal laughter.

"He was picked up by the cops last night. He's in jail waiting on an arraignment."

The fact that someone named Carlucci was involved in something the police might not cotton to was nothing new. The fact a Carlucci had been *caught* doing it was uncommon.

"What was he arrested for?" I asked, wondering why in God's name Tony Carlucci thought it was any of my business.

"For stealing a Coupe de Ville," Tony said, and after a short but dramatic pause threw in, "and murder."

"Oh," I said. Even if I wasn't hung over and had all of my mental faculties intact I couldn't have articulated my feelings any better.

"They found a dead body in the trunk of the Cadillac," Tony explained, and before I could say a word, if I'd had anything to say, added, "Benny says he didn't off the guy."

"Tough break," I said, before I could stop myself.

"Yes it is," he agreed.

It was very close to a grunt.

"So what do you think I can do for you, Tony?" I said, with no clue how I could have been foolish enough to ask.

Carlucci told me exactly what he expected me to do.

I telephoned Joey as soon as I could manage to get Tony Carlucci off the line.

Tony had been rambling, and the only way I could cut him off was by giving some him ill-advised assurances.

Darlene had been listening in on the conversation with the rapt attention of an audience member at the staging of a Chekhov play. When I was done with Carlucci and punching in Joey Clam's telephone number, she offered me a familiar facial expression that said: *Way to go, moron.*

Joey was obviously waiting on my phone call because he answered, "Give me the good news first."

There was no good news.

"Carlucci wants me to find out who whacked the guy in the trunk," I said.

21

"Oh?"

I ran it all by him.

"Does Tony believe Benny did it?" Joey asked, not that it would make much difference.

"I'd say no," I said. "But Tony seems convinced they'll hold the kid until a better solution comes up. Tony may be crazy, but he's not stupid. Tony says the cops like to have a suspect in custody—it eases some of the pressure from the public and the mayor's office while they're trying to figure it out. Meanwhile, Benny rots in jail until the actual killer is found. Carlucci wants me to find the real killer."

"Tony lacks faith in the police department?"

"Tony said, and I quote, *The SFPD couldn't find Barry Bonds in a bowl of vanilla ice cream.*"

"What did you tell Tony?"

"I told him I would get on it," I confessed.

"Did you make any guarantees?"

"Did I have a choice? He asked me if he had to worry about it."

"And?"

"And I told him not to sweat it, or something as inane or insane."

"What's your first step?"

"If I was smart, my first step would be into the path of an oncoming streetcar. In lieu of that, I will stroll down to the Vallejo Street Station and see if they'll let me talk to Benny Carlucci. It's doubtful, since I never took the Bar Exam. Maybe if I walk in gnawing on a hunk of provolone they'll believe I'm one of the family. Then I'll try to see Lopez, though when the Lieutenant senses I'm in the building, and she always can, she does a marvelous job of making herself invisible."

"Let me know if I can help,"

"You'll be the first to know, Joey."

I cradled the receiver and Darlene caught my eye.

"Well?" she said.

"Well, what?"

"Did you catch the final episode of Lizzie McGuire on the tube last night? Are you heading over to Vallejo Street Station?"

"Not this minute, I think I need to procrastinate for a while."

"Procrastinate awhile sounds redundant."

"I'm going to sit at my desk for a time and feel sorry for myself."

"Jake."

"Yes, Darlene," I said, heading to my inner office.

"Stay away from open windows and street cars."

FIVE

Molinari's Italian Delicatessen on Columbus Avenue between Grant and Vallejo Streets had been offering the finest imported meats and cheeses and flawlessly prepared Italian dishes for more than a century. Molinari's was a delicatessen in the strict sense of the word—a storehouse of delicacies. The market opened at eight in the morning, every morning except Sunday. By ten the joint was jumping. Molinari's was exclusively take-out. San Franciscans and tourists alike picking up something special to take to a park bench for their lunch or something to carry home or to the hotel for dinner. For those who actually cooked, the shelves were lined with everything possibly needed for a home-prepared meal and the selection of fine wines was equally impressive.

Angelo Verdi filled the wire basket with more breaded calamari and he slowly lowered the basket into the hot oil. The previous batch sat beside the deep fryer on a layer of grease soaked paper towels. The bell above the front door of Molinari's Delicatessen jingled, announcing the arrival of a customer.

A man in casual attire moved to the soda cooler of the market and after a moment browsing the selections he pulled out a Manhattan Special.

Angelo, occupied with the squid, waved to his wife Antoinette to deal with the sale.

She met the customer at the cash register.

"Coffee soda," the man said. "What a concept."

"Much too sweet for me," Antoinette offered. "Will there be anything else?"

"This should do it for now." The man placed a couple of dollars on the counter, waited for his change, and left the shop.

Antoinette returned to the back counter where she had been busy preparing a large salad of tomatoes, fresh basil and mozzarella for the display case. Angelo had turned his attention away from the fryer long enough to watch the man who had just exited the shop cross to the opposite side of Columbus Avenue. The man stopped and stood sipping the Manhattan Special while looking up at the second story of the building. Verdi felt he had seen this man before, but he couldn't recall the occasion. Angelo quickly pulled the basket out of the oil just in time to keep from turning the squid into charcoal.

Norman Hall took another drink of coffee soda and lit a cigarette. And he stared up at the bay windows of Diamond Investigations above Molinari's.

Sergeant Johnson had been trapped in the high-rise apartment building for nearly two hours. He was feeling more like a traffic cop than a homicide investigator.

The body of the dead doorman had been moved to the morgue, but the building was still a world of commotion. Johnson had called in four pair of uniformed officers to canvass the building floor by floor, four more uniforms were interviewing tenants as they left to begin the day, the tall skinny kid and whatshisname were doing the best they could to keep pedestrian traffic moving.

The testimony of a dog walker who reported seeing an indescribable woman out in front of the building sometime after midnight was all they had to show for their efforts.

Johnson stood in the building lobby daydreaming. *Bad day* dreams. Wondering how long this ordeal would drag on, dreading another evening without a decent home cooked meal, another night alone in bed. Johnson was missing his wife already.

Johnson was thinking about the afternoon when he first shared time with Amy Singleton. She sat next to him in his sophomore biology class at the University of Pennsylvania. It took him two weeks to work up the courage to ask her to join him for a cup of coffee. The Singletons had been a very well-respected and influential Philadelphia family for generations, which was a bit intimidating to Johnson until he recognized how unaffected Amy was. Her father, Sterling Singleton II, was a different story completely—as Johnson would eventually discover. He was recalling that afternoon with Amy, at a bench on campus, sipping coffee from Dunkin' Donuts Styrofoam cups, awkwardly getting to know each other.

"I just have to ask you," Amy said, after telling him about the mighty Singletons.

"What?"

"About your name."

"What about my name?"

"It's not very common, at least not around here."

"I would think Johnson was a very common name around here," he said, smiling.

She smiled also. A beautiful smile.

"You know what I'm talking about. I've never met anyone with that name before."

"First time for everything, I guess."

"C'mon."

"I was named after the town where my father and my mother were born."

"Roxton?"

"Roxton."

"England?"

"Texas."

Albert Johnson had been a third generation Texan and a second-generation welder. When there was no longer work in the small northeastern Texas town near the Oklahoma border, Bert Johnson moved with his pregnant wife to California. A son was born six months after they settled in San Francisco and the proud father named the boy after the hometown where Bert, and *his* father before him, had been born and raised.

"Can I call you Rocky?" Amy asked, after the Johnson family history lesson.

"Sure, I'd like that."

Amy's parents' anniversary party was set for Saturday. She would be back in San Francisco late Sunday evening.

Two and a half days.

Johnson hoped he could make it.

"Sergeant Johnson."

Johnson suddenly found himself back in the building lobby. Officer Murdoch was trying to get his attention.

"Sergeant Johnson," Murdoch repeated.

"What is it?"

"We just received a radio call from the thirty-fifth floor."

"And?"

"And the officers canvassing up there found another dead body. Male Caucasian. In Apartment thirty-five-zero-one."

"Terrific," Sergeant Roxton Johnson mumbled, moving quickly to the elevators.

Angelo Verdi transferred the fried calamari into a hotel pan and dropped it into the steam table. His wife was in back, sliding a large pan of lasagna into the oven.

Angelo admired their morning accomplishments. The refrigerated display case was loaded with salads, fried eggplant, rice balls, and a wide array of other Italian dishes. There was fresh focaccia with tomatoes and basil sitting on the counter. Angelo glanced up to the front door when the bell tinkled and gave Darlene Roman a wide smile as she walked into the shop. As she approached the front counter a movement on the street caught Verdi's eye. He gazed out and noticed the man who had been in earlier for a soda. The man was standing across Columbus Avenue watching the shop entrance.

"Good morning, Angelo," Darlene sang.

Verdi turned to greet her.

"*Buongiorno*, pretty lady. What can I help you with?"

"I need two very large coffees and a couple of cake donuts."

"Donuts. Since when?"

"They're for Jake."

"I thought you were trying to keep Jake away from donuts."

"He needs something to soak up all of the whiskey he poured down his throat last night," Darlene explained.

"I have an extra roll of paper towels."

"I'll keep that in mind if all else fails," Darlene smiled, sharing the joke.

Verdi filled two paper cups with dark coffee, snapped on the lids, and placed them neatly into a white paper bag. He threw in sugar packets and creamers, wrapped two donuts in deli paper and gently laid them on top.

"How about a little taste of the tomato and mozzarella salad, Darlene? My wife just made it."

"Thanks, but I'll pass. It's a little too early in the day for me to handle that."

If Antoinette had used chunks of smoked tempeh in place of the oil soaked cheese, Darlene might have given it some further thought.

"Tell Jake I have fried calamari today," Angelo said, handing her the white paper bag.

"He'll know," she assured him. "Can you put this on our tab?"

"Done. Have a good day, bella donna."

"You do the same, Angelo," Darlene said as she turned away from him and toward the front door.

Verdi watched her as she moved out to the street.

Looking past her, Angelo saw that the man who had been loitering across Columbus Avenue was gone.

Sergeant Johnson moved up to the door marked 3501 with Officer Murdoch behind him. The door was partially opened and Johnson used his foot to push it open wider.

"Wait out here, Murdoch. Don't let anyone else in."

Johnson glanced at his wristwatch. It was exactly ten in the morning. He stepped through the doorway.

A uniformed officer who had been standing idly in the front room snapped to attention.

"How was the body discovered?" Johnson asked.

"We were going door-to-door. This door was propped open with a shoe. We rapped on the door and called out. There was no answer from inside, so we entered."

"Did you touch anything," Johnson asked, regretting that

these days you *had* to ask.

"Over there," the officer answered. He pointed to a plain white envelope inside a clear plastic evidence bag sitting on a solid oak coffee table. "It was lying on the carpet, right inside the door. I was afraid it would get trampled when the troops arrived."

"How did you handle it?"

"Latex gloves, sir."

"Touch anything else?"

"Only the victim, long enough to check for pulse, and then I called it down to the lobby."

"Where's the body."

"The bedroom, down the hall on the left. My partner is in there."

"Did *he* touch anything?"

"She. I begged her not to, sir."

"What's your name?" Johnson asked.

"Cutler, sir. Davey Cutler."

"Good work, Cutler. Stay out here, see that no one gets in," Johnson said, and he headed for the bedroom.

A very young female officer in uniform was standing at the foot of the bed staring down at the body. *They are all so young*, Johnson thought to himself.

"Officer."

She turned, a bit startled by his voice.

"Yes, sir."

"What do we have?"

"One gunshot wound to the back of the head, sir. He may have just come into the room when he was shot."

So young and so eager.

"I know this man, sir," she added.

"Oh?"

"Take a look. I'm sure you'll recognize him also."

Johnson looked down at the victim's face. A day that had started out badly suddenly looked a whole lot worse.

SIX

It was past ten if my ancient Timex had anything to say about it. I'd been sitting at my office desk like a zombie for more than an hour. If I had something to be thankful about after drowning myself in Jameson's Irish whiskey the previous night and the phone call from Tony Carlucci that morning, it was the chair. It was a large bulky leather monstrosity, but it was comfortable as hell.

The chair was a gift from Vinnie Stradivarius, often referred to as Vinnie Strings for the sake of convenience, saving breath or avoiding embarrassing mispronunciations. Vinnie Strings tried to help Darlene and me with our work, when he wasn't busy gambling. He rarely succeeded in the help department, but always earned an A for effort.

Strings had rolled the massive thing into the office two days before Christmas, saying it was worth four hundred dollars and he won it in a poker game. Strings rarely won at poker. I could only imagine the other treasures thrown into the pot when Vinnie and his poker gang got together. I pictured gold mine claims and land deeds. Vinnie said the chair I had been using since setting up shop above Molinari's eight years earlier was an ergonomic disaster.

I had no idea what that meant.

"Let me put it this way," Vinnie had explained while he moved the newly acquired chair behind my desk and pushed the old catastrophe out the door. "You sit on that thing much longer and your posture will make Walter Brennan look like a guard on duty at Buckingham Palace."

I'm not sure I knew what that meant either.

The scent of fried calamari floated through the window from Molinari's Delicatessen. It was generally an inviting aroma. This morning it only served to intensify my headache and cause my stomach to do cartwheels. I rummaged through my desk drawer and dug out the drugs. I washed two Tylenol down with a healthy swallow of Mylanta.

I stuffed a paperback copy of *The Hunchback of Notre Dame* into my jacket pocket, anticipating a long wait before making any progress at the Vallejo Street Police Station.

I lifted myself from the chair and ventured out front.

"If you're done wallowing in self-pity," Darlene said over her shoulder, "I brought you a coffee and a couple of donuts."

"Can't do it," I said, walking around to the front of her desk. "What I need to do is try to find out where Benny Carlucci stands before his father's cousin Tony begins to doubt my enthusiasm."

"You have a way with words, Jake."

"So I'm told."

"Do you think they'll let you see the kid?"

"I could get lucky. What does my horoscope say?"

"Think you'll get to see Lieutenant Lopez?"

"Maybe. Unless she sees me first."

"You need to be more positive, Jake."

"I am," I said. "I'm positive this is going to be a long unpleasant day."

I left the office and headed for Vallejo Street.

I made no progress whatsoever at the police station. The good news was that failing had taken me hardly any time at all. What I did learn I got from Desk Sergeant Yardley, a crusty old-timer who took to me like a fish to dry land.

Sergeant Yardley was best at yes or no questions and his answer was usually no.

I did manage to discover that Benny Carlucci had been shuttled off to a courtroom for an arraignment, Lieutenant Lopez had the day off, and Sergeant Johnson was downtown on a homicide call.

I probably wouldn't have gotten very far with Lopez or Johnson anyhow.

Lieutenant Laura Lopez could read me like a comic book and treated me with all of the reverence she might afford a cartoon character. Sergeant Johnson and I got along like Stalin and Churchill.

"Who got wasted downtown?" I asked Yardley.

"What makes you think it's any of your business, Diamond?" the desk sergeant replied.

"Sorry, I lost my head there for a moment."

I headed out onto Columbus Avenue to catch a streetcar over to the Hall of Justice on Bryant Street.

I tried avoiding the criminal courts building at all costs. It was a large gray edifice crawling with people who had nothing to be happy about.

I was going to fit right in.

To state the obvious, if a case forced me to visit the place, it was a case involving a crime. Trying to solve a crime is no picnic for a private investigator. Everything conspires against you, especially the police.

If it's true that, for a criminal, crime doesn't pay—it is equally true that for a private investigator, working to solve a crime doesn't pay very well.

My only consolation was I could usually slip into the building through the rear door.

Hank Strode was one of a kind. He was the only person I could think of who could spend five days each week in the building and always manage a smile. After ten years in an evidence room at the SFPD, where everyone came and went in a hurry, Hank had landed a position that was perfect for him. He controlled the rear access to the Hall of Justice where judges, prosecutors, and prisoners escorted into the building for court appearances entered and exited.

Strode was a talker. Everyone who came through his door had a thing or two to talk about, and he had some time to do it. Coming through the back door was a delight compared to the cold indignity of the street entrance. There were no metal detectors, no emptying pockets of loose change or Zippo lighters or cell phones, no having to explain to some self-important dim-witted security guard that the bulge in your jacket was a book even after you had showed it to him.

Hank was unique in another way—he was the only person I knew in town who wore a badge and tolerated me.

When Hank saw it was good old Jake tap-tap-tapping on the window he gave me a big smile and ushered me in.

"Too much to drink last night, Jake," Strode said, by way of greeting.

Yet another confirmation that I looked as bad as I felt, as if I needed more proof.

Hank asked how Darlene, Joey and Vinnie were doing and after my report I told him what had brought me there.

"And you came because Tony Carlucci asked you to?"

"He didn't give me much selection," I said.

"Where have I heard that line before?"

"Brando. *One-Eyed Jacks.*"

"Good one. Can you say it like Brando?"

Hank was one of the few who knew I had been a mediocre actor before becoming an average P.I.

I put all of the focus I could muster into my nasal passage and gave it a shot.

"Not bad," Hank said. "Did you hear about Sandoval?"

"Manny Sandoval, the bookie?"

"Roberto Sandoval, the shoe-in to win the election for District Attorney."

"What about him?"

"He was shot to death in his apartment last night."

"Oh, boy."

I could only hope Benny Carlucci had a good alibi.

I walked into the courtroom just in time to see Benny Carlucci and Lionel Katz standing before the bench as the judge said *next case* and two uniformed police officers moved toward Benny to take him away. I caught his eye as he was being cuffed and gave him a little wave and a smile hoping he might get a good impression of me to report back to his father's cousin Tony.

Benny looked at me like I was an idiot and they led him out through the side of the courtroom.

Lionel Katz walked up the aisle toward the door to the courthouse hallway. He didn't look too happy either.

"Let's talk," he said.

I followed him out into the hall.

"Can I buy you breakfast?" he asked.

By the look of his Kiton suit and his American Belting attaché, I imagined he could.

Katz's idea of breakfast was a sweet roll and a black coffee from the cart in front of the Hall of Justice and a park bench across Bryant Street. I passed on the roll.

"Nice day," he said, once we'd settled in.

I wasn't too sure. If Katz was talking strictly about the weather it was a little warm for my taste. It would eventually reach eighty-one degrees, a record high for the eighteenth day of March in the City by the Bay.

A pigeon and a squirrel sat stationed at opposite ends of the bench, eyeballing the sweet roll and eyeballing each other.

Lionel Katz was the attorney for the Carlucci family. They were his only clients.

It took Lionel Katz less than a minute to bring me up to speed.

Benny had stumbled across a Cadillac with no passenger and a set of keys and decided to drive home to avoid public transportation. Carlucci knew absolutely nothing about the body in the trunk.

"All Benny is guilty of is driving a stolen car under the influence of alcohol," Katz concluded.

That's all the kid did. A real choirboy.

"Tony and John Carlucci are counting on you to find out who killed the guy in the trunk," he added.

Great.

I could only hope I would be afforded the mandatory eight-count.

Katz tossed a big piece from the edge of his roll out onto the grass in front of the park bench. It fell between the squirrel and the pigeon. It was a standoff. I tried to identify with one or the other of the little creatures, but felt more akin to the hunk of crust. I really wanted to ask Katz where to start, but didn't want to jeopardize the confidence everyone in the Carlucci camp seemed to have in me. Katz unwittingly helped me out.

"I'd start by finding out whatever you can about the

victim, who he was and how he was killed," Katz suggested. "It might help if you knew someone in the coroner's office who feels like sharing."

I did know someone in the coroner's office and he owed me a favor. However, I suppressed my optimism.

"Couldn't they identify the guy in the trunk?" I asked.

"Eventually they may be able to identify him from fingerprints, but the condition of the fingertips is going to slow them down a bit."

"Condition of what fingertips?"

"The victim's fingertips. I am told they were burned, they're guessing some kind of acid."

"Oh, those fingertips," I stammered. I closed my eyes and wished myself to a Mediterranean beach holding on to a tall glass of George Dickel Tennessee sour mash whiskey on ice. I opened my eyes and I was still on a park bench with a mob lawyer.

The squirrel and the pigeon were both gone, as was the hunk of the sweet roll.

I had no way of discerning which critter had taken the prize.

"Good luck, Diamond," Lionel Katz said, as he stood up from the bench. "Be assured that both Tony and John greatly appreciate what you are doing for the Carlucci family."

"Don't mention it," I said, meaning it literally.

As I watched him walk away, I wondered if my day could possibly go any further downhill. Then I looked down at my hands and wiggled my fingertips.

Sure, I decided.

Things could always be worse.

SEVEN

When Kenny Gerard spotted Laura Lopez out in front of the apartment building approaching the entrance he nearly tripped over his own feet to get there first.

Gerard opened the door and leered at her as she moved past him into the lobby. She was drop dead gorgeous. She looked up at him and held his gaze.

"You can let go of the door now, kid," she said. "And get your eyeballs back in your head before I accidentally step on them."

Lopez crossed the lobby to the uniformed officer who stood at the mouth of the elevator bank. Lopez couldn't remember whatshisname's name.

"Where might I find Sergeant Johnson?" she asked.

"He should still be up in apartment thirty-five-oh-one, Lieutenant," Winger said. "Would you like me to radio the sergeant and let him know you're coming up?"

"I'd rather surprise him," Lopez said as she headed for the elevator.

Lopez found a uniformed officer standing like a sentry just outside the door to 3501. Lopez couldn't remember the tall, skinny kid's name either.

The nametag on his chest clued her in.

"Officer Murdoch."

"Lieutenant," he said, and opened the door for her.

She stepped inside and found another officer in the front room.

"Officer."

"Cutler," he quickly replied, eager for recognition. "Lieutenant."

"Where is everyone?"

"Sergeant Johnson, Dr. Altman and a couple of evidence guys are in the bedroom, down the hall on the left."

Lopez did a quick inventory of the front room, her eyes

resting for a moment on the oak coffee table.

"Would you join Officer Murdoch out in the hall," she said. She watched Cutler move out and then walked over to the coffee table. She then started for the bedroom just as Sergeant Johnson entered the room from the rear hallway.

Johnson *was* surprised to see her there.

"I thought you had the day off," he said.

"Death is what happens when you're busy making other plans. What do we have?"

"Sandoval was at the Omni Hotel at a dinner and dance to raise money for the Crossroads Irish American Festival. The festival runs for a week each March and is followed by a fundraiser to kick off planning for the following year. Sandoval's boss, Duffey, is on the festival board. Duffey is giving up his District Attorney seat to make a run for the Mayor's Office. Duffey was backing Sandoval to take *his* office, mostly because Sandoval isn't Italian, so he dragged Roberto along to drum up Irish support. Stop me if you've heard any of this before."

"Go on."

"Sandoval left the hotel by taxi. I tracked down the driver. He said he dropped Sandoval out front at midnight. The doorman came to open the door of the taxi and Sandoval went into the building. The doorman chatted with the taxi driver for a minute or two and returned to the lobby. The cabbie drove off.

"A tenant passed through the lobby at about ten after midnight with his dog. Ethan Lloyd, strange bird. Anyway, he noticed the doorman was not at his post. At twelve-thirty he saw a woman come out of the building and rush off toward Market Street. He did not recognize her as a fellow tenant and could not describe her in any detail."

"Nothing?" Lopez asked. "Height, weight, hair, eyes."

"Average, average, hair covered by a scarf or a shawl, dark sun glasses, a canvas shoulder bag, nothing," Johnson answered. "At seven this morning the day doorman shows up and finds the night guy stuffed behind the security desk. A few hours later they find Sandoval. He lives here with his wife who is in Florence for two weeks, taking an art class. She left on Tuesday afternoon."

"Has the wife been notified?"

"Should have been by now. They were trying to track her down in Italy."

"What went down here? If you had to guess?"

"Okay. If I had to guess. The cabbie leaves, the perpetrator follows the doorman into the lobby and then snaps his neck, comes up here and shoots Sandoval."

"How does the perp get into the apartment?"

"I don't know. Sandoval lets the perp in, or leaves the door unlocked. Maybe he's expecting someone. By the position of the body, the perp may have led Sandoval back there at gunpoint and then shot him execution style in the back of the head. The M.E. and the forensic techs are back there now. An ambulance is on the way over for the body."

Johnson spotted the corner of a plastic bag peeking out of the lieutenant's jacket pocket.

"Did you bring me lunch?" he asked.

Lopez followed his eyes and stuffed the bag further down into her pocket. She caught him glancing over to the oak coffee table.

Johnson and Lopez had graduated from uniforms to plain clothes detectives around the same time. And if there were those in the department who questioned Lopez's rapid rise to lieutenant, resented being outranked by a woman, or implied her ascendancy was motivated by gender considerations— Johnson was not one of them.

In his opinion the lieutenant had won her position the old-fashioned way. She had worked hard for it.

Johnson and Lopez had been working together for a long time. Side-by-side in the trenches. And Johnson had known very few law enforcement officers, woman or otherwise, who were as cool and clear headed as Lopez in the most volatile and life threatening situations. But when Johnson turned back from the coffee table to meet her gaze he saw an uneasiness he had never seen in her eyes before.

"What gives, Lopez?" he asked.

"I need you back at the station, Sergeant," she said without blinking.

"When?"

"Now."

"Are you kidding?"

"Do I sound like I'm kidding?"

She didn't. Not at all.

"What on earth for?"

"I need you to work the homicide from last night. The victim found in the trunk of a Cadillac, shot in the temple, fingertips burned off. We need to find out who he was and who killed him."

"They already picked up the doer, driving around with the body. He was supposed to be arraigned this morning."

"The kid they picked up didn't do it."

"I heard he was a Carlucci. It's genetic with them."

"Not this particular Carlucci. The kid has no priors. He's a second cousin or something as removed. The kid was so drunk I doubt he could have found the trunk of the car with a roadmap. And he is frightened to death. The kid is just incredibly unlucky. He stole the wrong car."

"Lieutenant, there's a roomful of detectives sitting on their hands down there."

"I want *you* down there, Sergeant."

"What about this mess? Sandoval and the doorman?"

"I'll take it from here."

It had been a very long time since Johnson had been dismissed so summarily, and never before by Lopez.

He wanted very badly to complain, to argue with her, but he decided against it.

Something was telling him not to push her.

"I'm on it, Lieutenant."

"Thank you."

"Good luck with this mess," Johnson said, walking to the front door. Then he silently left the apartment.

Lopez sighed deeply and headed for the back rooms.

Johnson found Officers Murdoch and Cutler just outside the apartment door.

"Murdoch, remain here, don't let anyone in except the

ambulance guys," Johnson said. "Officer Cutler, please walk with me to the elevator."

"Yes, sir," Cutler said, and he followed Johnson down the hallway. At the elevator, Johnson turned to the young officer.

"Cutler, I need your assistance."

To Davey Cutler, the sergeant looked and sounded very sober.

"However I can help, Sergeant."

"I need a witness re-interviewed. His name is Ethan Lloyd, he lives in the building. Lloyd nearly ran into a woman who was coming out of the lobby last night. He was out front with his dog. He gave us nothing, claimed she was covered up— long coat, scarf, dark glasses. He had to notice more. He's just not trying hard enough. The woman's skin tone, approximate height and weight, her hands, shoes, jewelry, hair length or color. Get him to put his thinking cap on, to try seeing her in his mind, whatever the fuck it takes to shake something loose."

"What if he's not in?"

"Then you wait for him to come in, for as long as it takes. I need more on the woman."

"Yes, sir."

"You will report back to me, Cutler, and only to me. Understood?"

"Understood, sir."

"About the envelope you found."

"What about it, sir?"

"You handled that very well."

"Thank you, sir."

"I need you to forget it."

"Forget it, sir?"

"Yes, forget you ever saw it. At least for the time being."

"Isn't it evidence, sir?"

"Yes it is. It might be very important evidence and, for that reason, we need to keep it quiet at this stage of the investigation."

"Oh, I get it, Sergeant," Cutler said.

"You do?"

"It's like something only the killer might know about and

if it stays out of the media it could help identify whoever murdered Sandoval."

"That's exactly it, Cutler," Johnson said, thankful for all of the crime books and movies most of these young police officers were raised on. "I can see a very promising future for you in the department."

"Thank you, sir."

The elevator arrived and Johnson held it open with his foot.

"Get on the Lloyd thing right away. I'm counting on you, Cutler."

"I won't disappoint you, Sergeant."

"I'm certain you won't, Davey," Johnson said as he stepped into the elevator car.

Davey Cutler watched the doors shut.

The kid was beaming. Lit up like a Christmas tree.

As the car descended, Johnson could think of only one thing.

What the fuck was going on with Lieutenant Lopez?

Lopez ran into the forensic team in the hall, moving in the opposite direction.

Michael Gordon and Joe Beggs had been collecting crime scene evidence together for years, and for the third time in less than twenty-four hours. They worked quickly and meticulously. Wasting time was not something either Gordon or Beggs knew how to do.

"Done back there?" Lopez asked.

"Done," Gordon said.

"Get anything?"

"Nothing to jump up and shout about, we're going to do the front room," Beggs answered.

And they were gone.

Lopez found the M.E., Steve Altman, and a young female officer with the late Roberto Sandoval.

"Officer," Lopez said.

"Knapik, Lieutenant. Joanna Knapik."

"Officer Knapik, I need a word with Dr. Altman. See if the

evidence techs can use your help out there. If not, just try staying out of their way."

"Yes, Lieutenant," Knapik said and left the room.

"Johnson thought you had the day off," Altman said.

"So did I."

"Where is Johnson?"

"I had to send him back to Vallejo Street. So. Tell me everything you know."

"Not much to tell. They found the body here," Altman began, pointing down to the floor just inside the bedroom. Lopez noticed the bloodstains on the carpet. "We moved him to the bed to clear the doorway. One gunshot wound to the back of the head. Looks like a thirty-eight caliber, but I wouldn't swear to it until I pull the slug out. I'm guessing eight to twelve hours ago for time of death, but again I need to run tests before I sign off on it."

Lopez glanced at her wristwatch. It was a few minutes before noon.

"Could have been around midnight," she said, almost to herself. She walked over to the bed, stared down at the body, and stood silently for almost a full minute.

"You okay, Lieutenant?" the Medical Examiner asked.

"A cab driver has Sandoval arriving here at midnight and the doorman still breathing," Lopez said, ignoring his question. "Another witness notices the doorman was missing from his post shortly thereafter. So both Sandoval and the doorman could have been murdered between twelve and twelve-thirty."

"That's how it appears to me," Altman said.

"Lieutenant." It was Knapik calling from the hall.

"Yes?"

"The ambulance guys are here."

"Are you done with him?" Lopez asked Altman, looking down again at the body on the bed.

"I've done all I can here, I'll be doing the rest down at the morgue," Altman answered.

"Knapik."

"Yes, Lieutenant?"

"You can send them in," Lopez called. She walked over to

the north-facing window of the apartment. The panoramic view took in all of Nob Hill, Russian Hill, Telegraph Hill, the North Waterfront and Alcatraz Island. Lopez loved the city. She considered it one of the most beautiful spots on earth— even on those days when it got ugly.

"You okay, Lopez?" Altman asked a second time.

"Did you hear it's going to hit eighty today?"

"Too damn hot for March, if you ask me."

"Well, Doc, as Mark Twain so aptly phrased it," Lopez said, turning from the window as the ambulance guys walked in, "Everyone complains about the weather, but no one does anything about it. Get in touch with me right away if you learn anything else."

Lopez felt the bagged envelope like it was burning a hole in her jacket pocket. She left the room and then the apartment.

The weather was the least of her concerns.

Officer Davey Cutler wasn't quite sure what to do.

Davey was excited about getting the special assignment from Sergeant Johnson, a secret one at that. After parting with the sergeant, Cutler had quickly located Ethan Lloyd's apartment and knocked on the witness' door. The only answer he received was from the dog inside. Now he was back down in the building lobby, wondering how long he might have to wait before Lloyd turned up and what to do in the meantime. He considered calling Johnson, but worried about appearing indecisive in the eyes of the sergeant who had put so much faith and trust in him.

Kenny Gerard was somewhat at sea also. The lobby was usually his realm, but today he was feeling totally out of place. Kenny had been pushed around the lobby all morning, by all sorts of cops and other city officials, like a piece of furniture no one knew what to do with. Kenny was trying to fade into the woodwork when he suddenly saw Davey Cutler standing beside him.

"I wonder if you could tell me when Ethan Lloyd might be back," Cutler said. "He's one of your tenants."

"I know who he is," Gerard answered. "I take pride in

knowing who my tenants are."

"I'm sure you do," said Cutler politely. "When might he be back?"

"He should be back in a few hours. He's always here by two or so to take the dog out."

"That was easy. Thanks. You've been a great help."

"It was an easy question. Do you have anything more challenging I could help you with?"

Cutler thought about it for a moment, feeling the need to come up with something.

"Are there other ways in and out of the building?" he finally asked.

"Only through the parking garage," Kenny replied. "But you would need the access code."

"What's the access code?"

"It's a four digit number followed by the pound sign."

Gerard was trying the young officer's patience.

"I mean, what *is* the code?" Cutler plowed on.

"Is it important that you know it?"

"It could be very important," Cutler suggested, though he really didn't know exactly why. "And your help would be greatly appreciated and duly noted."

"Two two five three," Gerard said.

"Two two five three," Cutler repeated, quickly jotting it down.

"Don't forget the pound sign."

EIGHT

I opened my eyes to the noise of a clanging in my head which then became the sound of a church bell announcing the noon hour. I expected to find myself beside Quasimodo, him looking at me as if *I* was the Pope of Fools. Instead I was sitting on a bench across from the Hall of Justice.

Alone.

The last thing I could remember was watching as Lionel Katz walked away. I realized I had dozed off on the bench. I did that occasionally, particularly when I was badly hungover and I was having trouble deciding what to do next. And, as I also did quite often when confronted with the need to choose a course of action, I asked myself: *What would Jimmy Pigeon do?*

There was a time when I really thought I could make it as a movie star.

Not because I possessed movie star charisma or matinee idol good looks, since I didn't possess either—but because I believed I was a good actor and I thought that counted for something. However, the leap from stage to film acting was a long one, and I always fell short and landed harder every time I fell.

And then, on a film set in Los Angeles some years ago, I met a private detective named Jimmy Pigeon.

Jimmy was on location as a consultant, giving the lead actor pointers on ways to walk and talk like a private eye, and then tips on how to look convincing when the fictional private eye had to confront and ultimately kill off *my* character in the first reel.

I very rarely made it past the first reel.

Watching Pigeon fascinated me, intrigued me enough to approach Jimmy and ask him to tell me more about his work. I remember Jimmy telling me that what he did for a living was a lot easier than what I did.

"I could never be an actor," he said. "There are some things we are able to master, and some we can't. It's not a matter of intelligence. It's more about personality."

If he was trying to tell me not everyone could be a private investigator, he never said it straight out and I chose to ignore the inference. And before too long, Jake Diamond the Hollywood hopeful became Jimmy Pigeon's protégé and partner.

It had been four years since Pigeon was murdered, but as I listened to the twelfth peel of the church bell and I sat trying to figure out my next move, I asked myself, as I did again and again: *What would Jimmy advise?*

And the answer was always the same: *Do Something.*

Get your ass up off the bench, Jake, and do something— even if it's wrong.

Steve Altman was a San Francisco medical examiner, the man in the Coroner's Office who might help me get going. I believed Altman owed me one. I could only hope he agreed.

A while back I had helped Altman with a problem he had involving his daughter. He never mentioned who recommended me. I only knew it wasn't Lieutenant Lopez or Sergeant Johnson. I would be at the bottom of their lists of problem solvers, somewhere far below tarot cards and coin tosses.

Altman's daughter, Sara, a twenty-one-year-old senior at San Francisco State, had a new boyfriend who Altman had some doubts about.

"Just a gut feeling," Altman had told me. "Something I can't quite put my finger on, something not right with the guy. I worry about my daughter, she's gullible."

Not much to go on, maybe more about an over-protective father than anything else, but I decided to try to find out what I could about the boyfriend.

Bob Harper.

Jimmy always said if you wanted to learn about a person, the best course was to watch. So I watched Harper, for almost a week. It was a lot like watching episodes of *Seinfeld.*

Nothing happened. And in most of the episodes, Sara Altman made guest appearances. And from what I could tell, Sara thought Bob Harper was the cat's meow.

Then one evening, Vinnie Strings begged me to take him along on the surveillance and I couldn't say no because he was way down in the dumps over losing a huge bunch of money on an NFL playoff game and I was afraid to leave him alone as much as I knew that bringing Strings along on a stakeout was like wearing a sign around my neck saying *peek-a-boo*.

And, because Murphy's Law was sometimes made to be broken, taking Vinnie along paid off.

"I know him," Strings announced as we watched Harper come out of Sara Altman's apartment with Sara hanging on his arm.

Small world, I thought, though I wouldn't want to have to paint it.

"I don't know the doll," Vinnie added, "but I wouldn't want to be her father."

Vinnie knew of Harper from his Los Angeles days, where Bob had built up a reputation for quick, medium-take con games.

"He specializes in scamming unsuspecting college girls for a quick and easy grand or two," Strings said. "Gullible college girls. Then Bob stops sending flowers."

Perfect.

I took my findings to Steve Altman later that evening.

"What should I do?" he asked.

"Tell her."

"She won't buy it. She'll think it's just me, that I never believe any guy is good enough for my little girl."

I wondered where she might have got that notion.

"I have an idea that might work," I told Altman.

The following evening, I enlisted the assistance of Sonny "The Chin" Badalamenti, Joe Vongoli's son-in-law.

Sonny and I followed Harper to Sara's apartment and waited nearly two hours before they came out. Sonny moved to them very quickly and confronted Harper in front of the girl.

"I know you've been messing with my wife," Sonny said,

getting right into Bob's face, "and that you tried to take her for three thousand dollars. Don't say a word or I'll smack you."

Bob began to speak and Sonny decked him with a right uppercut. Harper sat on the ground and buttoned his lip.

"I'm giving you a chance to get lost, because I don't want to embarrass my wife. If you ever get near her again, I'll kill you," Sonny said, and then he turned to Sara. "Watch your ass, sweetheart."

Sonny walked off and Sara Altman looked down at Harper and yelled, "You bastard."

"I don't know what that maniac is talking about."

"Is that why you asked me for fifteen hundred dollars to put down on a beach house rental at Stinson Beach," Sara screamed, kicking him in the leg. "If you're not out of my sight in one minute I will call the police myself."

Harper dragged himself to his feet and quickly took off up the street.

Sonny came up beside me where I had watched the final episode from across the avenue.

"How did I do?" he asked.

"Worthy of an Emmy," I said. "Thanks."

"You're welcome," Sonny said, and disappeared into the night.

I called Steve Altman and told him to stop worrying.

He told me he owed me one.

I was hoping he would remember he'd said it.

I stood up from the bench, pulled out my cell phone, and tried reaching Altman through the Coroner's Office. I found myself trapped in a loop of automated telephone instructions that had me pushing buttons like a lab rat. Since I knew from experience where it was all headed, I cheated and pressed zero. I was rewarded for my cleverness with two words. No and no. *Is Dr. Altman in?* No. *Do you know when he might be back?* No. So much for the benefits of a live voice on the other end of the line.

A nod is as good as a wink to a blind horse.

I didn't relish the idea of calling Altman on his cell phone, fearing he might have his hands tied up examining a corpse. But I had decided on a course of action and didn't want to have to come up with Plan B. I had to do something, even if it was wrong. I was about to hit the END button after four rings when Altman answered.

"Jake Diamond. Long time," he said.

The fact that he knew who had called and still picked up was mildly encouraging.

"Steve, how are you?" I said, lamely. "How is your family? How's your daughter, Sara?"

Okay, I'll admit it, the shameless reminder.

"Everyone is fine, Jake, and you?"

"Good, Steve," I said, and then I cut to the chase. "I could use a favor."

"Can it wait several hours? I'm just finishing up at a murder scene and releasing the body to the ambulance," he said. "Roberto Sandoval. I need to do an autopsy as soon as possible and then get back to one I was working on when this call came in. I can give you a ring when I get done. It should be around three, maybe four this afternoon."

It would have to do.

"Sure, Steve, as soon as you have a minute. Thanks."

"Later," Altman said, and he was off the line.

Killing time for three or four hours was no difficult task for me. I was good at it. And there were some handy options. Some of them involved food. My whiskey headache was dissolving into serious hunger pangs.

I could cross back to the Hall of Justice and listen to a couple of hours of Hank Strode's worldview. I could grab a hotdog from the corner vendor, return to the bench, and see if the squirrel and pigeon returned for another round. I could head over to Molinari's for calamari, where Angelo Verdi could talk for hours without taking a breather, then walk the squid up to the office for a lecture from Darlene about the horrors of fried foods.

But none of these mildly promising time wasters was in the cards. With three or four hours on my hands, there was no way I could avoid Tony Carlucci any longer.

The good news, if there was any, was that I would find Tony at a place where I could get something to eat.

Mama Carlucci was true to form.

She piled a large bowl sky high with enough baked ziti and sausages to satisfy Pavarotti. I was expected to clean my plate. Tony Carlucci would not talk business, or sports for that matter, while you were still eating. I managed to finish the dish, keeping everyone happy for the moment.

A waiter who could have been a hundred and twenty years old cleared my plate and a minute later Tony appeared. He walked up to my table with two porcelain demitasse cups in one hand, a small silver pot of espresso in his other hand, and a bottle of Anisette tucked under his arm.

I was tempted to ask him for a match.

I was certain I wasn't Tony Carlucci's personal choice to get his cousin Guido's son Benny out of the jam he'd put himself in. Tony and I didn't exactly like each other. To put it politely, we were mutually ambivalent. Carlucci was no fool. He wasn't the sharpest knife in the drawer either. The sharpest knife in the Carlucci drawer was Tony's older brother John. "Johnny Boy" Carlucci called the plays from the side-lines and Tony executed them.

In John's case, the sidelines was a cell in San Quentin, where he was expected to reside for a very long time.

John had warmer feelings for me than Tony did, albeit for all the wrong reasons.

Frank Slater was a former mob lawyer who I finally identified as Jimmy Pigeon's murderer. He was also the man whose testimony put John Carlucci behind bars. Once I found Slater, I handed him to Tony Carlucci. Since that time, John Carlucci has continued giving me much more credit than I deserve.

So I knew I had been chosen by John, and the knowledge made it a little easier to sit at the table with Tony. If Tony called the shots, the man would be an impossibly scary Italian.

"So," Tony said. It was his way of initiating a meaningful conversation.

"Thanks for lunch," I said. It was my way of trying to avoid one.

"Benny didn't do it," Tony said as he poured espresso and anisette.

"I got that, Tony," I said.

"The guy's fingers were burned off. You think we teach our kids weird shit like that?"

More likely, the Carlucci family lesson plans included instructions on chopping fingers off entirely.

"Tony, I'm waiting to hear from a guy who may be able to help identify the dead man in the trunk. Lionel Katz agrees that's where we should start."

"I heard Katz bought you breakfast. You realize that greedy fuck is going to charge me for it."

I let that pass.

"What can you do while you're waiting to hear from your guy?" Tony asked.

"I'm wide open, Tony."

"Don't get cute, Diamond. You weren't exactly my first choice for the job."

Sometimes I have to admire my keen perceptions.

"I'm working on it, Tony. Give me a little time."

"Don't disappoint me, Diamond."

A horrible thought.

"Don't worry, Tony." I said, biting my tongue.

"It's my job to worry. Johnny Boy has enough to deal with handling the daily cuisine at Quentin."

Thankfully, the conversation moved to small talk as we sipped our coffee. Tony expressing his singular opinions on how the Giants would fare in the upcoming season, after the humiliating loss to the Marlins in the Division Series, and on how the Democrats could possibly think about choosing a loser like John Kerry for their candidate in November.

Before Tony Carlucci could move on to the subjects of gun control and abortion, I managed to cut loose, claiming I was very anxious to get back to work trying to clear cousin Guido's son Benny's murder charge.

I walked out onto Columbus Avenue with nothing to do but wait to hear from Dr. Steve Altman, hopefully my *ace-in-the-hole* at the morgue.

I decided I would wait it out back at the office, where no one but Darlene could catch me twiddling my thumbs.

NINE

Officer Davey Cutler was working the lobby, helping to interview residents as they entered or exited the building. Many had been questioned earlier, during the first sweep of officers doing door-to-door. Officer Winger was to collect notes from all the canvassers and check names off a list of tenants, until everyone in the building had been questioned at least once. Only Ethan Lloyd, who saw the *woman in blue* rush away from the building after midnight, had anything to contribute when interviewed on his way out in the morning—and his description of the woman had been sketchy at best.

Officer Cutler was anxiously awaiting Lloyd's return, hoping he could impress Sergeant Johnson by inducing Lloyd to come up with something more specific about the woman.

It was a few minutes after two in the afternoon when Kenny Gerard stepped up beside Cutler, pointed to a small rotund character coming into the lobby and said, "There's your man."

"Mr. Lloyd," Cutler said, swooping in like a hawk.

"I already spoke with an officer this morning, and I'm running late."

"It's important I speak with you further, sir. Often when we look at something a second time, we remember things we may have overlooked the first go around. I won't take much of your time."

"I need to run up and get the dog, before he redesigns my Persian rug again. I'll be down in a few minutes and we can talk while we walk."

Five minutes later, Cutler and Lloyd were walking the dog down Third Street toward the highway. The canine was a poodle, as short and round as his caretaker.

"Was the rug all right?" Cutler asked, trying to break the ice.

"It was unblemished today, thank heaven. A few weeks

53

ago he left a large brown circle in the upper right corner. I've been running home from the office in the middle of the day ever since to get him out in time. I can only hope if he loses it again he chooses the lower left, to maintain the integrity of the pattern."

Cutler was sorry he had asked.

"What's his name?"

"For the past two weeks I've been calling him fuck-up. How can I help you, Officer?"

"About the woman you saw last night. Is there any more you can add?"

"As I told you, I've been over this before. Long blue coat, long blue scarf, dark glasses, in a hurry."

"Try to see her again, in your head," Cutler offered, paraphrasing something Johnson had suggested. "Try closing your eyes, it might help."

"Are you going to hypnotize me next?"

"No, sir," Cutler said, attempting a smile. "Please try. Could you see her hair at all?"

"I'll close my eyes if you'll hold the dog."

"Sure," said Cutler, taking the leash.

"Reddish blonde," Lloyd said, after a moment or two. "Peeking out below the back of her scarf."

"You see, that's what I'm talking about," Cutler said, trying to restrain the dog while he scribbled notes. "Did you notice her shoes?"

Lloyd squeezed his eyes shut tighter, Cutler stifled a grin. "White, clean. Running shoes I'm guessing. New."

"Very good. Was she carrying anything?"

"Yes. It's amazing. I see it quite clearly now. A large, blue canvas bag with a long shoulder strap. There was a logo of some kind, it looked like a flower, maybe a rose," Lloyd said, opening his eyes. "That is all I recall, I did not ask to see her driver's license and I do need to get back to work."

"You've been very helpful, sir. Not everyone who have talked with has been as patient."

"I am sure they would all like to help, and I am also certain most of them are very frightened," Lloyd said, taking the leash. "Don't forget two men were murdered last night, in the place we all call home. Please try to be as patient with them as you would like them to be with you."

"Thank you for the reminder, sir."

"Good luck, Officer," Ethan Lloyd said, returning his attention to the dog. "Come along, Bonaparte."

Cutler watched the two walk off, realizing he had a lot to learn about police work and that his compact with Johnson could be the beginning of his higher education. He pulled out his cellular phone to call the Sergeant.

Cutler felt prepared to turn in his first homework assignment.

Marco Weido sat in the shade leaning against a tree in the Panhandle near Fell and Lyon Streets. Weido chewed the last bite of a Philly cheese steak from Jay's on Divisadero Street and washed it down with a long pull of Coors Light. The temperature had peaked at a record-breaking eighty-one degrees.

Weido watched a longhaired kid in torn jeans stop at a spot twenty feet away and take a guitar from a beat up case covered with decals. The kid placed the case opened at his feet and began to strum the instrument. He played a feeble imitation of a Pink Floyd song that was barely recognizable only after he began approximating the lyrics.

How I wish you were here, we're like two lost souls living in a fish bowl...

Weido took a Marlboro from a hard pack, placed it between his lips, and reached into his pants pocket.

"Fuck," he almost shouted, remembering he had misplaced his prized Zippo cigarette lighter.

Running over the same old ground, and have we found, the same old fears, wish you were here...

"Hey," Weido called.

The kid stopped singing and looked over.

"How I wish you weren't here," Weido said.

"Excuse me?"

"Go slaughter that tune somewhere else, beat it."

Weido tossed the Coors beer can and it landed in the open

guitar case. The kid looked into Weido's eyes and he was afraid of what he saw there. He took the beer can out of the case, placed in on the grass, returned the guitar to the case and turned toward Golden Gate Park.

"Hey," Weido called, stopping the kid in his tracks. "Don't fucking litter."

The kid picked up the beer can and quickly walked off as Weido's cell phone rang.

Weido knew who it was without having to look at the caller ID display.

"Warm day," he said.

"What the hell happened?"

"What you wanted to happen," Weido answered.

"A doorman was killed."

"Collateral damage. The shooter was a total fuckup. I gave him the access code for the parking garage, but the idiot decided to walk right in through the lobby."

"Jesus. Where did you find the guy?"

"You don't find these guys on fucking Craig's List. And they don't come with letters of recommendation. You get what you pay for."

"And if he fucks up again, gets pinched and decides to talk?"

"He's not talking to anyone anymore. I picked him up after he hit Sandoval and before he realized I wasn't reaching into my pocket for his payoff, I put a bullet into his ear. It was your brilliant idea to use an outside man. I told you I would take care of Sandoval myself, and then I wouldn't have had to deal with ditching a body."

"What about the body?"

"I took everything that could possibly ID him, wallet, jewelry, all of it. Then I dumped him in the trunk of the vehicle, after dipping his fingers into a jar of sulfuric acid."

"Why in God's name would you do that?"

"It'll take longer to ID him. Give the evidence guys a challenge. They get lazy and complacent at times."

"You carry a jar of sulfuric acid around with you?"

"Not all the time."

"What about the weapon?"

"I left the weapon in the trunk with him. I ditched the car under the James Lick."

"What if they connect the gun to Sandoval's murder?"

"Why would anyone even think of it? And besides, what does it have to do with me or you or the price of beans?"

"Whose car was it?"

"Some yahoo left a Cadillac running in front of a news stand on Masonic. I jumped in and drove off."

"Have they found the vehicle?"

"Yes, they did, and this will tickle you. A member of the Carlucci family was behind the wheel. I left the keys and the luckless bastard took the car for a joy ride."

"It will be much more than ticklish if the Carluccis ever connect us to it."

"I told you, no one is connecting anything to anyone, unless there's something you're not telling me. Is there?"

"Keep me informed."

Marco Weido made a highlighted mental note that the question had been ignored.

"I certainly will," Weido said.

It took Sergeant Rocky Johnson all of five minutes in an interrogation room with Benny Carlucci to feel convinced Lieutenant Lopez's assessment had been correct.

Benny might be a Carlucci, but he was not one of "The Family" and the scared kid at the interrogation table was definitely no murderer. All that connected Carlucci to the corpse in the trunk of the Caddy was incredible bad luck.

Benny nervously told Johnson everything he could recall from the night before. He claimed he was literally thrown out of the Chieftain Irish Pub after midnight and he stumbled upon the car some time later. He added there were three teenagers further down on Third Street who might have seen him get into the vehicle.

Johnson told Benny to try and relax and he would check it out. He assured Benny he would clear it up as soon as possible, and the kid might possibly be released on bail in time for lunch the next day.

If the kid was innocent, then someone else was guilty. So before following up on Benny's alibis, Johnson opted to see the Medical Examiner about the victim.

Johnson found Steve Altman at the morgue, leaning over the body of Roberto Sandoval.

"I just started," Altman said. "I can't tell you any more than what I suspected at the scene."

"I'm actually here about the fellow they found in the trunk."

"Mind if I work while we talk?" Altman asked, reaching for a scalpel.

"Go for it," Johnson said.

"The gentleman in the trunk was shot once in the ear, certainly died instantly. He hasn't been identified yet. The condition of his fingers is slowing down the process. The fingertips were mutilated post-mortem, which is either a strong hunch or my reluctance to envision it otherwise. They will eventually get something to work with, and then it will be a question of finding the prints on file somewhere. The body's on that gurney," Altman said, pointing it out to the Sergeant. "Personal effects are laid out on the adjoining table."

Johnson walked over to the gurney and he uncovered the victim's head. A thirty-eight caliber bullet hole through the victim's ear had done considerable damage. From what he'd learned from the forensic report on the vehicle, there was enough blood on the passenger seat and passenger window to alert anyone except a very drunk car thief like Carlucci. There were a number of different prints lifted, not yet all identified. The owner of the Cadillac had been located and questioned and reported the vehicle had been lifted out front of a newsstand, well before midnight—another fact that would most likely help Benny Carlucci's chances of exoneration, at least on the murder rap.

Johnson moved to the table and he looked down at the personal effects of the dead man.

Pants, shirt, underwear, socks, shoes, no wallet, no jewelry, no money, no keys.

Nothing.

"That's all they found on the guy?" Johnson asked, moving back to Altman.

"And the thirty-eight Special. They found it in the trunk with him," Altman said. "Recently fired."

"Oh?" Johnson said, hearing about the weapon found in the vehicle for the first time. "Where is the gun now?"

"It was sent down to ballistics. Maybe they can ID him through a firearm registration."

"That would be too easy."

"Somebody definitely went the extra mile to challenge us with the identification. I'll give you a phone call as soon as I know something more about Sandoval and the doorman."

"Call Lieutenant Lopez," Johnson said. "It's not my case anymore."

"Lopez took it over? Why would she?"

"Thanks for your time," Johnson said as he left the room, wondering the same thing.

Why would she?

Lieutenant Laura Lopez decided she needed to run. She drove back to the Vallejo Street Station to change into her jogging gear. It would be hours before all of the evidence collected in the lobby, and in Sandoval's apartment, would be put into a meaningful report. Altman was still working on the bodies. All they had was approximate times of death and the sighting of a woman leaving the building at roughly the same time, a woman who could not be clearly identified by the sole witness. Lopez had been summoned to meet with District Attorney Liam Duffey in his office at four and she knew what she could expect. The pressure from the Mayor's Office would have the D.A. frantic for a quick resolution. Sandoval was heir apparent to Duffey's throne, and Duffey had his eyes set on the Mayor's seat. Lopez did not look forward to going in to see Duffey with nothing to contribute. Rather than worry about it, Lopez slipped into a green running suit and her new running shoes, dropped two bottles of water into a canvas shoulder bag, and headed out of the station for a long jog in Golden Gate Park.

. . .

Officer Davey Cutler had been unable to reach Johnson by phone, so he decided to run over to Vallejo Street and try to catch the Sergeant at the station. As he turned toward the entrance, he caught sight of a woman walking away from the spot where he stood. Strawberry blond hair, tied back in a ponytail, bright white running shoes, carrying a blue canvas bag strapped over her shoulder.

Davey Cutler moved quickly and came up behind her.

"Excuse me," he called.

The woman turned, surprised to find an officer there.

Cutler noticed an embroidered rose on the shoulder bag before he looked up at her face.

"Officer Cutler, isn't it?" Lieutenant Lopez said.

"Yes, Lieutenant, thank you for remembering me. I'm sorry if I startled you."

"You're the one who appears a little startled. Can I help you with something?"

"No. Yes. I was wondering if you knew where Sergeant Johnson was."

"Anything I should know about, Officer?"

"No. Lieutenant. He asked me to give him a hand with the case he's working on."

"The Carlucci case?"

Carlucci? Davey almost said aloud. *The* Carlucci?

"Yes, I believe that's the one."

"Last I heard Johnson was down at the morgue, touching base with Dr. Altman."

"Thanks, Lieutenant, I'm sorry to have bothered you."

"No problem," Lopez said as she turned away, wondering why the kid looked like he had seen a ghost.

Darlene Roman was through waiting for the phone on her desk to ring.

She had spent the best part of the day sitting in the office alone, without Jake or the dog to talk to.

She had gone over the *Examiner*, cover-to-cover, and it was mostly bad news.

The crossword puzzle only made her feel more useless.

She had creatively juggled with the company finances, and was feeling fairly confident her ingenuity would hold off the creditors until the first of the month.

If the deadbeats who owed Diamond Investigations for services rendered all came through any time in the near future, they might manage to remain solvent until the beginning of May.

The phone had remained silent. No millionaire called, offering a fortune to find a missing son. No bank magnates called to offer bags of cash to discover who at the branch was embezzling funds. No furious wife called, offering to empty out her husband's savings account to find out who the bastard was sleeping with. And Jake hadn't called all day, although Darlene thought no news might be good news if it had anything to do with Tony Carlucci.

Darlene had told Jake she would be leaving the office early and she felt it was about time she did just that.

When Officer Cutler reached the morgue, he discovered he had missed Sergeant Johnson.

Again.

It was his first visit there, and he found it creepy as hell. Not the mention the aromas, which threatened to reintroduce him to his lunch.

Dr. Altman was busy, but, as usual, he was willing to chat while he worked.

"Is it true the Sergeant is working on a case involving the Carlucci family?" Cutler asked.

Davey Cutler was both thrilled and terrified about the possibility of getting invited onboard *that* roller coaster. He avoided watching Altman cut on Sandoval and he strolled around the large, brightly lit room. He stopped in front of a table covered with men's clothing.

"Johnson walked out of here fairly convinced the Carlucci kid didn't kill anyone," Altman said. "Johnson is off checking the kid's alibi. What you're looking at, by the way, are the effects of the dead guy the Carlucci kid was chauffeuring around, whether the kid knew it or not."

Davey Cutler had no clue as to what Altman was talking about.

"Nice shoes," Cutler said, lifting one off the table.

"Don't touch anything," Altman said.

Cutler quickly replaced the shoe. As he did, a small piece of notepaper slipped out of the shoe onto the table.

There were four numbers written on the paper.

2253.

Followed by a pound sign.

TEN

I made it back to the office from lunch at Carlucci's Restaurant without incident.

Darlene had high-tailed it for the day. It was a blessing perhaps. I was spared in depth commentary regarding my spicy Italian sausage induced complexion.

I had nothing to do but wait for the Medical Examiner, Steve Altman, to phone. I settled into my ergonomic desk chair and I picked up the sad tale of Quasimodo where I had left off. The homely bell ringer was having a bad day.

One of the hunchback's many problems, a dilemma not uncommon before or since, was looking up to a flawed dad.

As an abandoned, deformed child, Quasimodo had been adopted and raised by Claude Frollo, Archdeacon of Notre Dame Cathedral in Paris.

After setting his eyes upon the gypsy girl, Esmeralda, all of Frollo's righteousness went straight out the window. The Archdeacon recruits Quasimodo to help kidnap Esmeralda and when the attempt is thwarted by Phoebus and the King's Archers, Frollo remains hidden and leaves Quasimodo to take the rap. Quasimodo is put to the torture wheel and Frollo joins the jeering crowd in condemnation.

Nice role model.

Steve Altman phoned just as Esmeralda was giving the hunchback a drink of water at the wheel, and Quasimodo in turn made her an offer of protection I had a feeling he might one day come to regret.

"Sorry to keep you waiting, Jake," Altman said. "I've been tied up all day. I can give you a few minutes. How can I help you?"

"Benny Carlucci. He was picked up in a stolen car with a corpse in the trunk and he's looking at a murder rap. Tony Carlucci has the misguided notion I'm the man to fix it up. I'm hoping you could help me get started with some

63

information about the deceased."

"Don't worry about it, Jake."

I wanted to say, *I won't, thanks, have a nice day.*

"Oh?" I said instead.

"Sergeant Johnson dropped in to see me earlier. He's still checking out a few things, but seems convinced the Carlucci kid simply chose the wrong Cadillac to steal. The kid should be out of the slammer by morning, latest."

"You've made my day, Steve."

"Of course, he still has grand theft auto and driving under the influence to contend with. I hope Tony Carlucci doesn't expect you to fix that."

"So do I, Steve. So do I."

"If there's nothing else, I'm elbow deep in the remains of Roberto Sandoval."

I tried not to picture it.

"Why is Johnson on the Benny Carlucci case?" I asked. God knows why. "I would have guessed he'd be all over the Sandoval homicide."

"Lopez cut him loose."

"Trouble in paradise?" I asked, knowing Lopez and Johnson were like two peas in a pod.

"Couldn't say."

Okay.

"I'll let you go, Steve. Thanks for the good news."

Joey Vongoli walked into the office just as I replaced the telephone receiver.

"I'm off the hook with Tony," I said. "I think."

"How did you work it out so fast?"

"It worked itself out. I'm waiting on the final word."

"Take the credit anyhow," Joey suggested. "It never hurts to score points with Johnny Boy and Tony Carlucci."

"I wonder if it might be better if they didn't have so much faith in me."

"Did you remember to have lunch?"

"Yes. Plenty of lunch. But I could drink some George Dickel for dessert."

"Bourbon? After what you did to yourself last night?"

"It might be the only cure."

"Did you drive down here?"

"No. Couldn't find the car keys this morning."

"I'll give you a ride home and have a quick drink with you. Then I recommend you get some rest. And tomorrow you can start the day with a hug and a kiss from a grateful Tony Carlucci."

"I can hardly wait."

We settled in the kitchen at my house in the Presidio and Joey stayed for a few drinks. We steered clear of any talk of Carlucci's appreciation, and addressed the subject of the Giants instead.

Joey Clams' beloved Giants had blown the World Series to the Angels in 2002 and Joey was still bitter a year-and-a-half later. Joey was always quick to suggest where Mike Scioscia could shove the rally monkey.

Joey reminded me I was invited to join him for the Giants' home opener, less than four weeks off. An annual tradition.

"Any chance of getting an extra ticket for Vinnie?" I asked. "Strings is always depressed for days after we go to an opening day game without him."

"As a matter of fact, I scored four seats. We'll take Sonny *and* Vinnie along," Joey said, glancing at his watch. "Jesus, I have to run. I'll be late picking Angela up at her hairdresser. My wife finds one gray hair on her head and she acts like she's seen a mouse. Give Lionel Katz a call. Carlucci's mouthpiece can handle it from here."

With that, Joey Clams was out the door.

I called Katz with the glad tidings.

I moved into the living room, settled into my well-worn armchair, and opened the Victor Hugo paperback.

Quasimodo, indebted to the gypsy girl Esmeralda for bringing him water to quench his thirst, promises to give her sanctuary at the cathedral if ever the need arose.

Kind of like a *get out of jail free* Monopoly card.

I hoped Lionel Katz would have one handy for Benny in the morning.

And I felt thankful I might get out of this one without

having to play the *you tell me what you know and I'll tell you what I know* game with Lieutenant Lopez or Sergeant Johnson.

After reading a few pages, I became distracted. I found myself looking around the room I was in. I was still not quite accustomed to living in the large house, with its spectacular vista of the Golden Gate, after nearly a year.

Nearly a year since I had moved into the house Sally French and I had shared before our marriage fell apart.

Almost a year since I had courted my ex-wife like a teenage kid with a schoolboy crush.

Nearly a year since Sally died in an explosion, a booby-trapped bomb meant for yours truly, and I found out, when her last will and testament was read, she had left the large house to me.

The house often reminded me of Sally.

Memories both pleasant and painful.

As I surveyed the living room I felt my eyes getting blurry and I closed them. And, as I found out some hours later when the screaming telephone summoned me to St. Mary's Hospital, I fell asleep in the chair.

ELEVEN

Norman Hall took another look at his wristwatch. If he didn't get moving, he would be late for the appointment with his parole officer. As much as he wanted to stay, he was forced to miss watching Darlene Roman complete the last few laps of her run through Buena Vista Park.

If he was lucky, maybe he could watch her sitting on her front porch later that evening.

Norman wondered if Darlene Roman would like him when they finally met. Like him as much as he liked her.

And again he wondered where the mutt was, and how much more relaxed and pleasant his first personal encounter with Darlene Roman would be without the dog underfoot.

So, what are you waiting for, Norman? he thought.

The thought brought on a grin.

Norman Hall gave Darlene a loving parting glance and headed out for the street.

A few minutes after Norman left the park, a woman came up from behind Darlene and began running alongside.

"I wish this was as easy as you make it look," the woman said.

Darlene turned to the woman as they continued jogging side by side.

She was very attractive and in good physical shape, close to Darlene's age and appeared non-threatening.

"I've been at it for a while," Darlene said.

"How often do you run?"

"Four or five times a week."

"I'm a beginner. I'll be lucky if I can walk after today," she said, straining to keep up with Darlene.

"You'll build up your stamina before long," Darlene assured her. "Where's your water bottle?"

"Water bottle?"

"You need to carry water. It's extremely important. You

need to avoid dehydration," Darlene said as she began slowing down to a brisk walk. "Let's stop in the shade and take a drink before you overdo it."

They gradually came to a stop under a large tree and Darlene passed the woman her water bottle.

"Drink slowly," she said.

The woman took a long, slow drink and she passed the bottle back to Darlene.

"Thanks." She pulled a printed card from the pocket of her running shorts and handed it to Darlene.

"Megan Nico..."

"Nicolace. Rhymes with Liberace. It's Italian."

"Was Liberace Italian?"

"I doubt it."

"Darlene Roman. It's international."

"I wonder if you could do me a huge favor, Darlene."

"I'd have to know more before I could say."

"Can we walk and talk for a while? I can tell you how you can help me and you can decide if you're game."

Darlene took another look at Megan's business card and then a quick look around the park. Buena Vista was teeming with people enjoying the unseasonably warm day.

"Sure," Darlene said, taking a drink before recapping the water bottle. "We can walk and talk for a while."

Marco Weido knocked off the last can of the six-pack of Coors Light on his way back to his apartment in Oakland to shower and change for his meeting at four-fifteen.

The clock above the recliner in his living room told him he had lots of time. The La-Z-Boy looked very inviting.

After one more beer from the refrigerator and a few Marlboros, Weido leaned the chair back as far as it would go and was promptly asleep.

Detective Sergeant Roxton Johnson of the San Francisco Police Department sat silently behind the steering wheel of an unmarked motor pool vehicle parked on Third Street below

Interstate 80. Johnson gazed out across Third, to the spot where Benny Carlucci claimed he had come upon the abandoned Cadillac the night before.

He imagined he might simply cross the street and find something, in plain sight, which would clearly identify the villain who had left the vehicle sitting there with a dead body in the trunk.

Johnson imagined, as he crossed the street, that one or two or three teenagers would suddenly materialize to report to him that *yes, we saw a drunk guy climb into the Cadillac and drive away and, yes, the car had been sitting there for a while before the drunk stumbled along and, by the way, if you'd like a detailed description of the cat who dumped the Cadillac there in the first place and hurried away up Third Street back toward Market Street, Sergeant, all you need to do is ask.*

Johnson thought about his wife.

Amy would be in Philadelphia until Sunday evening. He was thinking about how much he would prefer to be dining on her meatloaf and mashed potatoes—complaining about the Golden State Warriors and confessing to her how much he had really missed her—than to be sitting in an unmarked police car underneath the highway entertaining fantasies of clear logical solutions to muddy senseless crimes.

Johnson glanced at his watch. He'd been sitting there in the car, daydreaming, for nearly thirty minutes.

The realization unsettled him.

As he climbed from the car, he thought about the white envelope in the plastic evidence bag peeking out of Lopez's jacket pocket, and he felt a queasiness in his stomach that even meatloaf and mashed potatoes smothered in gravy with a couple of bottles of Samuel Adams Boston Lager on the side wouldn't soothe.

He found no critical evidence on the pavement.

He met no adolescents with case-breaking news.

And Johnson was standing there trying to rationalize Lopez's behavior, with no luck at all, when Officer Cutler finally reached him on the cell phone.

Cutler was excited, trying to spill it all out at once over the telephone. He was talking so quickly Johnson couldn't follow him.

The roar of the traffic from the highway above didn't help. Johnson cut him off abruptly.

"Meet me at the Chieftain Irish Pub on Howard Street," Johnson said. "You can tell me everything you discovered over a bottle or two of Sam Adams."

If it takes that long to tell, Johnson left unsaid.

As Johnson turned back toward his car he caught sight of something on the ground. Something shining. He moved to it, reached down and picked it up. It was a Zippo lighter. He placed it into his jacket pocket and he crossed to the unmarked police vehicle. He headed over to the Chieftain to meet Officer Cutler.

The Hall of Justice in San Francisco is a seven-story L-shaped concrete building erected in 1958 and taking up a large portion of the city block bordered by Seventh Street and Harriet Street, west and east.

The main entrance sits on Bryant Street, on the south side. The north side of the building rests up against the Interstate 80 overpass known as the James Lick Skyway.

The building houses the police department's Southern Station and administration, patrol and investigative headquarters, criminal courts and the offices for prosecutors, probation officers and medical examiners.

The top two floors are home to more than eight hundred inmates, including, that particular afternoon, Benny Carlucci.

Eighteen hundred city employees work in the building each day and another fourteen hundred citizens visit.

The structure has for some time been cited as a place you do not want to be during an earthquake. Geological experts claimed that a minor quake could split the structure at the corner of the L, where the police administrative offices and the parole offices as well as some of the criminal courtrooms were located.

Lieutenant Laura Lopez could have ignored all of these

seismic concerns, and been perfectly at ease strolling into the Hall of Justice, if her presence had not necessitated a visit to the office of Liam Duffey.

The lieutenant had rushed to the Hall of Justice after an invigorating run through Golden Gate Park, followed by a very long, cold shower.

The lieutenant felt clean and refreshed, but wondered how long the feeling would last. As she climbed the stairs to the third floor, her sense of wellbeing was beginning to wane already.

Lopez was not looking forward to the meeting with the San Francisco District Attorney.

On top of that, Lopez was very worried about Sergeant Johnson. She knew the sergeant would not let her forget the envelope she had slipped into her jacket pocket at Roberto Sandoval's apartment.

Not because Johnson was interested in busting her for improper police procedure, but because the sergeant really cared about her and was honestly concerned.

Sergeant Johnson was an extremely competent partner and a good man, but Lopez feared that in this particular case, his admirable qualities might prove problematic.

Lopez walked into the District Attorney's office a few minutes before four in the afternoon. Lopez was cheerfully greeted by a young woman who she had never seen before, but who looked much like the four or five cute, perky girls who had occupied the same seat in the six years Duffey had held the office.

Lieutenant Lopez understood why Duffey might like the type. His wife was a former Miss California Pageant third runner-up and even now, pushing forty, Charlotte Bradford Duffey could have easily slipped behind the desk and been mistaken for any one of her husband's parade of adorable receptionists.

And, knowing a little about Liam Duffey's character, Lopez might also venture a guess as to why this position boasted such a high turnover rate.

The current incarnation flashed a broad smile exposing perfect bone white choppers.

"Mr. Duffey is expecting you, Lieutenant," the girl said. "Please go right in."

Lopez entered the D.A.'s inner sanctum to find Duffey peering through his large office window out toward the bay.

Duffey turned from the window and invited her to take a seat. He remained standing as Lopez settled into one of the two plush chairs facing his desk, and then he began to pace back and forth behind the enormous piece of furniture. He finally stopped moving, placed both of his hands on the back of the large burgundy leather desk chair that was his throne, and he began to speak without inflection.

"There is not much I could say about the fervor caused by Roberto Sandoval's murder last night that you could not guess yourself, Lieutenant. From the Commissioner's office to City Hall to every news desk in town," Duffey said. "So, why don't you talk and I'll listen."

Though Lopez was accustomed to Duffey's arrogance, and was long past being offended or intimidated by the man, she still found herself, from time to time, fighting the fierce urge to slap the pompous smirk off his face. If Duffey had addressed her as Laura, as he sometimes did, she might have lost the battle this particular afternoon.

Fleeting thoughts of simple diplomatic disclaimers ran through Lopez's head, such as *don't take this personally* or *I'm just covering the bases*, but she decided if Duffey was inclined to take offense, who was she to inhibit him.

Duffey had invited her to talk.

Lopez would oblige.

"Sandoval's body was discovered only four hours ago," she began. "The doorman was found earlier. We are guessing it was the same perp. The autopsy reports and the forensic findings are pending. The tenants are being questioned, so far nothing vital. I've been dodging reporters since noon, and trying to organize my protocol. I haven't been able to speak with Sandoval's wife. She is running around somewhere in Italy. I have no answers, only questions. So I thought I would begin right here, where Sandoval worked. I am hoping you can help me out."

"Me? How?"

"I understand you were one of the last people to see Sandoval alive."

"Well, I suppose you could say that."

I did say that, Lopez thought, as she flipped through the pages of a pocket-sized notepad that suddenly appeared in her hand.

"We spoke to the cab driver who drove Roberto Sandoval home from the Omni Hotel last night. He said you gave Sandoval a firm handshake and what the cabbie referred to as a bear hug before Sandoval got into the taxi."

"A bear hug?"

"Just quoting, sir. I wrote it down. Give me a second and I can find it."

"The fundraiser was a great success. Roberto charmed the entire congregation. My impulse, which the taxi driver so colorfully described, was celebratory in nature. It was a show of congratulations."

Lopez tried imagining the grandson of Irish immigrants and the grandson of Mexican immigrants wrapped up in a warm embrace. She was having trouble picturing the scene.

"I expected your visit this afternoon would be more a progress report than an interrogation," Duffey added.

"Don't be silly," Lopez said, feeling silly saying it. "I need a little information to help me get started. Maybe it would be more comfortable and more informal if you took a seat. I won't take much of your time, and the sooner we get through this, the sooner I can get back on the job."

"Fine," the District Attorney said, as he reluctantly settled into his desk chair. "What do you need to know?"

"How did Sandoval seem last evening?"

"How did he seem?"

"You indicated the event was very successful, in that it raised a worthy amount of money for the Crossroads Irish American Festival or in that it was good for Roberto Sandoval's campaign for this office?"

"Well, both actually. Those goals need not be mutually exclusive, Lieutenant."

"Of course not," Lopez granted. "And you appeared, by your actions outside the taxicab, to be exuberant over both outcomes."

"Very pleased, yes."

"Did Sandoval seem as pleased?"

"Why wouldn't he be?"

"I guess what I am asking is did he seem preoccupied with thoughts which may have dulled his enthusiasm? Did he seem to have something other than the great success of the evening's festivities on his mind? Did there seem to be something troubling him?"

"Your inquiry calls for a good deal of speculation, so I'll speculate," he said, with an air of condescension that had Lopez wishing she hadn't asked. "With hope it will lead to a line of questioning with more probative value."

Lopez flashed her most ingenuous smile.

"It's my hope as well, sir. Please bear with me."

"Roberto Sandoval *seemed* at ease the entire evening. He *seemed* to genuinely enjoy the occasion. If there was something distracting or distressing on his mind, it was not evident."

Wow, thought Lopez, *if you looked up "lawyer" in the encyclopedia there would be a picture of Liam Duffey with the same smug look on his face.*

"How about recently, the past few weeks or months, could you say if there was anything troubling him?"

"You need to be more specific."

"Were there any problems in his personal life?"

"Although I liked and respected Roberto a great deal, I didn't know much about his personal life. I've met his lovely wife on a few occasions, but beyond that we did not spend much time socially."

"Would you say he had a happy marriage?"

"I have no opinion whatsoever about their matrimonial state."

It was unusual that there was anything Duffey had *no* opinion about.

"What about his work here? Was he troubled or having problems with a case he was prosecuting, or preparing for trial?"

"Roberto Sandoval was a very competent and confident prosecutor. He avoided problems with diligent preparation and faultless execution."

Getting answers from Duffey was like pulling teeth.

Lopez pictured a large pair of pliers in her hand, but she quickly shook the image off.

"Have any felons Sandoval successfully prosecuted been released from prison recently?"

"I couldn't say off-hand. I would have to look into that."

"Please do. I'm looking for a motive—it really helps move an investigation along. I would appreciate everything you can provide concerning Sandoval's current cases and all you can find out about convicts he put away who may be back out on the street," Lopez said, rising from her seat. "As soon as possible."

"Where are you going?"

"I need to get back to Sandoval's apartment building, to check on how the canvassing is going. There will be a good number of tenants returning home from their work day soon who haven't been questioned yet."

"I was hoping you could stay a while longer. I wanted you to meet someone," Duffey said, checking his wall clock. "He's running late, but he should be here very soon."

"Some other time."

"But it's important. You will be working very closely with him on this case."

"Oh?"

"My new lead investigator. A decorated homicide detective we were very lucky to lure away from the Oakland Police Department. This investigation will need to be a joint effort, of your department and our investigative division. All information gathered will be shared, openly. I don't want any compromised evidence getting in the way of nailing whoever did this to Roberto Sandoval."

"Have you ever known me to compromise evidence?"

"No, but it's best to be doubly safe."

"It's not how I work. I use my own people."

"It is how you will work on this case, Lieutenant. So please wait a few more minutes to meet your partner."

"I really need to go. Have him meet me at my office tomorrow at noon. He and I can bond over a pastrami sandwich. Please send me the material I requested, at least as much as you can put together by that time."

"Talk to my secretary. She can help you with what you need."

Lopez quickly turned and left the office.

Duffey looked up at the wall clock and cursed his lead investigator's lack of punctuality.

Lopez stopped at the front desk and told the new girl what she wanted.

"Also, do you have a record of Mr. Sandoval's appointments in the past few weeks?" Lopez asked.

"Yes. At least any related to his work here."

"Please send that information also."

The term "wildly enthusiastic" would not come close to describing Officer Davey Cutler's condition. He was sitting on a bar stool in the Chieftain Irish Pub with his back to the bartender, staring intensely at the front entrance, as if expecting notification that he was the latest ten million dollar winner of the Publishers Clearinghouse Sweepstakes.

When Sergeant Johnson finally entered the bar, Davey nearly jumped out of his skin. He then froze, unable to decide whether to hop off the stool and meet Johnson half-way, or wait for the sergeant to reach him. Johnson solved the dilemma by waving Davey over to a booth in a far corner of the saloon.

Cutler slid onto the bench seat across from Johnson and tried speaking immediately. Johnson cut him off at the pass.

"Hold that thought," the sergeant said.

Johnson captured the attention of a girl carrying a busing tray. She wore cutoff jeans and a Golden Warriors T-shirt that was high and tight. He held up two fingers, much like a peace sign, and she skipped over to the bar. Watching her move, Davey forgot for a moment why he was there.

"Okay," Johnson said, bringing Cutler around. "What do you know?"

Davey's eagerness and enthusiasm kicked back in full-throttle.

"I accidentally found this," Cutler said, opening his right hand to reveal a slip of paper he had been clutching for more than thirty minutes. It sat in his palm looking as if it had been pulled through a straw.

"Accidentally?"

"I was down at the morgue, looking for you, and picked up a shoe belonging to the guy they found dead in the trunk of the Cadillac last night. And this fell out."

Davey was trying to unravel the paper and smooth it out flat on the table in front of him as he spoke.

"And you accidentally removed it from evidence?" Johnson asked.

The wind went out of Cutler's sails and he would have capsized and went under if Johnson hadn't rescued him with a broad smile.

"Just don't make a habit of it," Johnson said, picking up the slip of paper and giving it a quick glance.

2253#.

"Okay, I give up," the sergeant said.

"It's the access code to the parking garage of the building where the doorman and Mr. Sandoval were killed."

"Are you serious?"

"He looks totally serious," the waitress said, suddenly appearing with two bottles of Sam Adams Boston Lager. "Do you care for anything else, Sergeant," she added, talking to Johnson but looking straight at Officer Cutler.

"We're good, Amanda. Thanks."

She set the bottles down and bounced off.

Johnson was emptying the contents of his pockets onto the table looking for his cell phone. He took a drink of beer and invited Cutler to do the same.

"Don't know if I should be drinking on duty, sir," Davey said.

"Just don't make a habit of it."

Johnson pulled out a ring of keys, a money-clip, a Zippo lighter, and finally the cellular phone.

Sergeant Johnson punched in a phone number he knew from memory.

"Ballistics, Yeatman speaking."

"Tommy, Rocky Johnson here, did you get anything on the thirty-eight they pulled out of the trunk of the Cadillac?"

"All I can tell you is it wasn't the thirty-eight that put one in the victim's ear."

"What about prints?"

"I don't know prints. Check with Gordon or Beggs in forensics. They went over the gun before it came over to us—and the Cadillac inside and out."

"Okay, I need a favor. Could you check the piece against the bullet that killed Sandoval?"

"Wow, Rocky. Some kind of wild hunch?"

"Sort of. And I would like to keep it between us for the time being."

"It may take a while."

"Let me know as soon as you can. I'll owe you one."

"One like the other two or three you already owe me?"

"Yeah, like those, Tommy. Thanks."

"Don't mention it," Yeatman said, "and I won't."

The call ended.

Johnson placed the phone down and turned his attention to Cutler.

The movements in Cutler's shoulders, arms and hands could only be described as *fidgeting.*

"What?" asked Johnson.

"There's something else," Cutler choked out.

"What?" Johnson repeated.

"It's probably nothing. I'm reluctant to even bring it up."

"If you are done with the disclaimer, Cutler, please spit it out."

"I talked with Ethan Lloyd again, the dog walker, did what you asked, tried to jog his memory about the woman he saw in front of the apartment building last night."

"And?"

"I got him to flesh out his description."

"Cutler, don't torture me."

"Reddish blond hair, white running shoes, looked new, long strapped shoulder bag with an embroidered flower logo, maybe a rose."

"Well, that's a needle in a smaller haystack."

Cutler couldn't keep his hands still.

"What is it, Cutler?" Johnson had to ask. "You look like the cat that ate the Mercedes key."

"That's not all of it," Davey said.

"Oh?" said Johnson, trying to get Amanda's attention for another round of beers.

"Alright, here goes," said Davey Cutler, taking a deep breath. "I saw a woman outside the Vallejo Street Station earlier today. Strawberry blond hair, clean white running shoes, a shoulder bag with an embroidered rose. I came up behind her and she turned to me. It was Lieutenant Lopez."

"I am going to forget you said that, Cutler, and I would really like you to do the same. Terrific work on the parking garage connection. It could be a break in the case. I think we've done enough for one day. I'll give you a yell tomorrow morning and we can pick it up from here."

"Sure, Sergeant, thanks," said Cutler, gracefully accepting the dismissal.

Davey watched as Johnson peeled a twenty dollar bill from his money-clip, dropped it onto the table, and began gathering all of the items he had pulled out of his pockets earlier.

"Were you OPD before San Francisco?" Cutler asked.

"Come again."

"The cigarette lighter. The OPD inscription. That's an Oakland Police Department logo."

"I'll call you in the morning," Johnson said, slipping the lighter into his pocket, quickly rising and heading for the exit.

"What scared him off?" asked Amanda, showing up at the table with two more beers.

Cutler looked away from Johnson and up into Amanda's sky blue eyes. Suddenly, cigarette lighters and shoulder bags were the furthest things from Davey Cutler's mind.

On the other hand, a Zippo lighter and an embroidered shoulder bag was all Johnson could think about as he walked out onto Howard Street.

Darlene Roman and Megan Nicolace stood side by side on the western edge of Buena Vista Park. Darlene was pointing across the avenue and up Frederick Street.

"That's it," Darlene said. "It's the third house on the left."

"Very nice," Megan said. "You must enjoy being so close to the park."

"Love it, so does McGraw."

"Boyfriend?"

"Best friend. Four legs, long sloppy tongue, a tail that won't quit."

"Protective?"

"Very protective when near," Darlene replied. "He's away until Sunday, gets to spend the weekend at the beach. Do you want to come in for a cold drink?"

"Thanks, but I need to be somewhere. Keep what we talked about in mind."

"It won't be difficult."

"And you have all my phone numbers, don't hesitate for a moment."

"Roger that."

"Thanks."

"Thank you," Darlene said, and started across Buena Vista Park Avenue West toward her house.

Nicolace watched Darlene until she entered the house, and then she took a seat on a bench in the park and she watched the house for quite a while longer.

"Dr. Shepherd."

The doctor turned to the voice.

A young nurse, Jessica Sanders, moving quickly down the hall.

"Your mugging victim is awake. The police want to have a word with him," Jessica said. "I told them they still had to wait for your okay."

"Good. Did he say who walked all over him?"

"Nope."

"Shy boy?" asked the doctor.

"Not shy at all. He wasn't conscious two minutes before he began hitting on me like a ping-pong paddle. Sounds like he picked up most of his lines from a dime novel. When I squeezed in a question about what happened to him, he answered in three words."

"Which were?" asked Shepherd.

"Call Jake Diamond."

TWELVE

The first ring of the telephone woke me.

The phone had lately become a very effective means of delivering me from dreamland. At least as efficient as the alarm clock, if not as predictable—and instead of being greeted by a ceiling projection of large green numerals ticking off the remaining moments of my life, I found myself surrounded by some of my favorite things.

Camel cigarettes, George Dickel bourbon, and classic French literature close at hand.

By the third ring I was done romanticizing and picked up the receiver.

The caller identified herself as Dr. Justine Shepherd of St. Mary's Hospital, hoping to reach Jake Diamond.

I reluctantly admitted she had succeeded.

Dr. Shepherd called to inform me that a young man had been admitted to the Emergency Room with multiple bruises, lacerations and a fractured rib. The apparent victim of a serious beating inflicted by fists and pointy shoes.

Upon arrival, the victim had been heavily sedated and treated. He had finally regained consciousness.

When asked about the circumstances leading up to his landing in the hospital, the victim refused to elucidate.

Instead he asked that I be notified.

"Does the victim have a name?" I asked Dr. Shepherd.

"Vincent Stradivarius."

"I'll be right down."

I hopped in and out of the shower, threw a suit over a fresh, clean, wrinkled shirt, and I drove the Toyota out to St. Mary's.

I had tried to reach Darlene, settling for her answering machine.

I located Dr. Shepherd and she escorted me to Vinnie's room. Two SFPD uniforms stood outside the door impatiently waiting their turn.

Vinnie Strings attempted a smile as he watched me move to his bedside.

"What happened, Vin?"

"I fell, Jake."

"Like out of a third floor window?" I asked. "Or like under the wheels of a streetcar?"

Vinnie was a mess.

"It's nothing, Jake. Don't worry about it. I'm fine."

"Humor me, Vinnie. I was having a really good dream when the hospital called."

"Nothing, Jake, honest," Vinnie repeated. "I'm just really glad you came down."

And that was it. Vinnie Strings could stonewall with the best of them. If he didn't want to tell me who or what trampled all over him, he wasn't going to. He looked very pathetic so I decided he didn't need to be beat up further.

"Can I get you anything?" I asked.

"I could eat a horse."

"I'll run down and check the stable," I said, and left to look for something Vinnie might be able to chew.

Dr. Shepherd followed me out of the room.

"Can we talk with your patient, doctor?" a police officer asked.

She gave me a quick glance and got the message.

"Not yet," she said. "I'll let you know as soon as he is ready to answer questions."

"Thanks," I said as we walked down the hall.

"The food in the cafeteria isn't bad."

"I think Vinnie would appreciate something a bit more exotic. I know just the thing. I'll be back in fifteen minutes."

"Is your friend always so stubborn?"

"He seemed scared to me," I answered.

When I returned, Darlene was standing outside the door to Vinnie's hospital room. The police officers were not.

"Are the uniforms in with him?" I asked.

"Hello to you, too, Jake," Darlene answered. "They have been in and gone."

"Did he talk?"

"He said he was ambushed at an ATM machine."

"Since when does Vinnie have an ATM card?"

"I'm joking. Vinnie played possum. What's in the bag?"

"A couple of Polish hotdogs with the works."

"Too bad. He would have loved it."

"Oh?"

"The doctor gave Vinnie something very strong for the pain. He went out like a light," Darlene offered. "Vinnie mentioned Sandoval to me."

"The dead Assistant District Attorney? What about him?"

"The other Sandoval."

"Manny Sandoval. The bookie?"

"It seems Vinnie is behind on gambling debts. Manny and a couple of his goons gave him a harsh reminder and an unambiguous ultimatum."

"How much behind?"

"Vinnie claims it's only a few hundred, but..."

"But?"

"Vinnie's physical condition suggests his estimate is conservative."

"How did you pull all of this information out of him?"

"I walked in after the cops left and he just started blabbing."

"Did he happen to blab about where I might find Manny Sandoval?"

"Jake, get the needle out of your arm. Vinnie didn't talk with the cops because he was strongly advised against it. And he didn't talk to you because he doesn't want to see you lying in the adjoining bed. You don't want to find Manny Sandoval."

"Maybe I just want to see Sandoval to cover Vinnie's gambling debt."

"Try again. Maybe you need to give Sonny the Chin a call."

"Sonny took his wife and kids down to Joey's place in St.

Martin. He probably won't be back until the Giants' home opener."

"In that case, you might want to call Travis Duncan," Darlene said. "And please lose the bag, Jake, the Polish dogs are beginning to growl."

Darlene could be very charming at times.

And sometimes not.

"Are you all right, Darlene?"

She said: *I'm fine, Jake.*

I heard: *Back off.*

But I can be stubborn, too.

"I know when something is bothering you, Darlene."

Darlene did the thing she does when she is trying to control her emotions. Something like closing your eyes and counting to ten, only quicker.

"It hasn't been a lovely day, Jake. I spent most of it trying to juggle Diamond Investigations' finances like a one-armed, blindfolded circus clown. I miss the pooch, and I am not thrilled to see Vinnie looking like something you mold into a patty and throw on a grill. And I'm late."

"Late?"

"I promised Nicolai I would let him beat me at chess tonight. No reason to stick around here, by the look of the injection the doctor gave Vinnie he'll probably be out for quite some time. You should get going too, Jake. You still look like you need to recover from last night. Not to mention that shirt. We can come back to see Vinnie first thing in the morning. Maybe you wouldn't mind walking me to my car."

"Since when do you need an escort?"

"Let it go, Jake."

"I just want to be sure you're okay, Darlene."

"The biology experiment in the paper sack," Darlene said, pointing to a nearby trash can. "Let it go."

I took a few steps over to the receptacle, dumped the Polish hotdogs, and followed Darlene as she headed for the elevator.

. . .

As I watched Darlene drive away, I was tempted to take her advice. Head back home and lay low for the rest of the evening. But I felt I needed to do something quickly about Vinnie's dilemma. Travis Duncan only phoned or visited me at the office, so I pointed the Toyota out to North Beach.

At the office, I called Duncan using the only number I had for him. As always, it went straight to voice mail.

The greeting was short and sweet.

Leave your name.

Then you waited to hear from him. If he knew your name and cared to return the call.

The good news was I had slipped the Victor Hugo novel into my jacket before leaving home for the hospital, so I would at least have the bell ringer's company while I waited for a response from Duncan.

If I was going to get a response at all.

The office of Diamond Investigations was a modest two-room affair. Darlene's domain was off the hallway entrance, and my hiding place was a smaller room separated by a wall. It featured a three-paned, curved bay-window looking out onto Columbus Avenue.

There was only one fairly comfortable place to sit in the front room—an upholstered armchair against the wall facing Darlene's desk. This was where Darlene would invite clients to *please have a seat. Mr. Diamond will be with you as soon as he can.* It was meant to create the illusion that I might be tied-up with other important business.

I thought it was a nice touch.

Darlene insisted it was lame.

I was just about to settle into the chair with the hunchback when the phone rang. I expected Travis Duncan. I got Lionel Katz.

"Diamond," Katz began without ceremony. "Benny Carlucci is no longer a murder suspect. He will be released on bail in the morning. Of course, he has other legal problems to deal with, but I can handle it from here."

I took that to mean my services were no longer required.

"Good to hear."

"Tony Carlucci and I appreciate your help."

"I didn't really do much," I reminded him.

"Your time has value. Please let me know what you feel your effort was worth, and Tony will be more than happy to compensate you."

"Please tell Tony it's on the house, Mr. Katz. And thank him for the tasty lunch earlier today."

"I certainly will."

"Any word on who *did* snuff the guy in the trunk?"

"Not my concern, Mr. Diamond."

Lionel Katz was all business. A cold fish. I wondered if he would be more interested if it was his mother tied-up and gagged in the trunk.

I resisted the urge to ask.

I thanked him for the update and ended the call.

I eased myself into the armchair and located the bookmark.

Quasimodo was losing status fast. The bell ringer had gone from King of Fools to just another everyday sap in two easy steps. First, look up to the wrong man. Second, fall in love with the wrong woman.

Esmeralda was not faring much better. She had a crush on Phoebus, Captain of the King's Archers. Captain Phoebus was a shameless womanizer, and the Gypsy girl was about to make the biggest mistake of her young life.

And then there was the Archdeacon.

Lust for Esmeralda was tearing Frollo apart.

As Jimmy Pigeon noted more than once, "Whoever said all is fair in love was delusional."

I am always awed by the lessons that can be derived from classic literature, and amazed at how these lessons can be ignored time after time after time.

The phone rang—sparing me the journey further down that road. I expected Travis Duncan. I was thankful it was Joey Vongoli.

"Surprised to find you at the office, Jake," he said.

"I'm waiting for a phone call."

Joey didn't ask. He had told me many times that if there was something I thought he needed to know, he shouldn't *have* to ask.

"I'm calling because Angela would like you to join us for dinner tomorrow evening," Joey said. "In celebration of St. Joseph's Day."

Being part Italian, I knew about St. Joseph's Day. It was generally forgotten. Only two days after St. Patrick's, St. Joseph's was treated like the luckless kid whose birthday fell on the day after Christmas.

"Count me in, Joey. And thank Angela for thinking of me."

"She would like Darlene and Vinnie to join us also."

"Darlene might be a hard sell, especially if there is anything on the menu that was alive recently. And I'm not certain if Vinnie will be available. He's lying in a recovery room at St. Mary's. He had an accident involving Manny Sandoval and a couple of Manny's gorillas."

"Will he be all right?"

"He's resilient, but it could take a while."

"Anything I can do?" Joey asked.

I knew what he was asking and tried to act dumb.

"If you have the time, come with me to visit him in the morning. I'm sure he'd be happy to see you."

"I would be glad to visit him, Jake, but you know that's not what I was asking."

It was no wonder my acting abilities never took me very far in tinsel town.

"I'm waiting to hear back from Travis Duncan."

"You're planning to set Duncan loose on Manny and his boys?"

"That will be entirely up to him. I'm just wishing Travis can work something out."

"Call me in the morning when you're ready to go to the hospital," Joey said in parting, "and Jake."

"Yes, Joey?"

"Be careful what you wish for."

THIRTEEN

Lieutenant Laura Lopez left the Hall of Justice and took a deep breath of air. The short meeting with Liam Duffey had been stifling. Lopez had told Duffey she needed to check out the progress of the questioning at the apartment building where the doorman and Roberto Sandoval had been murdered and decided she should at least make an appearance. Lopez would much rather have been on her way to a beach in Barbados.

The lobby was as busy as it had been hours before, maybe more so as tenants began returning home from their workday. Joanna Knapik, the uniformed officer Lopez had met earlier, was doing her best to keep the interviews moving along with some semblance of order.

"Have there been any earth shattering revelations, Officer?" Lopez asked.

"Not a thing, Lieutenant," Knapik reported. "I'd guess the tenants here are used to feeling safe, so we have encountered a great deal of surprise and shock and concern, but nothing to help in the investigation."

"Hearing your fortress is not impregnable is not very good news. Is that a tenant list?" Lopez added without a beat, referring to the clipboard Officer Knapik held in her hand.

"Every resident, listed by apartment, floor-by-floor. We have been checking off names all afternoon, every tenant who has been questioned either going out, coming in, or in his or her apartment. It's a big building, Lieutenant. We still have a way to go."

"Can you keep it moving along without my supervision, Knapik? I need to check in with the Medical Examiner and the forensic team. Find out if there's anything new there."

"Sure, Lieutenant, I can handle it."

"Great. Thanks," Lopez said, and then added, "You are doing a great job, Officer."

"Thank you, Lieutenant," Knapik said, beaming.

Lopez stepped through the lobby door and out onto the street, where she nearly collided with a man trying to keep his dog from dragging him into the building.

"Excuse me," Ethan Lloyd apologized. "He's anxious to get inside. It's dinnertime."

"No problem," Lopez said. "Here, let me get the door for you."

"Thank you. Terrible what happened here last night. Do I know you? Are you a tenant?"

"No, I'm not."

"I feel I've seen you before," Lloyd went on, the dog straining to pull him along, Lopez holding the door.

"You may have. I've been in and out all day. Lieutenant Lopez. I'm heading the investigation."

"I see. It's shocking, Lieutenant. It makes one re-evaluate one's sense of security."

"I imagine it would," Lopez said, wishing *one* would get *one's* mutt into the damned building. "If you will excuse me, I need to be going."

"Of course," Lloyd said, letting the dog lead him into the lobby, allowing Lopez to release the door.

As Lopez moved away from the building, Lloyd could not help thinking he had seen the woman before today.

When Sergeant Johnson left Officer Davey Cutler at the Chieftain Irish Pub, he felt a strong need to talk to Lopez. And soon. Johnson thought he might find her at the Roberto Sandoval murder scene.

The apartment building was just a stone's throw away, but the prospect of confronting his superior made him think it would be more like throwing a boulder. He left his motor pool vehicle at the Chieftain and walked over to the high-rise. He was greeted by Officer Knapik with the news that the lieutenant had been there and gone. He had missed her by minutes. Johnson tried to reach Lopez on her cell phone and the call went straight to voice mail.

Johnson called Beggs at forensics. They had checked every

fingerprint they could lift from the Cadillac. Benny Carlucci's prints were all over the interior—the steering wheel and the radio and the driver's side door handle—but not anywhere near the trunk. Other prints in the interior matched the vehicle owner.

"I would say the Carlucci kid is clear," Beggs said.

"Seems to be the consensus already," Johnson said.

"Here's the good news," Beggs went on. "We identified the victim."

"I thought his fingertips were ruined."

"They were, after he got into the car. We ran prints from the passenger side door handle and got a hit. Salvatore DiMarco—convicted felon, gun for hire. No question. The mug shot matched the victim's mug exactly, minus the bullet hole in the ear."

"What's a guy like that doing out on the street?"

"Been out on parole for less than two weeks," Beggs reported.

"So, DiMarco entered the Cadillac from the passenger side."

"Exactly," Beggs said. "I'm guessing someone picked him up, then shot him, did a job on his fingers and dumped the vehicle."

"Did we get a residential address for DiMarco?" Johnson asked.

"His parole officer put him in a flea bag rooming-house in downtown Oakland. That's all we have, and I'm elbow deep in work down here, Rocky."

"Okay. Thanks, Joe," Sergeant Johnson said, and let the crime scene investigator get back to it.

Johnson tried reaching Lopez again.

No dice.

He walked back to pick up the car and drove over to the morgue to revisit Dr. Steve Altman. Altman gave Johnson what he needed, an eight-by-ten glossy black-and-white photograph of Salvatore DiMarco from the M.E.'s impressive collection of portraits of the dead.

"Suitable for framing," Altman said.

On his way back to the car, holding onto the glossy of the

late Salvatore DiMarco, Johnson pulled out the Zippo lighter that had been burning a hole in his pocket since he left the Chieftain Pub. He climbed into the vehicle.

His cell phone rang as he slipped behind the steering wheel.

"Johnson."

"Bingo," said Tommy Yeatman.

"Bingo?"

"The thirty-eight in the trunk of the Cadillac killed Roberto Sandoval, without question. It looks as if this DiMarco character was the shooter."

"Not necessarily. But at least we have a suspect. Can you keep a lid on this for a while?"

"Not for very long."

"Can you give me until noon tomorrow?" Johnson asked.

Can you give me time to talk with Lieutenant Lopez about a few things is what Johnson was thinking.

"Noon it is. No later."

"Thanks, Tommy. Good work," Johnson said. He fired up the engine and headed to the Bay Bridge to visit the Oakland Police Department.

Duffey finally heard from his man, who did not even offer an excuse or an apology for missing his scheduled appointment at four.

Duffey told his investigator where he needed to be the next day at noon, and he hoped the guy would be just a bit more diligent.

The D.A. wondered if he had made the right decision in recruiting the man.

But it was far too late to change horses now.

Sergei Romanov was born in the town of Khimki, Russia, twenty-four kilometers northwest of Moscow, in 1887. In 1914, while a student of Philosophy at the University of Bern in Switzerland, Sergei was among a crowd of students witnessing a fiery oration on the university campus. The speaker was a Russian exile named Vladimir Ilyich Lenin.

The speech changed Sergei's life.

Sergei became a disciple, and although he had the same surname as the royal family, he was soon transformed into an anti-monarchist to the core. In 1915, Sergei Romanov traveled with Lenin to Zurich and he assisted in the writing of Lenin's *Imperialism: The Highest State of Capitalism* in 1916.

In February, 1917, Tsar Nicolas II abdicated the Russian throne. Upon hearing the news, Lenin was determined to return home as quickly as possible. Russia was at war with Germany, but it was the Germans, hoping to stir up more turmoil in Russia, who helped Lenin get back into the country. Sergei Romanov was among the thirty followers who accompanied Lenin by train and boat from Zurich, through Germany and Sweden, and finally to Finland Station in Petrograd. During the historic journey, Lenin drafted the *April Theses*, his programme for the Bolshevik Party.

Sergei remained a member of Lenin's closest circle up until Lenin's death in 1924. He was then forced to choose allegiance to Josef Stalin or Leon Trotsky. Sergei supported Trotsky. It was a losing bet. Stalin seized power. Trotsky and his followers were branded enemies of the state. Trotsky ultimately settled near Mexico City, via Istanbul, France and Norway. Sergei Romanov escaped Stalin's purges, landing in Cuba in 1926. He obtained work at a sugar plantation outside of Havana, became a favorite of the plantation owner, and he married his employer's daughter in 1927. He was forty years old. The young bride was nineteen.

Upon news of Josef Stalin's death in 1953, Sergei Romanov decided to return to his homeland. He left Cuba with his wife and twenty-two-year-old daughter in 1955. Their twenty-seven-year-old son, Alexander, now married, felt much more Cuban than Russian. Alexander chose to remain in Cuba with his wife and two young children. It was at that time that Alexander Romanov became Alex Roman.

On the first of January, 1960, after New Year's Eve celebrations in Havana, Cuban President Fulgencio Batista fled the country.

By 1964, following the Bay of Pigs invasion, the missile

crisis, and the assassination of the American President, Alex Roman was unsure about a future for his family in Cuba. Alex decided to abandon the island with his wife, fifteen-year-old son, Nicolai, and thirteen-year-old daughter, Carmella, while they could still get away. After a brief residence in Miami, the family travelled across the country to California and settled in San Francisco.

Nicolai Roman was a strong, healthy and handsome fifty-five-year-old. Nicolai lived alone in a house in Concord, in the East Bay, which he had built himself from the ground up. He had constructed homes throughout the San Francisco Bay area for nearly thirty-five years and he could still walk a roof rafter and pound a sixteen penny nail with the best of them.

Nicolai was just twenty-two when he lost his wife to leukemia in 1971, only three years into their marriage. Though he always remained very popular with the ladies, Nicolai never remarried. His wife had left him with a two-year-old daughter, who he cherished above anything else in the world.

Nicolai Roman peered across the old chess board, brought over from Russia to Cuba to America, and watched his daughter contemplate her next move.

And he knew something was troubling her.

She moved her king's bishop to king's rook six and called *check* just as Nicolai had expected. Nicolai countered with knight to king's bishop seven, to block the threat against his king.

"Tell me again, about how your grandfather beat Lenin in a game of Durak on the train to Petrograd, Papa," she said as she studied the board.

"Tell me what is upsetting you," Nicolai responded.

"Upsetting me?"

"Please," Nicolai insisted.

Darlene Roman had avoided answering the same question from Jake Diamond earlier at St. Mary's Hospital.

It would not work with her father.

Darlene told Nicolai what was troubling her.

. . .

Indecision is not necessarily a bad thing at times.

Blake Sanchez had been standing in Marston Campbell Park at 17th and West Streets in Oakland for nearly twenty minutes casing the liquor store across West Street. In all that time, only two customers had entered and exited the store. Blake looked up and down the deserted intersection, and then finally decided to make his move. It was not a good decision.

Sanchez entered the store and quickly moved toward the man behind the counter, holding the gun in his right hand, his right arm fully extended.

"Don't look at me," he said.

The man behind the counter looked down without hesitation.

"Empty the cash register into a bag," Blake said. "And make sure I can see both your hands at all times."

"The bags are *under* the counter," the man said.

Give me a break.

"Forget the bag. Paper money only, stacked in a neat pile. Don't forget the large bills underneath the change compartment."

The man began pulling all of the bills from the register, and then he involuntarily looked up.

"I said don't look at me," Sanchez warned.

But the man was not looking at Blake Sanchez. He was looking past him.

Blake turned to see what the guy was gawking at and found himself face-to-face with a boy, no more than thirteen years old, trying his best to level a gun at Blake's chest. The gun was a lot bigger than the one Sanchez held. He tried to say something like *PLEASE, DON'T!* —but it was too late.

The .44 went off like a cannon and the impact blew Sanchez backwards, clear over the counter, taking the cash register with him.

Sergeant Johnson drove across the Bay Bridge, picked up the Nimitz Freeway to Broadway, and took Broadway over to 7th Street. Johnson stopped the first uniform he saw after entering the Oakland Police Department building and asked for the officer in charge.

"That would be Lieutenant Folgueras," the uniform said. "That's him there, on his way out the door."

Johnson hurried to the well-dressed man the officer had pointed out, catching up to him just as he was about to climb into a squad car beside a uniformed driver.

"Lieutenant Folgueras?"

"Yes?"

"Sergeant Johnson, SFPD."

"Well, what a surprise. Don Folgueras," he said, offering a handshake. "What brings you across the pond, Sergeant?"

"A murder case we're working on," Johnson said, accepting the handshake. "I'm hoping you can help us out with some information."

"I'm on my way to a shooting scene, attempted liquor store robbery."

"Anyone hurt?

"Only the perp."

"Could I ride along?"

"Sure, hop in," Folgueras said, opening the back door of the cruiser. "We can chat on the way."

As the patrol car pulled away from the police station, Johnson handed the photo to Folgueras from the back seat.

"Know this guy?" Johnson asked.

"Sal DiMarco—he's looked better," Folgueras answered. "What happened?"

"Found him stuffed into a Cadillac trunk under a freeway overpass across the bay last night."

"It just isn't safe for Italians on St. Patrick's Day. Wish I could say I'm sorry, but DiMarco was a bad man."

"Did he have any connections to your department?"

"May have been busted by a few of our people over the years, if you consider that a connection."

"Was he ever used as an informant?"

"Not that I know. What are you driving at?"

"I'm not really sure. Can you tell me anything about this?" Johnson asked, handing Folgueras the Zippo lighter.

"The original owner of this lighter would have been an Oakland homicide detective, couldn't get one like this any other way. And I can tell you it has been around for some time. This is an old logo, they stopped using it in the late nineties."

"How many lighters like this one are out there?"

"No clue."

"Is there any way to find out? How many were made? Who may have received one? And if DiMarco ever informed for any of your detectives?"

"Possibly. But there would be no way of telling where any of the lighters turned up afterwards. Things get lost, stolen, sold and given away. And you know as well as I do police detectives don't like talking about their snitches."

"I realize that. And I know it's a lot to ask of you."

"You're looking to connect the lighter to DiMarco's murder," Folgueras said, "and to a present or former Oakland police detective. I don't like the sound of it."

"It's probably a wild goose chase, but I have nothing else to go on. One of our assistant district attorneys was murdered last night. The murder weapon was found in the trunk with DiMarco. DiMarco may have been the trigger man, but I feel certain there was someone else involved. Someone who may have killed DiMarco and dropped the lighter."

"How about the gun that killed DiMarco? Did it turn up?"

"Not yet."

"I'll see what I can do," Folgueras said. "Here we are."

The cruiser stopped in front of the liquor store on West Street and they climbed out.

Folgueras quickly located Bruce Perry, one of the two uniformed officers who had been first on the scene.

"What do we have?"

"I recognized the perp, Blake Sanchez, neighborhood kid, sixteen years old. He's been in trouble a few times, but never armed," Perry said. "That's the owner. Blake ran in waving a thirty-eight in his face and demanded the cash in the register. That's the owner's son, twelve years old. Arrived on the scene like Dirty Harry and put a forty-four slug into Blake's chest. Sanchez was rushed over to the ER at Highland General."

"Real nice," Folgueras said.

"Here's the weapon Sanchez was carrying," Perry said,

holding out a plastic evidence bag containing a .38 caliber pistol.

Lieutenant Folgueras took the bag, opened the zip lock, and put his nose to it.

"Did Sanchez fire a shot?" the lieutenant asked.

"They say no," Perry said, referring to the owner and his son, who did not look as if they had enjoyed the experience.

"What do you make of this, Sergeant?" Folgueras asked, handing the bag to Johnson.

"I'd say it is a textbook throw-away. No serial numbers, taped grip and trigger, untraceable," Rocky said after taking a quick look. He also put his nose to the bag. "And I would say it has been fired recently, possibly within the past twenty-four hours."

"Where would a kid like Sanchez get a piece like that?" asked Perry.

"Very good question," Folgueras said. "Get this gun over to ballistics on the double. Have them check it against any shootings involving thirty-eight caliber weapons in the past few days."

"Yes, sir," Perry said, and hurried out of the store.

"Are you thinking what I'm thinking?" Folgueras asked Johnson.

"It would be one hell of a coincidence."

"Stranger things have happened," Folgueras said.

"Yes, they have."

"Can you get the bullet that killed DiMarco over to our ballistics guys?"

"I'm sure I can."

"Do it. And if it matches the gun Perry just walked off with I'll buy California State Lottery tickets for the both of us," said Folgueras. "And I'll see what I can do to help you out on the cigarette lighter question."

"I appreciate it."

"Do you know Laura Lopez very well?"

"She's been my boss for five years."

"Good cop."

"Great cop."

"You might ask her about the lighter. She was here with

Oakland Homicide, before she made the big move across the bay. Lopez would have been around when those Zippos were a fad in the department."

"I'll run it by her," Johnson said.

"Don't know that we can do much more here," Folgueras said. "I'll leave my driver to wait it out. A psychologist should be arriving any minute to talk with the boy. Let's blow, I'll give you a ride back to your car."

Norman Hall sat on a bench in Buena Vista Park, watching Darlene Roman's house on Frederick Street.

Waiting for Darlene to come home.

Hall didn't mind waiting.

Norman was a very patient man.

And Darlene was worth waiting for.

He did worry at times when she was out too late.

The meeting with his parole officer earlier that day had gone very well. Norman told his officer he had applied for a job at an Italian delicatessen on Columbus Avenue, and the prospects were good.

Norman had brought provisions for his vigil. A package of cookies, his favorite, Keebler fudge covered grahams. *You gotta love those elves,* he found himself thinking. And three bottles of Manhattan special. He was developing quite a taste for the coffee flavored soft drink.

As he continued watching the house, he was thinking tonight might be the night.

Sergeant Rocky Johnson stood at the stove trying to fan the smoke out through his kitchen window. He realized he was using a copy of *Travel and Leisure* magazine for the purpose. His wife, Amy, liked looking at the pictures of the exotic places they would most likely never visit. Johnson had been attempting to grill a cheese sandwich, and he had failed terribly. It sat in the frying pan looking like a square hockey puck.

Johnson had tried reaching Lopez again on his way back

over the bridge. The lieutenant was not answering her phone, and was not returning his calls. He decided to go home. He thought he'd had enough intrigue for one day.

And Johnson was out of ideas.

Except for the one that had to do with confronting Lopez.

And that was an idea he was trying very hard not to think about.

He dumped the ruined grilled cheese sandwich into the trash and wondered if he could fuck up a bowl of cereal.

He needed to talk to someone, but he was alone.

He thought he should telephone Amy, but remembered it was well after midnight in Philadelphia.

Johnson reached into the cupboard and pulled out a box of Apple Cinnamon Cheerios.

And he went to the refrigerator hoping to find milk.

FOURTEEN

I was waiting for a call or a visit from Travis Duncan.
Meanwhile...

Esmeralda was wallowing in the mire, and it seemed the hunchback had made up his mind he would not abandon the sinking gypsy.

The girl had agreed to a rendezvous with Captain Phoebus. Frollo caught them fooling around and he stabbed the captain in a fit of jealous rage. Esmeralda was tortured to the point of admitting it was she who stabbed Phoebus. She would have confessed to throwing the 1919 World Series. The Archdeacon allowed her take the fall. Frollo was deferring responsibility for his actions like a champ.

There was a soft tapping on the office door.

I hated having to put the book down.

The silhouette framed by the opaque window in the door was unmistakable.

Travis Duncan was a very scary man if he didn't care for you. He was an ex-U.S. Army Special Forces veteran of Desert Storm. On top of that, Duncan was a Texan.

The family had been Texans for generations, since Travis' great-great-great-great-grandfather, Joshua Duncan, moved his wife and two young sons from Duncan, Oklahoma, in 1835.

A year later, Joshua left his wife and boys in Austin and rushed down to San Antonio to die at the Alamo.

Joshua's oldest son rode with Robert E. Lee at the battle of Fredericksburg and *his* son rode with Teddy Roosevelt at San Juan Hill. Travis' grandfather fought the Japanese at Okinawa in 1945 and Travis' father was in Vietnam for the Tet Offensive.

After Iraq, Travis decided he was weary of dangerous places. He left the Lone Star State and landed in California.

Travis Duncan made Tony Carlucci look like a pussy cat.

I had helped Travis out of a jam. I'll skip the details— that's another story. In any case, Duncan's appreciation was boundless. He was the lion, I was Androcles.

I walked over and opened the office door. Duncan stood at the threshold, his right hand wrapped around the neck of a bottle of George Dickel Tennessee Sour Mash Whiskey No. 12.

For a tough guy, Duncan could be very thoughtful.

Travis held up the bag of ice cubes he gripped in his other hand. "Compliments of Mr. Verdi," he said, referring to Angelo in the deli below.

"Come in. I'll see if I can find a couple of clean glasses."

I fixed the drinks, straight on the rocks. We exchanged a few courteous preliminaries, and then he asked what he could do for me.

I sketched out the discord between Vinnie Strings and Manny Sandoval.

"I'm sorry this happened to Vinnie, tell him I said so."

"I will."

"I know a little about Manny Sandoval," Travis said. "He is a big talker, take away the apes Manny travels with and he loses his conversational edge."

"How do we do that?" I asked. "His gorillas are attached to him like Peter Pan's shadow."

"I have a few ideas. First I have to find the rock Manny hides under and convince him he needs crawl out and meet with you."

"Are you suggesting I can handle Sandoval one-on-one?"

"Not exactly. But taking his goons out of the equation will level the playing field somewhat."

"Okay." It was all I could come up with.

"How about tomorrow night?"

"I have a dinner engagement."

"Celebrating St. Joseph's Day?"

Travis Duncan was full of surprises.

"Uh-huh," I said, offering Travis another example of my superb vocabulary.

"Joseph. Patron Saint of Workers. He has always been one of my favorites. I mean, could anyone have been more humble? The early Christians were trying to persuade the pagans that Jesus was the son of God, and to do that they had to promote the verity of a virgin birth. It was a very hard sell, and the fact that Mary had a husband clouded the issue. So they played down the carpenter's importance, and it was centuries before Joseph was given his due. How about after your dinner tomorrow night?"

"Sure."

"Good. I have some research to do. I will give you a call tomorrow afternoon, and then we can get this business settled."

"Thanks," I said, Joey Clams' warning echoing in my head.

Be careful what you wish for.

Duncan left the office without another word.

He also left the bottle of Dickel.

A couple of nightcaps with Travis were not exactly the physical therapy I needed. The theory concerning *the hair of the dog* was highly overrated. I wondered for a moment where the expression originated, but let it go. It was definitely time to take Darlene's advice. A hot bath, a shot or two of Mylanta chased by a few quarts of water, and a good night's sleep might give me more than a snowball's chance in hell of feeling human in the morning.

I could hardly remember how it felt.

When I walked out of the building, Angelo Verdi was sweeping in front of the deli. I tried to tip-toe away.

"Jake, I need to talk to you for a minute."

Oh, boy.

Angelo couldn't talk for less than ten minutes if his life depended on it.

"Sure, Angelo, what's up?"

"Has Darlene said anything to you?" he asked.

"She generally has a lot to say to me. Are you referring to something specific?"

A quick getaway was looking very unlikely.

"I think someone has been watching her, watching the building, maybe following her."

Angelo ran his suspicions by me.

103

I recalled the scene at the hospital. Darlene insisting there was nothing on her mind when I knew there was.

"I need to check this out, Angelo."

"I hope I haven't worried you unnecessarily."

"Not at all. You did the right thing telling me."

And did it in record time.

"Let me know that everything is all right," he said.

"I will," I said, already rushing for my car.

I raced over to Darlene's house off Buena Vista Park.

Also in record time.

When I pulled up in front of the house, I spotted a man at the window to the south of the front door. He took off around the corner of the house, running to the rear. I double-parked the car. I left it running with the key still in the ignition and went after him. When I reached the back of the house and the alley behind, the man was nowhere in sight. Hoping I hadn't arrived too late, I scrambled back up to the front door like the place was on fire.

I pounded on the door until Darlene opened it.

She looked at me as if I was a raving maniac.

"Jesus, Jake, you look like a raving maniac," she said. "What are you doing here?"

"Angelo said he thought you were being followed. I got here as fast as I could. I think the stalker was peeping into your living room window."

"And you charged in like the Light Brigade and chased him away," she said, not sounding all that appreciative.

"Is there something wrong with that?"

"Yes and no."

Unless Darlene had honed her skills at ventriloquism, it was the voice of another woman behind her.

"My hero," Darlene said. "Maybe you should park the car. Then you can come inside and meet Megan."

I parked the car and I went back inside.

I found them in the kitchen, sharing a bottle of Pinot Noir.

"Jake, meet Detective Megan Nicolace. Megan, meet Jake Diamond," Darlene said. "He means well."

"Whoever Angelo is," Nicolace said. "He *is* perceptive."

"I'll be sure to let him know you think so," I said,

impatiently. "What's going on here?"

"His name is Norman Hall, a paroled sex-offender. Don't ask me. I would have thrown away the key. I've been watching him and he's been watching Darlene. I've been waiting for him to give us a good reason to revoke his parole," Nicolace said.

"The guy was at her window, Detective. How good a reason do you need?"

"Something that will put him away for a long time."

"Like assault?"

"Jake," Darlene said. "Quit it."

"So," I said to Nicolace, ignoring Darlene. "Norman is the wolf, you are the rancher, and Darlene gets to play the staked calf. No way."

"I will be watching Norman Hall and Darlene constantly," Nicolace said.

"I've heard that before. Get a restraining order. Get him off her."

"He'll just find someone else, Jake," Darlene said.

"Good."

"It's my decision, Jake."

"I don't like it."

"You don't like tofu either, but that never stopped me," Darlene said. "Don't worry. Go home, get some rest. Let me do this. I need to help get this creep off the street."

I conceded I was outnumbered.

"I hope you know what you're doing, Darlene," I said. And then to Nicolace, "If he messes a hair on her head I will see you're busted down to traffic patrol."

"Is that from a Jackie Chan movie?" Darlene asked.

"*Police Story 2.* I couldn't resist. Please be careful, Detective. Darlene is very important to me."

"That's sweet, Jake. Go home," Darlene said.

"I won't let anything hurt Darlene," Nicolace said. "The thought of directing traffic horrifies me. Go home."

I went home.

FIFTEEN

Marco Weido couldn't sleep.

The unplanned afternoon nap had lasted hours and now he was wide awake.

He had missed his appointment and his employer was going to give him grief about it.

He grabbed his pack of Marlboros and a book of matches, very unhappy about misplacing his prized Zippo lighter.

He stepped out onto his front porch and lit a cigarette. He stood on the doormat and felt something was not right. The mat was out of place, something he hadn't noticed coming in. He looked up and down the street, saw no one, moved the mat and removed the trap opening underneath. He reached into the opening and under the porch.

Nothing.

The gun was gone.

Laura Lopez couldn't sleep.

She was looking at three unsolved homicides cases.

Liam Duffey was breathing down her neck.

Lopez was looking forward to the meeting with Duffey's lead investigator with all of the enthusiasm associated with an appointment for wisdom tooth removal.

And then there was the matter of Sergeant Rocky Johnson.

It was not in Johnson's nature to let go when something about a case was nagging him, and the white envelope she had removed from Sandoval's apartment clearly fit the bill.

Lopez had managed to avoid the sergeant all day, but she couldn't hope to put him off much longer.

Nice going, Laura.

Lopez poured another Glenlivet on the rocks hoping that three would be a charm.

. . .

After leaving Jake Diamond, Travis Duncan had made a few inquiries. He was confident he knew where he could find Manny Sandoval and his two monkeys late the following night.

Duncan was actually looking forward to the get-together.

He slept like a baby.

Darlene Roman couldn't sleep.

As stubborn as she could be, she understood Jake's concerns were not unfounded.

She had confidence in Detective Nicolace, but it didn't negate the fact Megan had gone and Darlene was alone in the house.

Nicolace had assured her Norman Hall would not be coming back that night after Jake's wild pursuit.

It had sounded convincing, but—

Jake was concerned, her dad was concerned, even Angelo Verdi was concerned, and Darlene was sure if Tug McGraw was not off running up and down the beach with her 'nieces' he would be concerned also.

She was missing her trusty canine companion big-time.

Norman Hall couldn't sleep.

He had been diligent, patient and, above all, cautious.

Hall had waited in the park until Darlene arrived home. She was alone, the dog still mysteriously out of the picture. He watched as she entered the house and he saw the outside porch light go dark. Soon the light in the entranceway at the foot of the stairs leading up to the rooms above followed suit.

Norman saw the light in what he knew was the bedroom turn on and then the light in the bathroom. Hall wondered if she would shower before bed. He liked the idea. If she had showered, it was a quick one, since less than ten minutes later the bathroom went dark. A few minutes later the bedroom light went out.

Hall waited nearly thirty minutes before approaching the house, pleased by how well he had learned to take his time.

And now his time had come.

And then Diamond had arrived.

Charging after him like Rambo.

Norman knew who Jake Diamond was. He was the man Darlene worked with above the delicatessen. Hall hadn't worried that Diamond was a private investigator, he was just another loser who couldn't make it as a real cop.

In all the time he had watched Darlene, Hall had never seen Diamond at her house. Now Norman wondered if there was something going on between them, something dirty. It was the first time Hall had ever seen another man at Darlene's home.

The thought of another man upset Norman.

As Hall lay awake in his bed, he thought something might have to be done about Jake Diamond.

He did not want to be interrupted again.

It just wouldn't do.

Rocky Johnson couldn't sleep.

And as much as he missed his wife, it was thoughts of another woman that were keeping him awake.

Lieutenant Lopez.

Johnson was pacing his living room. Lopez was dodging him. The white envelope, Ethan Lloyd's description of the woman in blue, the Zippo cigarette lighter. Circumstantial but incriminating.

A quote from Henry David Thoreau came to mind: *We are always paid for our suspicion by finding what we suspect.*

He needed answers, and if Lopez refused to supply them he would have to try getting them some other way. He had an idea about that. An idea he found almost comical, but the only one he could muster. Johnson would try one last time with Lopez in the morning, if she continued to play deaf and dumb he would resort to Plan B.

He would need to go outside the department.

And he wouldn't sleep unless the alternate plan was in

place *before* he tried another go at Lopez.

Johnson could only think of one man for the job, and the thought was not a pleasant one. He hoped it wouldn't come to that, but he needed to know the option was there.

Johnson climbed into his car and headed out toward the Presidio.

SIXTEEN

On my way home I tried to replace thoughts of Darlene's possible peril with thoughts of a hot bath and a good night's sleep. When I pulled into the driveway, I saw a man standing at my front door. Easily recognizable and totally unexpected. The porch light lit him like a spot for a Puccini aria. The bald head, the slightly off-center facial features, the look of ruggedness and awkwardness that made him look like a cross between Telly Savalas and Mr. Potatohead.

"Sergeant Johnson, what a pleasure," I said as I joined him on the porch. "What did I do now?"

"I may need your help, Diamond."

I couldn't have been more surprised if he had said: *You are under arrest for murder.*

After all, I had heard that one from Johnson before.

Before I record my reaction, allow me to briefly recall my personal history with Sergeant Johnson.

Johnson and I were not what you would call buddies.

In fact, we got along like Tyson and Holyfield.

The very first time we met, four years earlier, he and Lieutenant Lopez had arrived at my apartment in the Fillmore. Uninvited.

They were there to take me in for questioning.

After beating on my door for a full minute, like a Ginger Baker drum solo, Johnson decided to try to break it down. He charged shoulder first and I opened the door as he was about to hit. He came through the doorway like a runaway freight train and his forward motion would have carried him across the room and out the window if my armchair hadn't stopped him cold halfway.

Our second meeting, not long after, was at the airport in San Francisco. Johnson and Lopez were there to meet my return flight from Los Angeles and take me in as a murder suspect. I sucker-punched Johnson and ran.

At our third meeting, Johnson knocked me to the ground, a perfect tackle. I went down like a piano from a twelfth-story window. He didn't apologize. He was there to prevent me from walking into an ambush. The sergeant was helping me out of a jam, I guess, but perhaps used a little too much force.

Since that time, I have done a very good job of avoiding Johnson, choosing to bother Laura Lopez instead when I needed to bother someone in the department. I decided I had as much chance of getting into Johnson's good graces as Pete Rose had of getting into the Hall of Fame.

Lieutenant Lopez wasn't exactly my buddy either, but she had a sense of humor at least. Which is to say I could often make her laugh even when it was not my intention.

So, when Johnson said, "I may need your help, Diamond,"—what else could I do but invite him in?

"Can I offer you something to drink?" I asked, as I led him to the kitchen.

"Scotch?" he said.

"Bourbon?" I said.

"Sure."

He sat at the kitchen table and waited as I fixed him up with a George Dickel on the rocks. I was tempted to join him, but I fought the urge. Instead I went to the refrigerator and pulled out a carton of orange juice. After I quickly checked the expiration date, I decided to put it back and save it for the next time I had need of paint remover. I opted for a tall glass of iced water and sat across from him at the table.

Johnson wasted no time.

After swearing me to secrecy the sergeant quickly listed his concerns about his lieutenant's uncharacteristic behavior, as he just as quickly finished his first drink and gratefully accepted another.

"So," he said in summation. "If Lopez can't give me an acceptable explanation tomorrow morning, I will need someone to look into this, unofficially. I don't want to create any doubt about the lieutenant's integrity within the department until I understand what's going on. I sincerely hope it will not come to this."

"So do I," was all I could manage to say.

"But if it does, I need to know if you are willing to help me."

In case you are wondering what a size ten shoe looks like stuffed into a private investigator's mouth—picture this.

"I'll try my best to help you, Sergeant."

With that he rose from his seat, thanked me for my time and for the drinks, and headed for the front door.

"I'll let you know," he said, as I followed him out onto the porch, and then he was gone.

Thirty minutes later, I lay in bed thinking about how much Johnson and Lopez reminded me of Quasimodo and Esmeralda.

The beautiful redhead and her homely protector.

The bell ringer had swung from the cathedral on a rope, scooping up the gypsy to rescue her from being destroyed by the mob.

I hoped I could offer Johnson enough rope to do the same for Lopez, without giving him enough rope to hang himself.

The large green numbers projected on the ceiling above me from the table-side alarm clock turned from 11:59 to 12:00.

My last thought before sleep welcomed me was that I had made it through another entire day without earning a cent.

Part Two

THE GOOD SERGEANT

One would have pronounced him a giant who had been broken and badly put together again.

—Victor Hugo

SEVENTEEN

Lieutenant Lopez woke up with a single-malt hangover that would have impressed Hemingway.

She had no time for holistic remedies.

The hot bath. The green tea. The artesian well water.

Lopez would have to go the plop-plop-fizz-fizz route for the sake of expediency. She watched the effervescent tablets dissolve and emptied the tall glass in one drink. The cherry flavored had been a poor choice.

She would try to remember to choose the Orange Zest next time.

She would try to avoid the need to ever use it again.

She would try to keep in mind how Hemingway had kicked the drinking habit.

She tried to recall her undergraduate days at Berkeley, when anything and everything was possible.

But all Laura Lopez could recall was yesterday, and the impossible mess today promised to be.

Lopez started a pot of coffee and jumped into and out of the shower. She slipped into a plush terrycloth robe with the embroidered inscription *Caesar's Palace.* She was a tall woman at five-foot-nine in bare feet, a fact that helped her survive in the male-dominated world of police investigation—still the robe swam on her.

It was one of the few things she had inherited from her father—a souvenir of her parents honeymoon in Vegas.

Victor Lopez had been with the Oakland Police Department for nearly thirty years, and although he was not killed on the job, the job slowly killed him nevertheless. It ruined his marriage, ruined his health, and ruined his bid for father-of-the-year honors. It wasn't until after her mother had passed away that Laura and Victor Lopez were able to investigate the possibility of developing a meaningful relationship. But the time allowed was too short. What she did know was he had been a clean cop, and although stuffing a hotel robe into your suitcase was not a capital crime, she never doubted Victor had paid for the keepsake.

She opened her front door, looked down at the headline of the *Examiner*, and left the newspaper lying there. She walked back to the kitchen, poured a cup of coffee, and settled into the living room sofa. The white envelope in the zip lock bag mocked her from its resting place on the coffee table.

She wanted to tear the envelope and its contents into a thousand pieces and flush it down the toilet with the rest of the cherry flavored Alka-Seltzer. But that was not an option. It had been found in Roberto Sandoval's apartment, it had been bagged as evidence by one or both of the first officers at the scene, and it had peeked out at Johnson from her jacket pocket.

Misplacing evidence in a murder investigation was one thing. Destroying it was something else entirely. If push came to shove, she would need to produce the envelope.

She could only hope Johnson wouldn't push too hard.

Lopez wondered if her timing could have possibly been any worse.

She wondered if she could ever hope to find anything to replace the pleasure of lighting up a cigarette and embracing the irony when the shit hit the fan.

Solving the case wouldn't hurt. A motive and a few leads would certainly help.

The lieutenant thought she knew what her father would have recommended, but she didn't feel quite ready for sound advice.

She didn't feel quite ready for the trip to the Vallejo Street Station.

Lopez elected to put it off for a few hours and decided on another cup of coffee.

Sergeant Johnson was at his desk at the Vallejo Street Station at seven Friday morning, drumming his fingers on his desk and trying to decide where to begin. He would strongly insist Lopez talk with him the moment she arrived, and try to keep focused on the work at hand while he waited.

Johnson called ballistics and asked for Thomas Yeatman.

"This is Officer Jimmy Chapman. Detective Yeatman is not expected until eight. Is there something I can help you with?"

The officer on the other end of the line sounded eager. He also sounded like he was in his teens.

Wonderful.

"Please ask Yeatman to call Sergeant Johnson at Vallejo Station as soon as he gets in."

"Yes, sir," Chapman said.

Johnson placed the receiver in its cradle and picked it up again almost immediately. He called Amy's parents' house in Philadelphia, hoping her father would not be the one to answer.

Her father answered.

"Sterling Singleton the second, may I help you?"

"This is Roxton, sir. Could I speak with Amy?"

"Amy and her sister are at the catering hall putting some finishing touches on the arrangements for tomorrow evening."

"Would you please tell her I called," Johnson said, and then before waiting for a reply that might never come added, "Thank you," and hung up.

It was seven-sixteen. Johnson was sure the day could only get better after such a disappointing start.

He was wrong.

Every morning, without fail, rain or shine, Darlene Roman took Tug McGraw for a walk through Buena Vista Park for twenty to thirty minutes. It was a routine hard to break. So Darlene found herself walking through the park on Friday morning, even though the dog was away frolicking in Marin County.

As she circled the park, alternating between a brisk walk and an easy jog, she thought about the previous evening.

She thought about Diamond. How, in spite of his stubborn concern, he had been sort of cute charging to her rescue, like a knight in wrinkled armor. She had first met Diamond through Jimmy Pigeon, who she had occasionally worked for in Santa Monica. When Jake decided to take a shot at starting his own investigation business and set up shop in San Francisco, he offered Darlene a job and she accepted. She had always liked Jake, and she was not one to spend time with anyone she did not like. But Diamond's dress habits and his eating habits and his complete lack of business acumen often drove her up the wall. And the benefit of computers was as foreign to him as the Mongolian alphabet. If you mentioned email to Jake, he thought you wanted to discuss Zola, and when you told Jake, time and again, that he could find an answer to his question by surfing the internet he was like a kid lost in a supermarket. In these areas he was not about to change. He would continue to fight tooth and nail against technology. He would never hope to balance a financial log, except perhaps on the top of his head. He would never get away from cigarettes or a terrible diet or Tennessee whiskey or mismatched outfits or wild-goose chases. But after Jimmy Pigeon was murdered and Sally French had been killed, he had changed in more meaningful ways. Jake became more sensitive and more compassionate, and he became much more adept at being a friend. At the same time he became tougher. He was impossible not to like, difficult not to care for, hard not to love, and he was very charming in his goofy way.

Darlene ended her walk through the park, absentmindedly expecting Tug McGraw to brush up against her legs.

She stood waiting for the traffic to offer her an opening to cross over to Frederick Street.

Darlene asked a man on a nearby bench for the time.

The young man wore dark glasses and a Giants ball cap.

"Seven-fifty-two," he said, not looking up at her.

"Thank you," she said, and then she crossed Buena Vista Park West toward her house.

Norman Hall removed the dark glasses and watched her all the way to her door.

. . .

At five after eight the phone on Johnson's desk rang. It was Thomas Yeatman from ballistics returning his call.

"Tommy, I need a favor," Johnson said.

"I'm already doing you a favor. Delaying identification of the gun in the trunk with DiMarco as the weapon that killed Roberto Sandoval is like sitting on a powder keg with a short fuse. And I can only sit on it until noon."

"I know, and I appreciate it. But I need another favor."

"I drink Johnnie Walker Black."

"Noted. Is it possible to have the bullet that killed DiMarco sent over to Oakland?"

"Not possible, Rocky. Why do you ask?"

"I need it compared to a thirty-eight used in an attempted holdup in Oakland yesterday."

"Was anyone shot with the gun during the robbery?"

"No. Not then. But it had been fired recently."

"Well, you might be able to get Oakland to send the gun here, and I can run the tests. The slug that killed DiMarco is evidence in a murder case. There is no way I could let it out of our hands. Are you working on another wild hunch?"

"I'm clutching at straws, Tommy," Johnson confessed. "I'll see if Oakland will send the weapon over. I really can't thank you enough for your help."

"Johnnie Walker..."

"Black. I'll let you know what Oakland decides."

Johnson ended the call and immediately phoned Oakland.

"Oakland Police Department, Perry speaking."

"Officer Perry, this is Sergeant Johnson."

"You were with Lieutenant Folgueras at the liquor store yesterday."

"That's right. Could I speak with the lieutenant?"

"He's not expected in until nine, Sergeant."

Terrific.

"Please ask him to call me."

"I sure will," Perry said.

Johnson slammed the receiver down into its cradle, picked it up and slammed it down again.

. . .

Tony Carlucci was sitting at the breakfast table with his wife, Carmella, and his son, Anthony Jr. He was scanning the front page story in the *San Francisco Examiner*.

"Jesus Christ," Carlucci said. "Is Liam Duffey one lucky bastard or what?"

"Tony, please watch your language," his wife said. "What do you mean?"

"Roberto Sandoval was murdered late Wednesday night."

"That's terrible," Carmella said. "But what does it have to do with Duffey and his luck?"

"Liam Duffey is planning a run at the Mayor's seat, and Sandoval was a shoe-in to move into the D.A.'s office if Duffey makes it to City Hall. Have you seen the latest polls? Duffey numbers keep falling. It's doubtful he can even win the *nomination* for mayor and he must know it."

"And?"

"And if Duffey can't be mayor, he at least wants to keep his job as head District Attorney, but if Sandoval ran against him in *that* race, Duffey would be back to chasing ambulances. So, I'm thinking what happened to Sandoval is a piece of luck for Duffey."

"Why are you so cynical, Tony?"

"It's my nature."

"Are you saying Duffey had something to do with what happened to Sandoval?" Carmella asked.

"How would I know? And frankly, I couldn't care less if these goddamn lawyers and politicians all killed each other."

"Tony, please don't talk that way."

"How is Cousin Benny?" Anthony Jr. asked, in an attempt to change the subject.

"Benny is an idiot. He's up on a grand theft auto rap," Tony said. "If you ever do something like that, Anthony, I will personally break both your arms."

"Tony, that's a horrible thing to say," Carmella cried.

"It is a horrible thing to say. So I hope I never have to say it again."

"Why would I ever steal a car, Pop," Anthony Jr. asked. "You already gave me two of them."

"This coffee is cold," Tony Carlucci replied.

. . .

At nine-fourteen Lieutenant Don Folgueras called from Oakland.

"Ballistics can't release the bullet that killed Sal DiMarco," Johnson reported.

"And you're wondering if we can send the gun to you."

"Yes," Johnson said.

"Give us a day to run it against recent shootings over here. I'll try getting it to you sometime tomorrow if I have to deliver it personally."

"Thanks."

"The odds that the hold-up gun also killed DiMarco would make Mr. Ed's chances against Secretariat look good."

"I have nothing to bet on but long shots," Johnson said.

"And if by some miracle we get a match," Folgueras added, "it might do you no good at all. The boy, Sanchez, is hanging by a thread in intensive care. He may not make it. And if he dies before he can say where he got the gun, you would be back to square one."

"I'll pray for the kid," Johnson said.

"Wouldn't hurt to pray for all of them," Folgueras said.

EIGHTEEN

I woke Friday morning feeling more rested and clear-headed than I had felt in nearly two days, back before St. Patrick had his way with me. I treated myself to a shower while coffee was brewing. I threw on a pair of sweatpants and a vintage New York Mets T-shirt. It was a cool morning, so I hid the T-shirt under a red plaid flannel. I carried a large mug of coffee and a Camel non-filtered cigarette out to the back yard and settled into an unusually comfortable piece of lawn furniture facing the Golden Gate Bridge. The air was crisp, the sky was crystal clear, and I had the feeling you sometimes get when greeted by a fresh new morning.

You know the one.

It's a beautiful day and it's great to be alive.

Once the caffeine and the nicotine kicked in I was able to see things more realistically.

I am not generally a negative person. Not the one to always expect the worst. But the words *Thank God it's Friday* were not exactly rolling off my tongue, and my prospects for a delightful time would have challenged the President of the Optimist Club.

The odds in favor of a beautiful day were slim to none, and Slim had already left town.

A mental list of what I had to look forward to in the next sixteen hours or so made it painfully obvious.

First would be a visit to St. Mary's Hospital to discover if Vinnie Strings looked more like Vinnie and less like a pile of purple mashed potatoes than he had the night before. I was sure Vinnie's mom would be up from Los Angeles. And I was sure Mrs. Stradivarius would not relent until I explained, to her satisfaction, how such a terrible thing could happen to her sweet innocent angel.

I would have no satisfactory explanation.

Next, I would need to sneak into my office and somehow

avoid being confronted by Angelo Verdi. Angelo would be prepared with twenty questions about Darlene and her stalker, which would only serve to remind me of the unappealing plan of action Darlene and Detective Nicolace had drummed up to trap Norman Hall, and would have me stealing quick looks out of windows and glancing over my shoulder to see if the creep was lurking about. I then realized I didn't need reminders from Angelo. I prayed I could tip-toe past him nevertheless.

I had no cases in progress and none expected. A condition that gave the term *private investigation* unwelcomed new meaning.

I thought if I spent some time in the office it would alert the cosmos to the fact I needed some work, and soon. The possibility that our next client might be a San Francisco police Detective Sergeant was not exactly the solution to a distressing lack of gainful employment I was hoping for.

The very thought gave me the unnerving feeling I would rather take up golf.

If an excursion to the hospital, an attempt to slip into my office like a thief in the night, and the dreaded probability of a call from Sergeant Johnson were not enough to look forward to, there was the matter of Travis Duncan and what he might have in mind for dealing with Manny Sandoval and his goons.

I could hardly wait to hear about it.

I remembered it was St. Joseph's Day, which in turn reminded me I had a dinner engagement with Joey and Angela Vongoli. I had told Joey that Darlene might choose to pass on the invite. Darlene would not eat meat, and my dining habits and the variety of cooked animals I regularly brought into the office often made it difficult for her to be in the same room. Angela's holiday dinner table would be a meat lover's dream, but her salads and vegetable side dishes were legendary and meatless. Joey would surely have the very best Chianti on hand. And the Zeppole di San Giuseppe, traditional fist-size golden pastry prepared traditionally for St. Joseph's Day, was a cannoli cream-filled miracle even Darlene found tough to resist.

I made up my mind I would use this ammunition to try

convincing Darlene to join us. I knew how much the Vongoli's enjoyed her company. Darlene Roman was infinitely more fun at social gatherings than I was.

And I wanted to keep Darlene in my sight, and out of Norman Hall's sight.

I was determined to do a great deal of arm twisting once I maneuvered past Angelo Verdi and reached Darlene at the office.

My coffee was gone, so I rose from my seat. I stretched my arms and took a deep breath. I could smell the ocean and I felt the Pacific mist in the air. I looked out to the bridge, the tops of its magnificent pillars partially hidden behind a parade of pure white clouds.

I could not help recognizing it was truly a beautiful morning.

And despite my endless complaining I was compelled to admit it was, in fact, not all that bad being alive.

NINETEEN

The phone on Johnson's desk rang at nine-fifty-six.

"She just walked in," the desk sergeant reported.

"Thanks, Yardley," Johnson said.

Laura Lopez climbed the stairs to her second floor office and found Johnson waiting at her door.

"Good morning," Lopez said.

"Good morning. We need to talk."

"Can it wait?"

"It would be better now."

"Well," she said, opening the door and hitting the light switch. "Let's talk."

Johnson followed her into the office. Lopez sat at her desk.

"Have a seat," she said.

"I've been sitting for three hours."

"What's on your mind?"

"Can you tell me about the evidence you removed from Roberto Sandoval's apartment?"

"No."

"No?"

"All I will say about it is I hope you can forget about it," Lopez said. "And please sit down, Sergeant."

Johnson sat.

"I only want to help you," Johnson said. "If you are in some kind of jam, let me help you."

"No."

Johnson had expected resistance, but he was unprepared for total dismissal.

"Is there anything else?" Lopez asked.

Johnson decided not to push.

"The murder victim in the trunk of the Cadillac Benny Carlucci took for a joy ride was identified."

"I heard. Salvatore DiMarco."

"There was a thirty-eight in the trunk with DiMarco. It

was the gun that killed Sandoval."

"Are you certain?"

"Yeatman at ballistics made a positive match."

"When was that?"

"Late yesterday. I tried reaching you. I asked him to sit on it until I could let you know. He can only wait until noon today."

"What clued you to the possibility that DiMarco might be a suspect?"

"The parking garage code to Sandoval's building was found tucked into DiMarco's shoe."

"And he didn't use it?"

"He may have used it, but on the way in or the way out he chose, for some reason, to use the lobby and kill the doorman. Or he killed no one and it is all an elaborate set-up."

"Anything solid on who killed DiMarco?"

"Nothing. Could have been anyone, with the exception of Benny Carlucci."

"I'll talk to Yeatman before noon and make it official."

"Let Yeatman know he's not in hot water."

"Anything else?"

"Have you ever seen one of these?" Johnson asked, pulling the Zippo from his pocket.

"A lighter?"

"I found it on the ground where Carlucci stumbled across the Cadillac."

Johnson handed the lighter across the desk to Lopez.

Lopez studied it for a moment and laid it on the desk.

"And?" she asked.

"These particular lighters were issued in the nineties to Oakland police detectives of merit. Lieutenant Folgueras over in Oakland is trying to get me a list of recipients."

"I know Don Folgueras," Lopez said.

"He mentioned it."

"Give the lieutenant my best. Let me know as soon as he has something. Anything else?"

"If DiMarco killed Sandoval, I doubt he had personal reasons unless Sandoval put him away sometime. It's much more likely DiMarco was a hired gun and was murdered by his employer. Discovering who killed DiMarco could be the key."

"I'm inclined to agree. So get to work."

And that was that.

Johnson left without answers and without the Zippo.

Less than a three minute walk from Vallejo Street Central Police Station, Norman Hall sat nursing his third cup of coffee at a window seat in Café Trieste. From his vantage point, Hall could easily watch Molinari's Deli across Columbus Avenue. He had been watching for more than an hour, since before Darlene Roman stepped off the Broadway bus, walked into the deli, came out a few minutes later carrying a small white paper bag, and disappeared through the entrance of the building that led to the offices above.

Norman nearly jumped out of his seat when Jake Diamond walked past the window, so close Hall could almost touch him. He couldn't understand why Diamond was walking *away* from the delicatessen and his office. He watched Diamond walk to the intersection of Vallejo and Columbus Avenue before crossing the avenue. Diamond approached the building from the north—it seemed as if he was avoiding a walk past the deli.

Fifteen feet away, at another table in the café, looking out of the same window with her back to Norman Hall, Detective Megan Nicolace found it odd also.

Alone in her office, Lieutenant Laura Lopez sat with her elbows resting on her desk and her head resting in her hands. Her hair fell across her face and forearms like a cascade of reddish-gold waves. The Alka-Seltzer cure had been temporary at best. The lieutenant had not eaten anything all morning. The thought of trying food as a remedy was repulsive. Lopez had consumed so much water in the past few hours she didn't think she could swallow another drop. The throbbing pain in her temples, neck and shoulders was back in full force. The fact that in less than two hours she would be required to team with Liam Duffey's lead investigator and pretend to cooperate for perhaps as long as it took to arrest, indict and convict Roberto Sandoval's killer only compounded her discomfort.

Lopez pushed her hair back away from her face and looked at the Zippo lighter sitting on the desk. She had been ready for Sergeant Johnson, had expected him, and had been prepared to deflect any question with a *yes* or a *no,* or with a question of her own. But she was totally unprepared for the lighter.

Johnson had asked, innocently or rhetorically, if she had ever seen one like it.

It had not been so easy to evade *that* question.

Laura Lopez had seen a Zippo lighter *exactly* like it.

Johnson sat at his desk, with Jake Diamond's phone number sitting by his telephone and his hand on the receiver. He had every intention of calling Diamond since Lieutenant Lopez had so effectively shut him down, but he was hesitating. He was trying to decide whether to make the call or wait.

He was saved by the bell when the telephone rang.

It was Joe Beggs from forensics.

"We found a key under the passenger seat of the Cadillac that the owner of the vehicle couldn't identify. It may have belonged to DiMarco or whoever killed him. Unless you have another idea."

"I might. Could you let it out of your hands for a while?"

"Sure."

"Good. I'll send someone over for it."

Johnson buzzed Yardley at the front desk.

"Could you locate Officer Davey Cutler for me?" he asked.

"He's out on patrol," Yardley reported. "I could radio him."

"Would you do that, ask him to call me."

"Sure."

Cutler called minutes later.

"I need you to pick up a key from Beggs at forensics and try it on the door to Roberto Sandoval's apartment," Johnson said. "Let me know as soon as you find out if the key is a fit or not."

"Yes, sir," Cutler said, thrilled to be back in the game.

Marco Weido paced his living room with the television on. He needed to be at an appointment in San Francisco in less than ninety minutes, but his missing gun was distracting him. Weido lit one cigarette after another with a red plastic lighter, the need to use the ninety-nine-cent piece-of-crap only aggravated him further. He was just about to head upstairs to shower and dress for his meeting when the TV program was interrupted by a news bulletin.

A thirty-eight caliber hand gun, discovered by the San Francisco Police Department in the trunk of stolen Cadillac, had been identified as the weapon that had been used to kill Assistant D.A. Roberto Sandoval late Wednesday night.

Also in the trunk was the body of ex-convict Salvatore DiMarco of Oakland, killed from a gunshot wound to the head. Ballistic testing had determined the bullet that killed DiMarco was also .38 caliber, but had not been fired from the same weapon. The evidence suggested there may have been more than one perpetrator involved in Sandoval's death.

Lieutenant Lopez, who made the announcement, declined to offer any additional speculation.

The lieutenant reminded reporters that the San Francisco Homicide Division was in the business of solid investigation, not in the business of playing guessing games.

Lopez assured the Press that further information would be made public when, and only when, it could be substantiated.

Marco Weido decided it would be a good idea to postpone the meeting until later in the day, whether his employer agreed or not. He made the phone call, and was very grateful when the call went straight to voicemail. He expressed his regret that he would not be able to make the appointment, and added he hoped the meeting could be rescheduled for later in the afternoon. He apologized for any inconvenience and he disconnected.

Weido was relieved to have that out of the way, at least temporarily, but there were much more troubling concerns. As much as he missed having it, he was not too worried about the cigarette lighter. There were a good number of those lighters around. The gun was an entirely different story. If found it could be connected to the bullet that killed Sal DiMarco.

And if the fuck who pinched the weapon led the police to his front door, Marco would have a lot of explaining to do.

Weido lit another Marlboro and threw the plastic piece-of-shit lighter against the wall.

Lieutenant Lopez had barely survived her statement to the press.

She had fought through the pain in her head, said what she had to say, and had quickly retreated.

Lopez had just forced down a couple of extra-strength Excedrin tablets when Yardley rang from the front desk.

"I have good news and bad news, Lieutenant. Would you like the good news first?"

"Shoot."

"I just received word that your noon appointment has been put-off until three this afternoon."

"That is good news. What's the bad news?"

"We located Roberto Sandoval's widow in Italy. She will be flying into San Francisco later today. Mrs. Sandoval is meeting Dr. Altman at seven to officially identify the body."

"And?"

"She insisted the lead investigator be there at that time."

"Terrific. You're batting a thousand, Yardley."

"No need to thank me, Lieutenant."

"I wasn't going to, Sergeant."

Cutler called shortly after eleven.

"Worked like a charm, Sergeant."

"Okay, bring the key back to Beggs and forget about it for a while. Go back to what you were doing. I'll let you know if I need anything else."

"Yes, sir."

"Good work. Thanks, Davey."

"You're welcome, sir."

Johnson put down the receiver, wondering whether it was all that helpful to be right about his hunches so often.

It was a new ballgame.

Obtaining the access code to the parking garage at Roberto Sandoval's building would not be exceedingly difficult.

Getting hold of a key to Roberto Sandoval's apartment was, on the other hand, a very impressive accomplishment.

He could not decide whether or not to go straight to Lopez with the news.

He wished Amy would return his call and help him, as only she could, work out what to do about Lopez. And what to do about Jake Diamond.

Johnson realized he was famished. He decided all other considerations could wait until after lunch.

Ralph Morrison was a police groupie, a police hound.

Since high school, Morrison had wanted nothing more than to be a member of the Oakland Police Department. He had signed up for the first Iraq war because he thought it would look good on his résumé. A wound sustained in Kuwait left his right arm and hand useless. Ralph's dreams of becoming a police officer and hopefully, in time, a plain clothes detective, were replaced by a monthly disability check.

Since then, Ralph had spent what could have been idle time with a studious daily examination of crime in Oakland and with what the police department was doing about it. He listened to dispatches on his shortwave radio, and he spent hours in and around police stations, talking with officers as they entered and exited, with endless inquiries about the state of the war on crime. Ralph knew them all by name, and many of them could tell you his name, although some of the tags they employed to identify Ralph *The Grinch* Morrison were not flattering.

When Morrison walked into the Buttercup Grill and Bar on Broadway, a five minute stroll from the Oakland Police Station on Seventh Street, he spotted a familiar face immediately. He moved quickly across the restaurant and sat in a booth opposite a man working on a large plate of pork chops and eggs.

"Hey," Ralph said.

"Roll Call Ralph," Marco Weido said. "How's it hanging?"

"I'm surprised to find you here. I thought you had a fancy new job across the bay."

"Haven't found a place there yet where I can get a Coors draft with my breakfast."

"Did you hear about Sal DiMarco?" Ralph asked.

"Which Sal DiMarco?" Weido replied.

"Salvatore 'Buttonhead' DiMarco. They found him dead in the trunk of a Cadillac over in Frisco."

"Good choice of vehicles. Roomy trunks. They have any idea who whacked him?"

"Nothing yet. They're working on a lead."

"Oh?"

"They found a lighter at the scene. And get this. It was a Zippo with an Oakland PD logo, old time. Don Folgueras is working up a list of anyone who may have owned one like it for a homicide detective in San Francisco."

"Homicide dick have a name?"

"Johnson, Sergeant Roxton Johnson," Ralph said.

"Nice moniker. Anything else?"

"Not yet."

"Then let me finish my breakfast," Weido said.

"Sure," Ralph said, rising from his seat. "Good seeing you."

Ralph Morrison headed for the restaurant counter.

"And Ralph," Weido called after him.

"Yes?" Ralph said, hoping to be invited to stay.

"If you hear anything else, be sure to let me know."

. . .

Johnson didn't want to stray far from his desk so he had ordered out from Mo's Restaurant on Grant Street. Mo's had a legendary reputation for huge portions and prompt delivery. The Belly Buster was a half-pound char-broiled hamburger smothered in sautéed mushrooms, caramelized onions and melted cheddar with a side of French fries and killer homemade chili, accompanied by a large Root Beer Float to wash it all down.

Rocky Johnson felt pleased with one of his decisions for the first time all morning.

His wife, Amy, would have been horrified.

The phone on Johnson's desk rang a few minutes before noon, just as he finished off the float.

Lieutenant Folgueras calling from Oakland.

"I worked up a preliminary list of Oakland police officers who were in possession of one of the Zippo lighters initially. It's not complete, I'll keep working on it, but I thought you might want to see what came up so far," Folgueras reported. "I can shoot it over."

"That would be great," Johnson said, giving Folgueras the fax number at Vallejo.

"We're working as quickly as possible on clearing the gun used in the attempted liquor store stick-up. If it doesn't tie into something more sinister over here, I might be able to get it over to you as early as tomorrow morning."

"Great, Don. I really appreciate your help."

"Anything else you need right now?" Folgueras asked.

"Just the fax, Lieutenant. Thanks again."

A few minutes later, Johnson retrieved the two-page print-out from the office fax machine and walked it back to his desk.

He quickly scanned the first page, and then went on to the next.

The name Victor Lopez jumped off the second page like a frightened jackrabbit.

Sergeant Johnson set the list on his desk and reached for Jake Diamond's phone number.

TWENTY

Call me Nostradamus.

The scene at St. Mary's was nearly a carbon copy of what I had predicted it would be.

Vinnie's mom had arrived early, in time to be at the head of the line when visiting hours began.

It had been some time since I had seen Mrs. Stradivarius, but she had not changed a lick. She remained a very attractive woman and she held herself with great dignity, despite the poor hand she had been dealt. Her husband had fallen or been pushed off the roof of a seven-story building when Vinnie was fifteen years old. The insurance company tried to withhold benefits on the grounds that Sarge Stradivarius' death was a suicide.

Jimmy Pigeon used all of his resources to convince the courts to rule the fall an accident and Sarge's wife and son ultimately collected the life insurance settlement.

Pigeon took Vinnie under his wing and became a substitute father for the troubled teen. Although Vinnie did not inherit his father's drinking problems, the boy did become heir to the gambling gene. Big-time. Jimmy Pigeon had always suspected the plunge from the roof had been aided by someone Sarge owed money to, unpaid loans to cover unsuccessful gambling wagers.

Now Vinnie was in the same sort of mess.

And with Jimmy gone, it was up to me to come to Vinnie's rescue.

Good old Uncle Jake.

In truth, Frances Stradivarius knew her son was not exactly an angel, but she also knew Vinnie was basically a well-meaning kid and she was totally devoted to her thirty-two-year-old *boy*.

When I walked into the hospital room, Frances was sitting at Vinnie's bedside holding his hand. His hand was one of the few parts of his body not covered with bruises. Vinnie looked better than he had the night before, which is like saying Rocky Balboa looked better than Apollo Creed after their first championship bout. And his speech was unimpaired, which isn't necessarily an improvement considering his impressive ability to talk a blue streak.

Dr. Shepherd had finally allowed a police officer to enter and question Vinnie after his mother arrived, and Fran insisted she be present for the interview. So Vinnie told both the same story.

He had been heading down the stairs to the Powell Street BART station when a man running to catch a train hit him from behind and sent him bouncing to the bottom of the stone steps.

Not bad.

At least it seemed Vinnie had convinced his audience.

Vinnie Strings liked to consider himself my "right-hand man." In reality he was more like a second left foot.

I tried keeping Vinnie busy helping Darlene and I with minor private investigation assignments, in the same manner Jimmy Pigeon had, in an attempt to keep him out of the kind of mess he had managed to get himself into.

To his credit, he tried very hard to assist us.

There was not much Vinnie disliked. The three things Vinnie did not like were losing bets, as good as he was at it, disappointing me, and color photography. I had the delusional notion I could find out more about his trouble with Manny Sandoval. How much he owed? How long he had to come up with payment? What Vinnie could expect if he failed to deliver?

I had ways of extracting information from Vinnie on those rare occasions when he was reluctant to talk, mostly involving assurances that he had not let me down or pissed me off.

I was hoping for anything that might aid negotiations when Travis Duncan set up a chit-chat with Manny Sandoval later that night, as Travis had assured me he would. But Strings was not about to admit to me he had totally screwed up, again, unless I walked into the hospital room in a jogging suit with a mutt on a leash and a paper bag over my head with a big smile penciled on it pretending to be Darlene. And even then, not as long as his mother was glued to his bedside.

So we ruminated on the upcoming baseball season and about the weather and I excused myself on the grounds I did not wish to further impose on quality time between mother and son.

Call me non-confrontational.

From St. Mary's Hospital I headed for the office to put that particular skill through a series of true challenges.

My route to the office might have raised some eyebrows had anyone bothered to notice. I went out of my way to approach my destination from the north, avoiding a stroll past the entrance of Molinari's and a chance encounter with Angelo Verdi.

Call me stealthy.

I made it into the building unscathed.

I wasn't as fortunate when I walked through the door of Diamond Investigations. Darlene looked up from her desk and got right down to it.

"Sir Galahad. Good of you to drop in. I brought coffee up for you. It's ice cold. I didn't want to bring you donuts so I didn't."

I let it slide.

"Angelo asked if you had taken care of my 'problem'. I wasn't quite sure which problem he was referring to, since I have more than a few. Nevertheless, I told him you had done so, admirably. Your reward is a free order of octopus salad his wife whipped up this morning."

I was tempted to run straight down.

Darlene didn't miss a beat.

"You had several phone calls," she said. "Interested?"

She finally let me get my first word in.

"Sure."

I thought it would be a good idea to wait awhile before I tried sweet-talking her into joining Joe and Angela for dinner.

"Travis Duncan called. He left a phone number."

"Did he say where he was?"

"I wouldn't dream of asking," Darlene answered. "There was a call from Ray Boyle."

Oh, boy.

"Did he say what it was about?"

"He said it was about wanting you to call him."

"I see."

Darlene was having way too much fun.

"Your mother called to wish you a happy St. Joseph's Day. She said she was sorry she couldn't have you over for dinner since, as you may or may not recall, your mother is down in Atlanta visiting your brother and her grandchildren, and she will be very disappointed if you fail to return her call."

I had entirely forgotten.

"Of course I know where my mother is. And I will call her. Did Sergeant Johnson call?"

"No. Why would Johnson be calling you?"

"To wish me a cheery St. Joseph's Day," I said, finally getting a jab in, but Darlene had me beat by points. "Thanks for the coffee."

End of Round One.

I picked up the paper cup from her desk and moved to my own desk in the back room.

I had three phone calls to consider, with no three-sided coin handy. On top of that, the thought of Mrs. Verdi's tasty *insalada di polpo* was distracting me.

I finally decided to call my mom first, and save the coin-toss to determine whether I would reluctantly call Ray Boyle or reluctantly call Travis Duncan next.

My brother Abraham was two years my senior. Other than both being born when Ike was President we had very little in common.

While I was failing biology in high school, Abe was eating it up. I aspired to be an actor, to gain fame and fortune and meet pretty girls; Abe wanted only to be a scientist and marry the girl he had dated since they were fifteen. They had two perfect children, and Abraham was devoted to his wife and offspring and to saving the world from contagious diseases at the Centers for Disease Control in Atlanta.

My father, Bernard, came to Brooklyn in 1955.

His Jewish, Russian born parents had immigrated to Israel in 1948. Bernie decided to try New York. He changed his name to Diamond for two good reasons. His father's surname, though starting with D, was followed by ten more letters only two of which were vowels. Not only was it impossible to pronounce or to spell, it made one dizzy just seeing it on paper. On top of that, Russian names were not very popular in 1950's America.

Bernie met, and quickly married, the daughter of Italian immigrants. Roman Catholics. Mary Falco was a public school teacher. The newlyweds took the ground floor apartment in the three-family house where Mary had grown up. Mary's sister and her husband lived in the apartment above. Mary's parents lived in the basement below.

The neighborhood was populated exclusively by Italians and Italian-Americans, with the exception of Bernie Diamond.

Abraham chose Judaism.

I chose baseball and the Catholic Church.

If I couldn't meet girls on the ball field, I could at least hope to charm one or two at Mass.

In that, and many other ways, Abraham was more my father's son and I was more my mother's son. My father seemed to understand Abe and to never quite figure out what I was about. I'm sure it had a lot to do with the fact that Jacob Diamond wasn't particularly self-aware while my brother was always sure about who he was. And who he would become.

My brother became Abraham Dykhovichny, and even learned how to spell and pronounce it.

The irony is I had adopted many more of my father's passions and preferences than Abe ever had. A love of classic literature, an undying devotion to the New York Mets, a true appreciation of fine Tennessee whiskey and the pleasure of an after-dinner smoke.

The finest moments my father and I shared were out on the back porch in Brooklyn, while Abe helped Mary with the dishes, talking enthusiastically about Dickens or the 1986 World Series, sipping sour mash and firing up a Camel non-filter or two.

The phone call was short and sweet. I spoke with Abe for a few minutes, gaining a good deal of knowledge regarding the climate in central Georgia. I then wished my mom a wonderful visit and a safe trip home and promised I would cross the Bay to see her in Pleasant Hill as soon as I possibly could.

With that taken care of, I dug into my pants pocket for a loose coin.

Heads Duncan. Tails Boyle.

George Washington's stoic profile sealed the deal.

The best way to describe the phone conversation with Duncan would be to transcribe the dialogue in its entirety.

"Good morning, Jake."

"Good morning, Travis."

"I was hoping to pick you up at your office around eleven tonight if that works for you."

"I can make it work."

"I'll see you then."

"See you then."

Over and Out.

I called Boyle.

Ray Boyle and I shared affection for each other that had evolved from frigid to ice cold to lukewarm.

Our earliest encounters could accurately be described as the interaction between a man trying to do his job and the oaf always getting in his way. I played the oaf to perfection. Boyle was a Los Angeles homicide detective who I first locked horns with when working with Jimmy Pigeon. Most recently, Ray had helped to put away a very nasty Chicago lawyer who had made my life a living nightmare. I was indebted to Lieutenant Boyle, and had even learned to like the guy, but news of his call had left me more apprehensive than curious.

Boyle wasn't in the habit of calling just to chew the fat.

"I need your help, Jake," Lieutenant Boyle said, after the very brief formalities.

I have never been big on conspiracy theory. The questions of who killed Kennedy and where Jimmy Hoffa disappeared to were moot to me. These were questions without definitive answers.

But being asked for assistance by police detectives in both San Francisco and Los Angeles in the span of two short days was a coincidence that had me worrying I may have somehow angered the gods.

"I would be happy to help if I can, Ray," I said, though the word *happy* was a blatant exaggeration.

"Does the name Bobo Bigelow ring a bell?" he asked.

As well as Quasimodo does.

"Unfortunately."

"Bigelow is holed up somewhere in the Bay area and I need you to find him."

Bobo was a small time con artist who would stab you in the back if he had to circumnavigate the globe in order to approach you from behind. Bigelow was someone you worked diligently at losing...not finding.

"What's it about?"

"Bigelow was witness to an incident down here I'm trying to sort out," Ray said, giving new meaning to the term *sketchy information.*

"Can you tell me more?"

"I could, but I won't. For now, I just need you to locate him and sit on him until I can ask the man a few questions he has been trying very hard to dodge."

Okay.

"Why not reach out to the troops up here?" I inquired, quickly regretting I had.

"If I wanted to involve the SFPD, Diamond, I wouldn't have called you."

Fair enough.

"Any hints as to where I might begin the search?"

"The Kit Kat Club in Oakland. Off Lakeshore, north of the MacArthur Freeway. Ask for Gloria. Try to charm her."

"I'll try my best."

"And, Jake, unless you have other pressing engagements today, please get on this right away."

I decided not to mention I could hardly have had a greater number of pressing engagements if I were campaigning for the Presidency.

"I'm on it, Ray," I said.

"Thank you, give my best to Darlene."

Over and Out.

My appointment calendar was filling in nicely. I might even be able to squeeze in a little time for Sergeant Johnson if he decided to call on me. The only thing missing was some gainful employment, but then I wouldn't have been able to fit it into my schedule anyway.

I threw on my jacket, armed with the Hugo paperback, and walked up front into the reception area.

"Would you care to join me for dinner at Joe and Angela's this evening, Darlene?" I asked, not missing a step.

"Sure," she said.

How about that.

"I can pick you up around five-thirty."

"Sure. Where are you headed?"

"Across the Bay."

"But your mother is still in Atlanta," Darlene said, trying to bait me.

"It's something else," I said, not biting. "If Sergeant Johnson calls, tell him I'll get back to him as soon as I can."

"Roger that. See you later."

"Five-thirty."

"Got it."

"Okay."

"Okay."

"Later."

Call me a master of repartee.

I left the office considering the unappealing prospect of successfully tracking down Bobo Bigelow.

TWENTY ONE

Darlene Roman answered the phone call.

"Diamond Investigations, please hold. I have someone on the other line."

"This is Sergeant Johnson."

"Oh. Sorry, Sergeant. Go ahead. I use that greeting to fool prospective clients into thinking business is booming."

"Can I speak to Diamond?"

"You missed him by ten minutes. Jake mentioned you might be calling. If you could tell me what it's about, maybe I can help."

"No offense, Ms. Roman, but I can't and you couldn't."

"No offense taken, Sergeant, would you like me to let Jake know you called?"

"I would like that very much."

"In that case I certainly will, Sergeant. Have a nice day."

"Thank you, Ms. Roman. I will certainly try."

Johnson placed the receiver down and the phone rang almost immediately. It was his wife Amy calling from Philadelphia.

"Is everything alright, Rocky?"

"Not exactly."

"Tell me what is troubling you."

"I miss you."

"I miss you. Now, tell me what is troubling you."

And he did.

Travis Duncan had put the word out on the street that he was looking for Manny Sandoval, and he didn't want Manny to know he was being looked for. Duncan stipulated he wanted to find Sandoval in a setting unencumbered by bystanders. He offered a handsome reward for useful information.

In no time he received a lot of useless information, but he did manage to get what he needed.

Sandoval ran a popular Mexican restaurant in the Mission. The eatery stopped serving at ten on Friday evenings. All of the diners, wait and kitchen staff, and the cleaning crew were gone by eleven or so. Manny religiously remained at the bar, washing down homemade salsa and tortilla chips with several bottles of Negra Modelo. Only his two bodyguards stayed on board with him.

Travis had scouted the restaurant, imaginatively called Manny's, during lunch hour. The bar was on the left side as you walked in. It ran nearly sixty feet and was lined with stools. Along the right wall were four small tables with two chairs at each. Further back was the dining room, and beyond the dining room were the restrooms and a locked door leading out to the alley behind the restaurant. After taking note of the layout of the establishment, Duncan had phoned Diamond to schedule a rendezvous at Jake's office at eleven.

Duncan would have Diamond call Manny at the restaurant and ask if it would be alright to drop over with some cash. He had learned Vinnie Strings was into Sandoval for four thousand dollars. Manny would gladly invite Jake to stop in. Travis had the cash handy, and he could be reimbursed at Jake's convenience.

Duncan thought catching a movie would be a perfect way to kill a little time. He chose one entitled *Taking Lives,* which had opened that afternoon. He thoroughly enjoyed serial killer films and was a serious Angelina Jolie fan.

Travis Duncan couldn't help feeling that, so far, he was having a good day.

Laura Lopez was feeling a lot better, at least physically. She had taken a short walk through North Beach and settled onto a bench in Washington Square Park with a dry toasted bagel and a cup of green tea.

Back at her desk at Vallejo Street Station, she glanced at the wall clock as she played with the Zippo lighter, turning it in her hand like Captain Queeg fiddling with his ball bearings on the *Caine*. The lieutenant stopped herself, and dropped the lighter into a desk drawer.

A stack of files had arrived from the D. A.'s office, in time for the noon meeting, which had ultimately been postponed until three. Files relating to cases Roberto Sandoval had been working on at the time of his death and jackets on all of the recently released convicts who he had helped put away.

Along with a copy of Sandoval's appointment planner.

It was ten minutes after two in the afternoon. In less than an hour, Lopez would have to contend with Liam Duffey's investigator, and then at seven she would need to deal with Roberto Sandoval's widow.

Thinking about it would only bring back the headache, so Lopez returned to the files.

Oakland police officer Bruce Perry stood beside a nurse looking down at the seemingly lifeless body of Blake Sanchez.

"Who is the other boy?" Perry asked.

"The younger brother, he's been sitting by the bedside for hours."

"What are the older boy's chances?"

"Fifty-fifty."

Lieutenant Folgueras had sent Perry to the hospital with the hope Sanchez might speak.

"We're hoping he can tell us where he came by the weapon he carried into the liquor store," Perry said.

"He hasn't said a word," the nurse repeated.

"You'll call us if he does."

"I will."

Perry followed the nurse out of the hospital room.

Raul Sanchez looked at his brother, attached to tubes and wires, missing the animated facial expressions that made Blake so special to the younger boy. Raul had listened to the nurse and the police officer talking. His brother might be unable to say where he had found the gun but, if someone made the information profitable enough, Raul could.

· · ·

Weido drove to his appointment across the Bay Bridge.

Marco had been told that delaying the meeting again would be totally unacceptable. He had been admonished as if he was a child and talked down to like an idiot. It made him angry and, for the moment, took his mind off concerns about the missing gun and lighter.

As much as Marco prized the generous monetary rewards for his services, there was a thin line between being valuable to an employer and being made to feel like a lackey.

On top of that, he had been asked to pick up a woman at the San Francisco airport and drive her into the city.

Now he was a fucking chauffeur.

Don Folgueras had some new leads and some new dead ends.

Office Perry updated Lieutenant Folgueras on the medical condition of Blake Sanchez. The prognosis had improved from heavy odds against surviving to an even chance, but the would-be liquor store bandit remained unable to speak.

The Oakland Police Forensics Department was not yet ready to release the handgun Blake Sanchez had used in the attempted robbery.

However, Folgueras had new information that could possibly be helpful to Sergeant Johnson in San Francisco.

He called Johnson, thankful he had a little more to offer than just disappointing news.

The logoed Zippo lighters issued to members of the Oakland police department had been produced in seven separate pressings between 1995 and 2001. Each of the lighters had been stamped with a particular serial number. The last two digits of the number indicated the year it was issued—a fact that would narrow down the search for the initial owner. The entire serial number could positively identify the original recipient, but only if it had be voluntarily registered within thirty days of the issue date. Some who received a lighter had registered their Zippo while others had not.

Johnson thanked Folgueras once again for his diligence.

. . .

Bruce Perry was big-hearted, which at times inspired him to have a big mouth. Whenever Perry ran into Ralph Morrison, Perry could not help but feel pity for *The Grinch*. He saw Ralph as a lonesome, unfulfilled man, the butt of cruel jokes from Perry's fellow police officers. When he returned to the police station from the hospital, Perry saw Ralph standing at his usual position out front, eagerly looking for interaction with members of the club he had never been invited to join.

Perry perceived Morrison as innocent and harmless. When Ralph greeted Perry warmly and asked what Perry had been doing lately to help make Oakland safer for its citizens, Perry was willing to talk, willing to satisfy Morrison's sad yearning to feel involved. He told Ralph about the attempted liquor store robbery, the weapon that might be related to a homicide in San Francisco, and the boy in the hospital who could possibly tell the police where he got the gun. Perry excused himself, saying he had pressing business inside. He entered the station feeling as if he had done a good deed. Shining a little light into one of Ralph Morrison's many dark days.

Morrison watched Perry walk away. The talk of a homicide in San Francisco, one the Oakland police department was helping to investigate, brought his earlier encounter with Marco Weido to mind. He had no way of knowing if Weido would be interested, but the opportunity to make points with a decorated police detective was worth exploring. And Weido *had* asked *The Grinch* to keep his ears open.

Ralph Morrison decided it wouldn't hurt to share what he had learned.

Talking with his wife had helped Sergeant Johnson a great deal, but now the calmness Amy had helped him achieve was beginning to slip away.

Johnson was waiting to hear from Diamond, to reluctantly ask for the private investigator's assistance.

The sergeant was also waiting for a fax from Folgueras, a list of numbers that could possibly identify the original owner of the cigarette lighter Johnson had discovered at the scene of Sal DiMarco's last stand.

Then he would need to work out how to get the Zippo back into his hands.

Darlene Roman finally reached Jake on his cell phone. She could barely hear his greeting over the loud background noise.

"Jesus, Jake, where are you, at a bull fight?"

"Something like that, something happen?"

"Johnson called. He would like you to call him back."

"Listen, Darlene. I can't right now. Please call him for me. Ask him to meet me at the office at ten tonight."

"What's going on, Jake."

"I can't talk now. I will fill you in when I pick you up for dinner."

The line went dead. Darlene replaced the receiver and the telephone rang.

It was Detective Nicolace.

"I watched Norman Hall watch your house for a few hours this morning. I followed him for a while when he left, I don't believe he will be back there again. When will you be leaving work today?"

"I plan to leave by four. Jake will be picking me up for dinner at five-thirty."

"I will be looking out for Hall outside your house until Jake arrives. After you leave I'll use the back door key and wait for you inside until you get home."

"We should be back between nine and nine-thirty. Jake has an appointment at ten."

"I'll see you later," Megan said.

After ending the short conversation with Megan Nicolace, Darlene called Sergeant Johnson to relay Jake's message.

"Bigelow called me. He wants to make a deal."

"What kind of deal?"

"The usual. Bobo gets enough cash to disappear and he forgets everything he may have seen here in Los Angeles."

"Boyle will find him. And Boyle will make him remember."

"I agree."

"Did Bigelow say where we could make the deal?"

"Not exactly. Bigelow said we could contact him through a friend of his, Gloria, works at the Kit Kat Club in Oakland."

"So you want me to drop by the club and talk to her?"

"I found out where she lives. Go there instead. With any luck she has Bobo stashed at her place."

"And if I find him?"

"Shut him up. Forever."

"No problem. Give me the address."

Johnson's patience was being tested, and the sergeant's patience was not an A student.

Johnson had been waiting for one thing or another all day. And each time it arrived, it led to more questions with answers just out of his reach.

He finally received word from Darlene Roman. The word being he would have to wait until ten to talk to Jake Diamond.

Just before three, Johnson finally received the list from Folgueras. Now he would need to get his hands on the cigarette lighter he had abandoned in Lopez's office. And he wasn't looking forward to being treated like a nuisance again.

Rocky Johnson felt like the pilot of a plane waiting for the clearance to land, with no permission coming. Trapped in an endless holding pattern, circling the runway.

He went over to Lopez's office and tapped lightly on her door.

"Come in," she called.

"Sorry to bother you again, Lieutenant," he said as he walked in.

"Can it wait? I have a meeting in a few minutes."

"I just need the cigarette lighter I left here earlier."

Lopez fished around in her desk drawer and came up with the Zippo. She rose from her seat and handed it to Johnson.

Simple as that.

"Something come up?"

"Could be something, could be nothing," Johnson replied.

"Keep me informed."

Dismissed.

"I will," he said, and hurried out of the office.

He nearly collided with a man moving to the lieutenant's door.

"Excuse me," the man said, offering Johnson a handshake and identifying himself by name. "I'm looking for Lieutenant Lopez. I'm District Attorney Duffey's special investigator. I have an appointment with the lieutenant."

Johnson transferred the Zippo from his right to his left hand and accepted the handshake.

"I'm Sergeant Johnson. This is the lieutenant's office. She's expecting you."

"Thanks," Duffey's investigator said. He watched Johnson walk off, his eyes glued to the cigarette lighter in Johnson's hand. He turned and rapped on the office door.

"Come in."

Lopez looked up from her desk as he entered.

"What a surprise," she said. "Mr. Duffey failed to mention his new investigator would be an old colleague."

"Good to see you, too, Laura," he said.

"Have a seat, Marco. Make yourself comfortable.

TWENTY TWO

According to the sign prominently posted at the entrance, business hours ran between noon and two in the morning. When I went through the door, and it closed behind me, there was no way of knowing what time it actually was.

The Kit Kat Club was dark and loud, no windows to let in daylight, no acoustics to mute the noise. It was designed to provide patrons with no clues to where they were or when, and it did the job very effectively.

I somehow managed to find my way to the bar through all of the smoke.

A tall, muscular bartender appeared immediately, in very tight blue jeans and a tighter tank top leaving nothing to the imagination, proudly displaying an upper-arm tattoo that read *Born To Be Wild*.

She asked me what I was drinking.

I asked for George Dickel sour-mash, doubting my chances.

"Mr. Dickel has left the house. Will Mr. Daniels do the trick?"

"I guess he will have to."

"Rocks?"

"Sure. I'm looking for Gloria."

"You're looking at Gloria," she said.

"My name is Jake Diamond. I'm looking for an old friend who might need my help."

"You came to the wrong place, Mr. Diamond. The majority of our clientele are beyond help."

"I'm looking for Bobo Bigelow."

"Sounds like the name of a circus clown."

Gloria looked me up and down and sideways. She placed a glass full of ice in front of me and reached behind her for a bottle of Jack Daniels.

Before she poured, she asked for I.D.

"It's been a long time since I was carded for a drink," I said, sporting an artificial smile.

Ray Boyle had asked me to charm the lady. Believe it or not, I was giving it my best shot.

"Don't flatter yourself. I just need to see if you are who you say you are."

I pulled out my wallet and I handed Gloria my laminated private investigator's license card, goofy photo and all.

"I can't imagine anyone else claiming to be Jake Diamond," I said, as she looked from me to the card and back to me again. "I have trouble admitting it myself a lot of the time."

"That's one goofy photo," she said, returning the card and pouring a healthy dose of Jack Daniels over the ice.

"Thanks for noticing."

"I'll be back in a minute," Gloria said.

She walked to a telephone at the opposite end of the bar.

I nursed the Dickel substitute.

True to her word, Gloria was back in a flash. She grabbed a cocktail napkin and scribbled an address and a phone number.

"Bigelow is at my place, here's the address."

"I'm a sucker for wild goose chases, Gloria."

"You'll have to wait for one. This is on the level. Bobo wants to see you. Call him at that phone number before you go in…he's easily spooked."

"Thank you."

I rose from the stool, dropped two twenties on the bar, knocked down what was left of my drink, and turned to leave.

"Watch your back, Mr. Diamond."

I pushed through the door and the daylight nearly blinded me.

I made it to my car and climbed in, but before I fired up the engine I called Ray Boyle in Los Angeles.

"Did you locate Bigelow?" Ray asked.

"I think so. I'm on my way to find out. Before I go, Ray, I would appreciate knowing what I might be walking into."

So, Lieutenant Boyle told me what I might be walking into.

. . .

A teenage girl, calling herself Katya, had stumbled into a Los Angeles police station four days earlier. The Ides of March.

She had been badly beaten and did not speak English.

With the help of a Russian translator, Katya told police she had been brought into the country from St. Petersburg with the guarantee of a position as a housekeeper for a wealthy Beverly Hills family. When she arrived, she found herself with a number of other young Russian women who had been promised the same opportunity, but were told they would need to work off the expenses of their relocation at a night club called The Volga, a Burbank establishment that doubled as a modern day bordello.

The girls were literally held hostage, and were strongly advised against failing to meet their obligations. Katya was sent into one of the club's private rooms with a client. She resisted and the man got rough. Two bouncers responded to the commotion and restrained the client. Katya bolted.

The Los Angeles Police Department responded swiftly. The police raided The Volga that night and made arrests. The girls were collected and transferred to the Department of Immigration and Naturalization in an attempt to sort it all out.

The owner of The Volga, Ivan Rimsky, was not found on the premises at the time of the raid. Detectives did not find Ivan at his home.

The following day, Ivan contacted the Los Angeles District Attorney's Office. He said he would agree to turn himself in, and name the man who supplied the girls to the night club, in exchange for immunity and protection. The D.A. agreed, but Rimsky never showed. Apparently Rimsky decided to run instead, and that is where Bigelow came into the picture.

Bobo had adopted a new career in a long line of nefarious enterprises.

. . .

"Bigelow was making ends meet forging papers," Boyle said. "Driver's licenses and the like. He whipped up a new passport for Ivan. When Rimsky went to Bigelow's office on Vine Street to pick up the passport, he was followed. Bobo stepped into a back room to collect the finished document and heard gunshots. Bigelow opened the connecting door and spied a man in an expensive business suit and a very large man holding a gun. Rimsky was bleeding all over Bobo's prized Moroccan rug. The big man turned the gun on Bigelow and squeezed off a shot, missing Bobo by inches. Bigelow slammed the door and escaped through a rear exit."

"And you know all of this how?" I asked Boyle.

"I heard it from your friend Willie Dogtail."

"Oh?"

"Bobo dropped in on Dogtail to catch his breath, spilled the works. Willie recommended Bobo call me. Bigelow said he had considered it but needed some time to think, mentioned he had a friend, Gloria, worked at the Kit Kat up in Oakland, who could help him lay low while he deliberated."

"And Willie called you."

"And Willie called me. I doubt there is any question the dude in the suit is the man Rimsky was going to name as the trafficker of teenage girls. I want this bastard, Diamond, for kidnapping and for murder," Boyle said, "and Bigelow can identify him. And I can't protect Bigelow unless he comes in."

"Gloria said Bobo wants to see me," I said.

"Then go see him, Jake. Before someone else does."

I started the car and headed for the address Gloria had written on the Kit Kat Club cocktail napkin.

I pulled in to a spot at the curb across the street from the apartment building. I called the phone number Gloria had also provided. She had given me the impression that if I went in without warning, Bobo might take a back door exit again.

There was no answer.

I was about to leave my car when a big man, the size of an Oakland Raiders defensive lineman, hurried out of the apartment house. He looked up and down the street, rushed down the front stairs, walked quickly to the closest intersection, turned left and disappeared. His face was vaguely familiar, but I couldn't quite put my finger on where I might have seen him before.

I waited a full ten minutes before going in.

I found Apartment 208 and rapped on the door.

Nothing.

I tried the door knob, the door was unlocked. I pushed it open as far as it would go, far enough for me to see Bigelow's body on the floor blocking the door.

The bullet hole in Bigelow's right temple and the pool of blood spreading around his head made checking for a pulse seem frivolous.

I closed the door and promptly left the building.

I was halfway across the Bay Bridge, parked on the side of a deserted road in Treasure Island, before I called Ray Boyle.

And I finally recalled where and when I had crossed paths with the gorilla fleeing Gloria's apartment building.

"Did you find Bigelow?"

"I recognized an ape coming out of the place before I went in. He used to be a strong arm for Crazy Al Pazzo. He drove Al around before Pazzo was locked away at California State Prison in Lancaster. The mook who was granted a *get out of jail* card for giving Pazzo up."

"Carmine Cicero?"

"If that was his name, Ray, I was never formally introduced. And I'm guessing it was Cicero who shot Rimsky and parted Bigelow's hair in Los Angeles. Do you have any idea who Carmine's latest employer might be?"

"What does Bobo say?"

"Bobo can't say anything, Carmine didn't miss his target this time."

"Dead?"

"Very dead. I was a little too late."

"Lucky you weren't a little too early. What's the address, I'll give the Oakland PD a head's up."

"Please ask them to clean up the mess before Gloria gets home, Ray."

"Will do."

I gave Boyle the address and asked if there was anything else I could do, hoping for a *no, thank you.*

"I'll let you know," he said. "Thanks, Jake."

Close enough.

"Anytime, Ray."

"If we can find Carmine, and identify his new benefactor, I think we'll have our man. You may have to testify you saw Cicero at the scene."

"No problem."

"Good. Thanks again."

"Good luck, Ray," I said in parting. I hoped if they found Carmine he would be considerate enough to be carrying the murder weapon in his breast pocket.

I restarted the car, slipped it into gear, and set out on the second leg of my return trip to San Francisco.

TWENTY THREE

Laura Lopez and Marco Weido had two things in common.

They had both graduated from the Oakland Police Academy ten years earlier and they shared a mutual dislike for one another.

All similarities ended there.

The meeting between the lieutenant and the D.A.'s special investigator lasted exactly eighteen minutes, and could not end soon enough for either participant.

Lopez dominated time of possession.

Weido remained distracted by the vision of his cigarette lighter in Sergeant Johnson's paw.

"Thank you for taking the time to meet today," Lopez said. "I hope it was not inconvenient. Please thank District Attorney Duffey for sending the information I requested. It is going to take me a while longer to study all of the material thoroughly, but there's something I came across you can help look into for the time being."

Lopez was laying the ground rules, letting Weido know, and letting Duffey know through Weido, who was running the show and who was there to lend a subordinate hand.

And she was doing it as politely as possible.

Weido did not like it at all, nor would Duffey, but Marco was in no position to argue at the moment.

"That's why I'm here, Lieutenant," Weido said. "To help."

"Roberto Sandoval had a meeting scheduled for yesterday morning at ten at the D.A.'s office with a man named Justin Walker. Walker never showed. He had probably heard the news of Sandoval's death. I'm interested to know who the man is, what he does, and what the meeting might have been about."

"You want me to find him and interrogate him?"

"Just find him, find out who he is. We can decide what to

156

do about him later," Lopez said. "It would be a great help, and I can continue going through Sandoval's case files."

"Any clues as to where I should start?" Weido asked.

"Just the name, Justin Walker, it's all we have."

"I'll get right on it."

"Thank you," Lopez said.

And the eighteen minutes were up.

Back at his desk, Sergeant Johnson waited impatiently for the updated list from Lieutenant Folgueras. It finally arrived at half-past three. Johnson quickly scanned the list, looking for the name Victor Lopez. When he found it, accompanied with a serial number, he checked the number against the one stamped on the bottom of the lighter.

No match.

The sergeant was relieved.

Johnson then proceeded to check all of the serial numbers on the list against that on the lighter.

No matches there either.

The sergeant was frustrated.

All he could determine from the number on the lighter was its year of issue, nineteen ninety-eight, information that was of little if any help.

Johnson decided it was time to go to Lopez with the news that a key to Sandoval's apartment was found in the Cadillac with Sal DiMarco's body.

"Be nice to know where the key came from," Lopez said.

"Very nice," Johnson agreed.

"Any ideas?"

"I'll speak to the building doorman. Find out if there is a record of all keys issued, and if the duplication of keys is permitted," Johnson suggested. "I understand you will be meeting with Mrs. Sandoval this evening."

"I'm not looking forward to it."

"You might ask her who, to her knowledge, may have had a key to the apartment—in addition to her and her husband."

"I'm not certain that's a good idea, at least not for the moment," Lopez suggested. "Let me know what you learn from building security as soon as you can."

"I will."

Johnson started for the door.

"Rocky."

"Yes, Lieutenant," he said, turning back to Lopez.

"The envelope I removed from Sandoval's apartment."

"Yes."

"I will explain as soon as I can."

"It's not idle curiosity, Laura. I'm only interested in your welfare."

"I know that. I am asking you to trust me on this, give me a little time. Can you do that?"

"Yes, I can."

"Thank you."

"I'll get back to you on the key," Johnson said, and he left the office.

He walked back to his desk. He did trust Lopez. He was about to call Jake Diamond to cancel their meeting.

But he decided it could wait until after he talked with the security guard at Roberto Sandoval's apartment building.

"Did you meet with Lopez?"

"Yes," Weido reported.

"And?"

"She's keeping me at arm's length, has me on a rabbit hunt while she goes over Sandoval's case files."

"Who is the rabbit?"

"Some character named Walker."

"*Justin* Walker?"

"That's the one," Marco said, wondering how the man knew. "Lucky guess?"

"Don't be cute, Weido. If you find Walker, I want to be the *first* to know."

"Sure. You're the boss."

"I am. Don't forget it."

"I'll be in touch," Weido said, disconnecting.

And fuck you, too.

. . .

Darlene Roman was tired of waiting for the phone to ring. She had managed to keep busy for a few hours, but she was out of ideas. If it had been the end of the month, she could at least have kept occupied trying to figure out how to come up with enough capital to cover Diamond Investigations' operating expenses for another thirty days.

Darlene was itching to know what Jake had been up to all afternoon. She wondered where he had been when they talked on the phone earlier. Judging by the background noise, it could have been a rodeo. Jake said he would fill her in later that evening. She hoped he would do so without prompting because she damn well wasn't going to plead with him to tell her.

She left the office at three-forty-five. She needed to get home with enough time to be ready for Jake at five-thirty.

Darlene scanned Frederick Street, up and down, before she went into the house. It was becoming a habit. She didn't spot Megan Nicolace watching her enter, but the detective *was* there at her post in Buena Vista Park.

Nicolace had also been watching for Norman Hall.

Norman was conspicuous in his absence.

Darlene set her mind to deciding what to wear for dinner with Joe and Angela Vongoli.

And Jake.

Lopez picked up her telephone on the third ring.

"Lieutenant Lopez," she said.

"Lieutenant, this is Juliana Lani."

"Who?"

"We met yesterday. I'm Mr. Duffey's Executive Assistant."

Lopez had to give the girl some credit, Lani had lofty ambitions.

"If you are calling to see if I received the material you sent, I did. Thank you. I appreciate your timely attention to my request."

"You're welcome, Lieutenant," Juliana said. "It's something else. I can't reach Mr. Duffey, he seems to have left for the day. I didn't know who else to call."

"Please tell me what's on your mind."

"A man came into the office a short while ago asking questions. It was odd."

"Go on."

"He said he was scheduled to meet with Mr. Sandoval and another man, a man named Justin Walker, yesterday morning. He asked me for Walker's address claiming that, in light of the circumstances necessitating the cancellation of the meeting, he needed to speak with Mr. Walker as soon as possible," Lani said. "I asked him who he was. He was a very big man, kind of scary, really. He said he was with the SFPD."

"Did you give the man an address?" Lopez asked, suddenly interested.

"I didn't have an address and, I'm not sure why, I didn't say so. Instead I asked him for identification."

"And?"

"And he said *forget about it* and walked out."

"He said *forget about it*?"

"I'm pretty sure that's what he said. He made it sound like one word."

"Can you describe him in more detail? *He was a big man* is a little vague."

"I can do better than that. I took a photograph of him leaving the building."

"You did?"

"Yes, from the office window with a telephoto lens. I think it's a very good shot."

"Can you send it to me?"

"I'll download the photo and email it."

"Great. And get a copy to building security in case he visits again."

"Will do."

"Thanks."

"Sure."

Lopez cradled the receiver thinking Duffey may have accidentally hired an assistant who was more than just another pretty face.

Kenny Gerard was not a happy camper.

James Bingham's untimely death had knocked Kenny out of his prized day-shift position. Building management had acted swiftly to solve the logistical problem of a murdered doorman. They brought in an employee from one of their other buildings who had seniority over Kenny. The new man had insisted on the day-shift and Gerard was forced to move to the swing-shift.

If Kenny was a glass half-full kind of guy, he might have been thankful he didn't land on the graveyard-shift. But here he was at four in the afternoon on a Friday, stuck inside the building until midnight, when he could have been at home getting prepared for a night on the town. Instead, he would have to look on as tenants left him stranded in the lobby as they began their personal quests for a memorable weekend.

When Police Sergeant Johnson marched in at half-past four with a list of questions about building security and apartment keys—Gerard was not in the mood for chit-chat. And if he had to be interviewed by the police again, he would have preferred shooting the breeze with the red-headed lieutenant.

In any event, Kenny decided cooperation would be the most expedient method of getting it out of the way.

To his credit, Gerard was well versed on the subject.

"Despite recent events, Sergeant Johnson, be assured the privacy and security of our tenants is a priority," Kenny said. "No one is allowed to pass this post unannounced."

Unless they kill the doorman, Johnson said to himself.

"Access to the apartments is strictly controlled," Gerard continued. "Each occupant is issued one key and one key only."

"So the Sandovals would have had only two keys."

"That is correct, Sergeant. They are laser keys, cut on a laser cutting machine. They cannot be duplicated at the local hardware store. They are also transponder keys, or electronic chip keys, equipped with a code that is recognized by the door lock specifically programmed to the key," Kenny reported. "The technology was originally developed for automobile ignitions, to help prevent car theft."

Gerard was on a roll, and Johnson didn't want to get in his way. So he did what good detectives do, he prodded just enough to keep Kenny going.

"I assume the door locks when it closes," Johnson said.

"Yes."

"And if a tenant is locked out, forgets or loses the key?"

"The tenant would need to call the security company, need to provide a password or social security number, and wait for a representative of the company to arrive and open the apartment door. There are no copies or pass keys on the premises."

"Have there been any cases of lost keys recently?"

"None that I am aware of, Sergeant, though you might check with the security company. Sleep Sound Systems," Kenny said. "There is a five hundred dollar fee for key replacement, an incentive for residents to keep track of their keys. Are you suggesting Roberto Sandoval's killer somehow got hold of a key to his apartment?"

"From what you have told me," said Johnson, classifying information, "it seems very unlikely."

"Well, then, you are looking for Houdini, or someone who Mr. Sandoval opened the door for."

"Thanks for your help, Mr. Gerard," Johnson said, turning to leave.

"You're welcome," Kenny said.

He resisted saying, *if there is anything else, I'll be here until fucking midnight.*

Weido was getting nowhere using unconventional methods, so he finally called the D.A.'s office. Juliana Lani answered.

"I'm looking for an address for a man who was scheduled to meet with Mr. Sandoval yesterday. Justin Walker."

"I'm sorry, Detective," Lani said. "I don't have an address, but it's funny you should ask."

"How's that?"

"Hold on, please, I have another call coming in. I'll be right back," Lani said, and took the other call. "District Attorney's Office."

"Juliana. Sorry I've been out of touch all afternoon. I had a late lunch meeting that wouldn't end. I won't be back in the office today. Just checking in to see if anything important turned up."

"I'm not sure if it's important or not, Mr. Duffey," she said.

"Well, then it probably isn't. I'm sure it can wait until morning."

"I have Detective Weido on the other line. Would you like to speak with him?"

"Sure. Put him through," Duffey said.

"Sorry to keep you waiting, Detective," she said, going back to Weido. The line was dead.

Marco's patience was short. He had decided *fuck this.*

"Mr. Duffey, Detective Weido disconnected."

"That's alright, I'll call him later. I'll see you in the morning."

"Have a good evening, Mr. Duffey."

"You do the same, Juliana," Duffey said, imagining for a moment the two of them having a good evening together.

It was just after five when Johnson reported back to Lopez in her office. He filled her in on all he had learned from the doorman at Roberto Sandoval's building concerning security.

"We have to assume there was another key floating around," Johnson said. "Sandoval used his key to get in that night, the key was found in the apartment. Sandoval's wife was in Italy. The key found in the Cadillac had to be a third copy. I will call the security company in the morning to see if anyone has any idea how that might be possible."

"Good."

"It's the shoe that really bothers me," Johnson said.

"Oh?"

"If Sandoval's killer lets the door shut and lock after him, it could be awhile before the body is discovered. Why does he prop the door open?"

"He wants the body found sooner?"

"What's the hurry?"

"A good question," Lopez said.

"It's lucky for Mrs. Sandoval she didn't arrive home in time to find the body herself."

"I don't know that lucky is the right word for it," Lopez said, "but speaking of the wife."

"Yes?"

"I need a favor."

"Okay."

"I'm meeting her at the Medical Examiner's office at seven for an official identification. I would like you to be there with me, if you are not in a rush to get anywhere."

"Amy is in Philadelphia. There is nowhere I need to be," Johnson said. "May I ask why you want company?"

"You know what it's like when a family member is shown the body of a murder victim, you have been there as many times as I have. I would prefer not being there alone."

"Sure," Johnson said. "I'll meet you there at six-forty-five."

"Thanks."

"You're welcome."

The sergeant returned to his desk puzzling over a key, a shoe and a letter-sized white envelope.

Darlene Roman was ready to go when Jake Diamond pulled up to her house in his 1963 Chevrolet Impala convertible at five-thirty.

"Do we need to bring anything?" she asked as she slid into the passenger seat.

"Strictly forbidden," Jake answered. "Joey assured me Angela would be insulted. She would consider it an implication she didn't have everything covered."

"Jake, don't you think it is a little unusual to attend a dinner party where bringing something for the host and hostess is considered poor etiquette?" Darlene said, understanding that asking him for an opinion about etiquette was like asking Emily Post for Joe Montana's lifetime passing percentage.

"Not at all. It's an Italian thing. Would you like to know what I was up to this afternoon?"

"Sure, why not," Darlene said, feigning indifference.

So he began filling her in on Ray Boyle, Bobo Bigelow and Carmine Cicero.

A wave of jealously ran through Norman Hall as he watched Darlene climb into Jake Diamond's car. He decided he would be changing his plans for the evening.

Detective Nicolace also watched the Impala pull away.

She spent another hour in and around Buena Vista Park.

Megan carried a large drawing tablet—she had been an art student in college, before deciding to go into law enforcement. She settled on a bench and chose something to sketch, while she kept an eye on Darlene's house and an eye out for Norman Hall.

Finally, she circled around to the alley behind the house, passed through the gate and across the small yard, and entered the house through the back door with the key Darlene had given to her. Nicolace had asked Darlene to leave the house as she normally would when going out for the evening.

The kitchen, the first room off the rear door, was lit. There was also a table lamp lit in the living room up front. The rest of the house would be dark.

Nicolace helped herself to a cup of coffee from a fresh pot Darlene had been kind enough to brew before leaving.

Megan carried the coffee into the living room and dropped onto an armchair beside the small lamp-lit table for what she expected would be long, tedious stake-out. She saw a copy of *Runner's World* on the table, set down the coffee, picked up the magazine, and began leafing through its pages.

It served to pass the time, but she didn't really get it.

. . .

Marco Weido had no trouble spotting the woman at the airport. He had seen her more than once before and been taken by her movie star good looks. Weido took her suitcase and he led her to his car. She sat silently in the passenger seat during the trip to the Hall of Justice downtown.

"Would you escort me in," she asked when they arrived.

"Of course," he answered.

They found Medical Examiner Dr. Steve Altman, Lieutenant Lopez and Sergeant Johnson waiting.

"I'm sorry for your loss," Lopez addressed the woman.

"Thank you," Theresa Sandoval said. "Can I see my husband?"

"Certainly," Lopez said. "Please follow Dr. Altman and Sergeant Johnson. I will be right behind you."

The three walked off, Lopez turned to Weido.

"I'm surprised again to see you, Detective," she said.

"Duffey asked me to pick her up and bring her here."

"Any luck on Walker?"

"None. I found an address through Motor Vehicles, but there was no one there. I'll stay on it."

"Take the night off, pick it up in the morning," Lopez suggested.

"Sure, I'll keep in touch," Weido said, and headed out.

Lopez went to join the others, they were already through with the identification.

Theresa Sandoval was signing papers that would release her husband's body to a funeral home to prepare for a wake and the subsequent burial.

"When can I return to the apartment?" Mrs. Sandoval asked.

"Whenever you feel ready," Lopez said. "We can take you to a hotel if you feel you need to wait awhile."

"Please do. I'll need to deal with getting a key in the morning."

"A key?" Lopez said.

"I misplaced my keys," Sandoval explained, "hopefully in my hotel room in Milan. In any event, building security will need to be called to let me in and arrange for a replacement."

"Sergeant, would you please take Mrs. Sandoval to the

Downtown Hilton. Mr. Duffey reserved a room."

"Sure. Please come with me, ma'am," he said, taking her suitcase.

"And, Sergeant."

"Yes, Lieutenant?"

"Would you please meet me back at my office afterward."

"Sure, I'll be there as soon as I can."

"Well?"

"Walker showed at his apartment, apparently to pick up a few things. He ran in, and then out again five minutes later with a suitcase. I followed him to a motel near the airport. He must have had travel plans."

"And?"

"Walker won't be going anywhere."

"Good. We have another problem."

"Run it by me."

Back at her desk at Vallejo Street, Lopez found a message from Ray Boyle asking that she give him a call in Los Angeles.

"Ray," she said when he answered. "How are things in the sunny south?"

"The bad guys never rest, Laura."

"Tell me about it. What can I do for you?"

"Does the name Carmine Cicero ring any bells?"

"I don't think so."

"He usually causes trouble in my neighborhood, but he was spotted in Oakland earlier today and may have been involved in a homicide. I talked to Don Folgueras," Boyle said. "I'd like you and Folgueras to keep an eye out for Cicero, in case he has reason to stick around the Bay area."

"I can put the word out, Ray. Do you want him picked up?"

"No. I just want to know where he is, Laura. I'm hoping to follow him to a bigger fish."

"We'll do what we can."

"Thanks. I'll send a mug shot over."

"I'll pass it around," Lopez said.

Relieved that his bullshit duties in San Francisco were done, at least for the day, Marco Weido hurried over the Bay Bridge to his favorite watering hole. Built from the timbers of a whaling ship, the First and Last Chance Saloon on Webster in Oakland had been a landmark drinking establishment since 1883.

Marco was a regular. Very regular. If you had the need to find Weido on any given evening, your chances were good at the saloon. And the saloon was where Ralph Morrison had been waiting since seven with the hope of finding the detective.

Marco entered the saloon and grabbed a stool at the bar.

The Grinch was at Weido's elbow in no time.

"I've been waiting for you, Detective," Morrison said.

"And here I am. If you have something to say, say it, and then give me some breathing room to enjoy my drink."

Ralph told Weido what he had learned from Officer Perry.

About Blake Sanchez, the unlucky kid who had tried to rob a liquor store and landed in the hospital.

About the gun he used, and how it might be connected to the Sal DiMarco homicide in San Francisco.

About how they were hoping Sanchez would survive to tell them where he got the gun.

"The kid is in real bad shape, he may not make it, and he hasn't been able to say a word," Ralph said.

"What in the world would make anyone think it was the same gun," Weido asked, as much aloud to himself as to Ralph.

"It's the sergeant from San Francisco who I told you about earlier, the one who found the Zippo with the Oakland PD logo at the DiMarco scene. I'm guessing this Sergeant Johnson has no good leads and he's stabbing in the dark. It would be a miracle if there was a connection."

"And you say this kid isn't talking."

"Like I said, not a word."

"Can you do me a favor, Ralph?"

"Sure. I would like that."

"Hang around the hospital, and let me know the minute it looks like Sanchez might be able to speak," Weido said. "I met Sergeant Johnson earlier today. He's dreaming, but I liked the guy and wouldn't mind giving him a hand if I can."

"Would you mind if I sit for a while and have a drink with you?" Morrison asked.

"Why don't you get over to the hospital instead, Ralph."

Weido watched Ralph leave the saloon. He knocked down the rest of his drink and slammed his glass on the bar.

Goddamn fucking son-of-a-bitch.

"Did you say something, Marco?" the bartender asked.

"Bring me another scotch," Weido said. "Better make it a double."

Jake Diamond and Joe Vongoli sat at the dining room table.

Darlene and Angela were preparing coffee and plating the Zeppole di San Giuseppe.

Watching Angela do her magic around food was the only time Darlene forgot how much she was offended by the adage *a woman's place is in the kitchen.*

"It's hard to believe Bobo Bigelow won't be dropping in unwelcomed anymore," Jake said.

"I'm surprised he lasted this long," Joey offered. "He was very good at making enemies. Are you sure it was Carmine Cicero?"

"I saw him coming out. It took me awhile to place him, I'd only had the displeasure of seeing him a few times—and that was three years ago when he was knocking people around for Al Pazzo, and before he dropped the dime on Crazy Al to cut a deal for himself. Luckily, Carmine and Al never learned we'd set them up."

"And Boyle thinks if he can get his hands on Cicero, the ape will give up his new boss?"

"Ray is counting on Carmine to be true to his nature."

Angela Vongoli carried a large tray into the dining room. A pot of espresso, four demitasse cups with saucers and spoons, a sugar bowl, and four plates holding the beautiful St. Joseph Day pastries.

"Joey," she said, "do you think you can get out of that chair long enough to fetch the anisette?"

Darlene had to suppress a smile.

When Ralph Morrison arrived at the hospital he spotted a young boy sitting on the front steps.

The kid was visibly shaken.

"Are you alright, son," he asked the boy.

"My brother died," the boy said, looking up at Ralph.

"Jeez, that's tough. I'm sorry."

"I told him not to try it, but he wouldn't listen to me. He said, *mind your business, small fry, and don't tell Mom.*"

"Where are your mother and father?" Morrison asked.

"I have no father," the boy answered. "Mom is in there. I'm waiting for the police."

"I'm the police," Ralph said. It just came out of his mouth without thought. He liked the sound of it.

"I know where Blake found the gun," the kid said.

"Blake Sanchez?"

"Yes. My brother, Blake. I know where he got the gun, but I want money before I tell."

"How much money?"

"A hundred dollars."

Morrison pulled out his wallet and checked the contents.

"Would you settle for sixty dollars?" he asked.

"I guess."

Ralph handed the boy three twenties.

"Tell me," he said.

"From under the porch of a house in our neighborhood."

"Do you know who lives in the house?"

"He's a cop, like you," Raul Sanchez said.

"Do you know his name?"

"Everybody knows his name, and nobody likes him. He's a real asshole. His name is Weido. We all call him *Weirdo* behind his back."

The blood ran out of Morrison's face.

"Are *you* okay?" Raul asked, thinking maybe he should have waited for a policeman with more pocket cash.

"I'm fine," Ralph managed to answer. "Do you think you can keep this between you and me?"

"Do you think you can get me more money?"

"Sure. I can meet you back here with forty dollars more," Ralph said. "How about ten tomorrow morning?"

"Okay," Raul said. "I better go in to be with my mom."

Morrison watched as the boy walked into the hospital.

Ralph was not quite sure about what to do next.

After dropping Theresa Sandoval off at the Hilton, Johnson headed to Vallejo Street to meet Lopez.

The sergeant stopped at his desk and found a message that Folgueras had called from Oakland.

"I can cut the gun loose. I can have Officer Perry bring it over to you first thing in the morning," Folgueras said.

"I forgot all about it. I'm sure it's a waste of time."

"You may as well follow it through," Folgueras said. "If only to get it out of the way so you can move on."

"You're right. Have Perry deliver the gun to Yeatman at our ballistics department. It won't take him long to run the comparison. We'll get the weapon back to you as soon as we can. Yeatman should be there by seven."

"Will do. There's something else."

"Yes?"

"Blake Sanchez didn't make it," Folgueras said. "He died earlier this evening. He was never able to talk."

"I'm sorry to hear it."

"Let me know if there's anything else I can do."

"Thanks."

The sergeant put down the telephone receiver and walked over to see Lieutenant Lopez.

"Did Mrs. Sandoval say anything?" Lopez asked when he walked into her office.

"Aside from thanking me, she said exactly one word. No."

"No?"

"I asked her the obligatory question," Johnson said. "*Can you think of anyone who may have wanted to harm your husband?*"

"That's the one."

"Are you thinking what I'm thinking?"

"That it is quite a coincidence Theresa Sandoval lost her key?"

"Yes. And there's something else."

Isn't there always, Johnson thought.

"Yes?"

"Mrs. Sandoval was originally scheduled to come back from Italy early Wednesday morning," Lopez explained. "She was set to accompany her husband to the event he attended the night he was killed. At the last minute she cancelled her return flight and delayed it until today."

"How do you know this?"

"I made a few calls. The airlines confirmed the flight cancellation and reschedule. An organizer for the Crossroads Irish American Festival fundraiser said she was on the guest list."

"Are you going to question her?"

"I don't know that I can," Lopez said. "Her husband was very popular and influential, and so is she. Duffey will not allow her to be interrogated unless we have a lot more to go on. I think all we can do for now is to keep an eye on her."

"Terrific. What made you think to look into her itinerary?"

"Something you said when we talked about the shoe in the apartment door. How it was lucky Mrs. Sandoval didn't return in time to find her husband's body. What I failed to mention then is I knew she wouldn't be returning until today."

"How would you have known that?"

"Roberto Sandoval told me," Lopez said. "I think it's time you see this."

The lieutenant removed a plastic evidence bag containing a white letter-sized envelope from her desk drawer and handed it across to Johnson.

The sergeant removed a hand written letter from the envelope.

After reading it, he gently placed the bag, the envelope and the letter onto the desk.

"I don't know what to say."

"I met Roberto Sandoval eleven years ago. He was brilliant, and handsome. We were both studying at Berkeley. Roberto was a pre-law student. I was among the many students with no idea what they wanted to be when they grew up. Roberto was the son of a diplomat and I was the daughter of an Oakland cop. It was love at first sight."

Lopez rose from her chair and began pacing. Johnson sat and listened.

"When Roberto was accepted to Yale Law School it was an offer he could not refuse. He asked me to go east with him. At the time, my father was not doing very well. I felt I couldn't leave him behind. On top of that, I was too much a California girl to believe I could survive in Connecticut. And that was that.

"Five years later Roberto returned to California, with a beautiful wife in tow, to take the job with the San Francisco District Attorney's Office. By then, I was a proud member of the Oakland Police Department, struggling to overtake all the boys in the race for a detective's badge.

"I ran into Roberto from time to time after I came over to the SFPD. We treated each other like old friends who were now colleagues in the fight against crime. We were what you might call *mutually respectful.*

"This past Sunday evening I was tired of sitting in my place, alone. I decided to run out for a drink. I ran into Roberto at the bar. He spotted me, so I walked over to say hello. He was sitting alone at a booth. I could tell he had already had a few. He asked if I would join him. So I did. He told me over several glasses of scotch he was having marital problems, and it was getting more and more difficult to pretend. He said he had brought up the subject of divorce and Theresa tried to talk him out of it. He had announced his intention of running for Duffey's office and she felt a separation could hurt his chances in the election. She recommended they think it over for a while, and decided to take the trip to Italy to give it some time. By then, we had both had too much to drink. We wound up at my place. He stayed until morning. I woke up knowing it had been a big mistake. I rushed him out—claiming I needed to hurry to work.

"He began calling me. A lot. When I couldn't dodge the calls, I told him it was no good. Wednesday, when I got home after work, I found that letter in my mailbox."

"He was going to tell his wife," Johnson said.

"You read what I wrote on the bottom, insisting it would not work between us, that I had no interest in pursuing it, and he needed to forget about it. I went over to his building with the letter. I covered up my appearance a bit. I intended to leave it with the doorman. But when I arrived the security desk was unattended, so I took the elevator up and I slipped the letter under his door. As I left the building, I nearly collided with Ethan Lloyd and his obnoxious dog.

"I saw no reason for anyone to see that letter. Sandoval was gone, and it would only serve to blemish his legacy. And there was no reason for his wife to see the letter. When I spotted it on a table in an evidence bag the next day, I picked it up and put it in my pocket. It was an impulsive action."

"Do you think Sandoval's wife had anything to do with his death?"

"I don't know what to think," Lopez said.

"Well, then, what we need to do is try to find out. And, Laura."

"Yes?"

"I agree. There is absolutely no reason for anyone to see that letter."

"Thank you, Rocky."

There was a light tapping at the office door.

"Come," Lopez called.

Officer Knapik entered with a photograph in her hand.

"This just came in from Lieutenant Boyle in Los Angeles," she said, handing the photo to Lopez.

"Thank you, Officer," Lopez said, and Knapik left.

"What is it?" Johnson asked.

"A mug shot. Carmine Cicero. Boyle asked if we could keep an eye out for the man."

Lopez studied the photo and then hurried to her computer.

"Son of a bitch," she said after a moment.

Johnson walked up behind her and looked at the computer monitor.

"Earlier today a man claiming to be one of ours came into the D.A.'s office asking about Justin Walker," Lopez said.

"Who is Justin Walker?"

"I don't really know. I only know he was scheduled to meet Roberto Sandoval the day after Sandoval was killed."

"Okay."

"Duffey's receptionist thought something was fishy about the guy, so she took this photograph of him when he left the building."

"Okay," Johnson repeated.

"Look at this," Lopez said, handing Johnson the mug shot Boyle had sent.

Johnson looked back and forth between the monitor and the mug shot.

"Is it the same guy?"

"It sure looks like the same guy."

"Son-of-a-bitch. Are we trying to find Walker?"

"I put Weido on it, more to get him out of my hair than anything else. I would like you to get on it yourself first thing tomorrow."

"Sure."

"I doubt we'd accomplish much tonight. I think we both need to call it a day."

"Damn."

"What?"

"I had an appointment for later tonight that I meant to cancel and I never got around to it."

"Something important?" Lopez asked.

"It's not important anymore," he said, knowing how angry Lopez would be if she knew he was thinking of asking Jake Diamond to spy on her.

Lopez was not a huge Jake Diamond fan.

"Get some rest," she said. "We'll hit it hard tomorrow."

"Sure. Good night," Johnson said, and left the office.

He tried calling Diamond, but got no answer.

Johnson decided he may as well keep the appointment. Tell Jake face-to-face the business with Lopez had been a misunderstanding.

The sergeant would not be needing Diamond's help after all.

San Francisco District Attorney Liam Duffey stood out in front of the Downtown Hilton, trying to decide whether to stay or leave. In normal circumstances, the fact the woman was now a widow should have made it much simpler, but that was far from the case.

Duffey finally admitted he needed to see her, that he could not wait any longer.

He pushed through the hotel entrance and into the lobby. He knew the room number, and headed straight for the elevators.

San Francisco private investigator Tom Romano followed Duffey into the building, watched him enter an elevator, noted the floor where the lift stopped, pulled a fifty-dollar bill from his wallet, and approached the young man at the reservations desk.

Jake Diamond pulled the Chevy up in front of Darlene's house just past nine-thirty.

"Exactly how many meatballs did you devour?" Darlene asked.

"I wasn't counting. It would have slowed me down. Is Detective Nicolace in there?"

"She should be watching us from my bedroom."

"I can't see her," Jake said, looking up to the window.

"That's the idea, Jake. Are you going to tell me what your mysterious meeting is all about?"

"Eventually. I'll wait until you get inside. Be careful."

"Thanks for taking me with you tonight."

"Thanks for coming. See you tomorrow."

Jake watched Darlene enter the house before pulling away. Norman Hall watched them both.

TWENTY FOUR

I dropped Darlene off at her house and headed over to my place in the Presidio.

Parking a car in North Beach on a Friday night would be impossible at best, so I decided to take a cab to the office.

Travis Duncan would be picking me up there at eleven and he could drop me back home after our date with Manny Sandoval.

I was not looking forward to the meeting with Johnson *or* Duncan—but if I only had to do what I really wanted to do, I might not have enough to complain about.

To compound my discomfort, Angela's meatballs were staging a Bocce match in my stomach.

I had called ahead for a taxi and, when I arrived home, it sat waiting at the curb.

I pulled the Chevy into the driveway, hopped into the cab, and we were off.

Expecting Sergeant Johnson at any moment, I left the door to the office open after walking in.

I reached down to floor to retrieve a printed flyer which had obviously been slipped under the door. It advertised next week's lunch specials at the deli below. I had little need for such information. If I wanted to learn what Angelo was whipping up for lunch, I only needed to poke my nose out the window.

I heard a sound behind me but before I could turn I felt an object pressed against the back of my head that could have been the barrel of a handgun or the neck of a beer bottle.

When a man's voice said, *get down on your knees,* instead of, *did you bring the potato chips.* I guessed it was the former.

I lowered myself to my knees.

Then I heard what sounded like Barry Bonds clobbering one over the right field wall into McCovey Cove. I heard a gunshot and I was knocked face down to the floor.

My head bounced once or twice and I was out cold.

Sometime later I opened my eyes. I found myself sitting in Darlene's chair.

There was a damp towel wrapped around my forehead.

In another chair, at the opposite side of the desk, a man I didn't recognize sat with his hands resting on his lap. I could see no restraints, but he sat there not moving a muscle.

I looked up and found Sergeant Johnson standing behind the man.

"He was about to take you out, execution style," Johnson said.

"Why?" I asked, pulling the towel off my head.

"You're messing with my girlfriend," the man said.

"Shut up," Johnson said, and he slapped the guy in the back of the head the way Mr. Rosiello, my Junior High School shop teacher, would slap me in the head when I left the wood plane resting on its blade.

"I clocked him with my elbow, he went down like an anvil in a swimming pool, the gun discharged, and he landed on you, hard," Johnson explained. "His name is Norman Hall. Have you been messing with his sweetheart?"

"This bastard has been stalking Darlene," I said. "A vice detective named Nicolace was using Darlene as bait to catch him doing something that would revoke his parole."

"It sort of worked," Johnson said. "Guess we should get hold of Detective Nicolace."

"That won't be difficult."

I picked up the phone and called Darlene at home.

"I want a lawyer," Hall said.

"Another word from you," Johnson said, slapping Norman in the head again, "and I will make you eat that three-hole punch sitting on the desk."

"Norman Hall is down here at the office," I told Darlene. "Would you send Nicolace over to pick him up."

"What are you talking about, Jake?"

"Seems Norman has a jealous streak, he came to eliminate what he perceived as a rival for your affection."

"Are you alright?"

"I have a lump on my head the size of one of Angela's meatballs, but other than that I'm fine."

"I'll be right there," Darlene said.

"No. Please, Darlene. I have a lot of other business to take care of tonight. I will explain it all to you tomorrow. Just send Nicolace here to get this creep out of my sight."

"She's on her way," Darlene said, and disconnected.

"While we wait," I said, addressing Johnson, "did you want to talk about what I can do for you?"

"I would rather not have an audience," Johnson said.

"Cuff Norman to the radiator, it will hold him. I've used the radiator before," I said. "We can talk privately back in my office."

Fifteen minutes later, Nicolace called out from the front room.

Johnson had been given enough time to assure me his suspicions about Lieutenant Lopez had been a misunderstanding, he would not need my help after all, and I should forget he had ever brought it up.

Johnson helped Detective Nicolace exchange his handcuffs for hers.

Nicolace read Hall his rights and she took him into custody.

"Can you come to the station to swear out a complaint?" she asked me. "Assault with intent to kill?"

"I'll swear he killed Cock Robin if you want me to, but I can't leave here now. Can you hold him until morning without my statement? I can come down first thing."

"I can sign off on the complaint," Johnson offered. "I witnessed the attempt."

With that settled, Johnson and Nicolace escorted Norman out of the building.

A few minutes later the telephone on Darlene's desk rang.

Travis Duncan.

"Jake, I've been sitting in my car across the street for twenty minutes," Duncan said. "It's been busier than Caltrain Depot out here. What's going on?"

"It's a long story that would bore you, Travis. Do we have a little time?"

"Some."

"I need a drink. I'm alone now. Why don't you come up and join me for a glass of Dickel, and you can fill me in on your plan for dealing with Manny Sandoval."

"I'll be right up," Duncan said.

I wasn't exactly jumping for joy.

I sat beside Travis as he drove to Sandoval's restaurant.

Manny was expecting me, alone. I had called him from my office before we left. It was a short telephone call. My end of the conversation scripted by Duncan. I asked Sandoval for permission to drop by to hand him a fistful of dollars.

Manny liked the idea.

Travis stopped a few hundred feet from the entrance of Manny's to let me out.

"Can you act tough?" he asked.

"I've done it more than once for bit parts in gangster movies."

"Good."

"Yes and no," I said. "I was always killed before the end of the first reel."

"I've got your back, Jake. Stay cool, act tough. When you ask for the bathroom be polite and insistent."

"Like Michael Corleone."

"Something like that. You will be frisked. Put this in your inside jacket pocket."

Duncan handed me a thick envelope. I slid it into my jacket.

"Let's do this," I said.

"Are you okay?"

"Sure," I said, and I climbed out of the car and I walked the short distance to the restaurant entrance. A sign hanging from a chain in the front door window read *CLOSED*.

I rapped lightly at the door.

A pair of simian eyes looked me over before the door was opened. The ape who stood there motioned for me to enter. A second man sat at a table close to the entrance, he could have been a twin. Manny Sandoval sat at the bar, closer to the far end of the room.

"Jake Diamond, I presume," Manny said.

I wanted to say, *No, Dr. Livingstone you fucking scumbag.* I bit my tongue.

"Yes."

"Do you mind if Hector checks you out?"

"Not at all," I said, and then to Hector, "be gentle."

Hector patted me down. Hector's clone watched closely from his seat nearby. Manny seemed mildly disinterested.

"What's this?" Hector asked when he came across the bulge in my jacket.

"Money," I said.

"Let me have it."

"I would prefer to hand it to Mr. Sandoval personally," I said, wondering how many of the words he could identify, "that is if you don't fucking mind."

"Hey, watch your mouth." Hector warned.

"Sure, do you have a mirror?"

Hector grabbed me by the lapels, I knocked his hands off, Manny intervened.

"Enough," Sandoval said. "Is he clean?"

"Yes."

"The boys take their jobs seriously. Join me for a drink, Jake," Manny said. "Hector, get Mr. Diamond whatever he likes."

I walked over and pulled up a stool beside Sandoval.

Hector moved behind the bar.

"Bourbon," I said, "whatever you have."

Hector poured a shot of Jack Daniels over some ice.

It would have to do.

"So," Manny said.

"So," I said, pulling the envelope from my pocket. "This is four grand in cash, which is what Vinnie owes you if I am not mistaken. Consider his debt paid, and don't ever take a bet from him again."

"What? No *please,*" Manny said. "And you are forgetting about the vig. Your friend is very late in his payment. He owes me closer to six thousand by now."

"I was hoping we could forego the interest, to defer some of Vinnie's hospital costs. Pretty please."

"It's not the way I work, Jake, and you are coming very close to being disrespectful."

"Sorry, it's been a rough day. Can I use the rest room?"

"It's in the back."

Hector made a move to follow me.

"I can find it myself," I said.

"Stay put, Hector," Manny said, "and get me another beer."

I walked to the back, opened the bathroom door and let it close, unlocked the deadbolt on the rear door leading out into the alley behind the restaurant, counted to sixty, played with the bathroom door again and returned to Manny at the bar.

"Okay. Where were we?" I asked.

Before Manny could recap, there was a loud crash. Hector started to move.

"Hector, stay," Manny said. "Tito, go."

Hector and Tito were like trained Dobermans.

The three of us at the bar looked toward the rear. Tito was taking his time investigating.

"See what's taking him so fucking long," Manny finally said.

Hector complied.

After a minute, a gun appeared in Manny's hand. My cue.

Before he could rise, I kicked the stool out from under him. He fell to the floor, the gun squirted out of his grip, and I kicked it across the room. We both heard the wails of pain coming from the back.

"What the fuck," he yelled, looking up at me with pure hatred in his eyes.

"I recommend you stay down, Manny," I said.

Tito was hurled into the room, followed by Hector. They were both gagged, but their cries of pure agony were not well muffled. I counted four broken legs.

Travis Duncan stepped into view a moment later wielding a Louisville Slugger.

"I'm batting a thousand," he said, looking down at Manny

who was looking up from the floor in horror.

"Don't," Manny choked out.

"What, no *please*," I said.

"Please," Manny said.

"Want to take it from here, Jake," Travis asked.

"Sure, fix yourself a drink," I said. "Manny, get the fuck up and have a seat."

Sandoval rose from the floor, set the fallen stool upright and sat. Travis had poured himself a whiskey and then asked if Manny would care for another beer. Sandoval politely declined.

Hector and Tito rested on the floor, uncharacteristically still.

"How about you, Jake? Ready for another?"

"I'll pass. Maybe if they stocked Dickel in this dump, I would become a regular."

I pushed the cash filled envelope until it rested in front of Sandoval.

"Please listen carefully, Manny," I began, "I am only going to say it once."

When Travis had suggested earlier that the meeting with Sandoval and his goons would be fun, I thought he was insane.

Now I had to admit it was very entertaining.

"Consider the debt paid in full," I continued. "If you ever mess a hair on Vinnie's head again, my friend behind the bar will pull out all of your fingernails before he pulls out all of your teeth. And he will love every moment. Am I clear?"

"Yes."

"Terrific. We'll get out of here now, let you clean up. You should get Hector and Tito to the veterinarian as soon as possible. Thank you for the drinks," I added, dropping a twenty dollar bill on the bar. "Keep the change."

Travis and I headed for the front. Duncan picked Manny's gun off the floor and tossed it across the bar. It broke the wall mirror and destroyed at least a dozen bottles on a shelf below. Manny didn't seem to mind.

We were both quiet during the short drive.

Travis pulled the car to the curb in front of my house.

"Thank you," I said, as I left the vehicle.

"Anytime," he said, and he drove off.

I was too wired to think about sleep, so I poured a Dickel and settled into my reading chair with the Hugo paperback.

Vinnie was saved from Manny Sandoval and his goons.

Darlene was saved from Norman Hall.

Lieutenant Lopez was saved from Sergeant Johnson's suspicions.

I was saved from having to snoop around for Johnson or Lieutenant Ray Boyle.

Esmeralda was saved, protected by Quasimodo the Hunchback within the sanctuary of Notre Dame Cathedral.

But for how long.

Part Three

THE BELL RINGER
or Cleared for Landing

The straight line, a respectable optical illusion which ruins many a man.

—Victor Hugo

TWENTY FIVE

Sergeant Johnson was at his desk at Vallejo Street Station by seven Saturday morning. He called Yeatman at ballistics at ten past.

"Officer Perry from Oakland PD was waiting for me when I arrived," Yeatman reported. "I have the weapon."

"How long before you have results on a comparison?"

"Give me an hour, maybe less. I'll call you as soon as I know one way or another."

"Good. Thanks again, Tommy."

"Johnnie Walker Black. You're welcome."

Next, Johnson called Sleep Sound Security to follow up on what he had learned from the guard at Roberto Sandoval's apartment building. A recorded message informed him the office hours on Saturday were eight until three and provided an after-hours emergency number. Johnson would call back at eight.

Then he followed Weido's suit and called the Department of Motor Vehicles for an address on Justin Walker. The DMV was closed Saturday, but in this case he had a privileged number at his disposal.

Johnson decided he would go to check out the address while he waited for the Sleep Sound Security office to open and while he waited to hear from Yeatman at ballistics.

The phone on his desk rang before he could get away.

"Yeatman?"

"Yardley," the desk sergeant said. "It looks like we have a homicide. The first officers at the scene just called it in. The Travelodge at the airport, cleaning lady found the body."

"Make sure the uniforms know not to touch anything without gloves," Johnson said. "Tell them I'm on my way."

. . .

189

"Vallejo Street. Yardley."

"I need to speak with Sergeant Johnson."

"Sergeant Johnson is in the field. You just missed him."

"When will he be back?"

"I have no idea. Tell me what you need. If I can't help, I will put you through to another detective."

"I need to speak with Sergeant Johnson, it's urgent."

"If it is an emergency, hang up and dial nine-one-one," Yardley said, beginning to lose patience.

"This is Officer Perry from Oakland. Can you give me a cell phone number for the sergeant?"

"I cannot. I will try to reach Johnson and give him the message that you called. Can he reach you at your station?"

"Please ask him to call me on *my* cell phone. Please tell him it is extremely important he contact me as soon as possible."

"What's the number?"

The caller gave Yardley a cell number.

"Got it. I'll do what I can, Perry."

"Thank you."

When Johnson arrived at the airport motel he found a uniformed officer waiting for him in the lobby.

"Charles Musman, Sergeant," the officer said, greeting Johnson.

"What do we have?"

"My partner, Derek Plewacki, is in the room with the murder victim. Room one-oh-three. Multiple gunshot wounds. We were instructed to wait for your arrival before calling in a forensics team or the medical examiner," Musman said. "Three additional officers have been canvassing the other guest rooms, nothing yet."

"Good. Join the others canvassing. Let me know if you get anything," Johnson said, and he continued on to Room 103.

Officer Plewacki led Johnson to the body. Three clustered gunshots to the chest, close range.

"You can call in the M.E. and forensics," Johnson said. "We can rule out suicide. Has the victim been identified?"

"We found his wallet, driver's license," Plewacki reported. "His name was Justin Walker."

"Jesus."

"Something wrong, Sergeant?"

"We have been searching for this man," Johnson answered. "Anything else?"

"It looks as if he was planning a trip. We found an airline ticket for Tel Aviv. And we also found this—an employee identification card," the officer said, handing it to Johnson. "It seems Walker worked for a company called Sound Sleep Security."

"Son-of-a bitch," the sergeant said.

Johnson pulled out his cell phone and turned it back on. His noticed there were two missed calls. It would wait until after he phoned Lieutenant Lopez.

Marco Weido was chugging a Coors Light, trying to remedy a colossal hangover at eight-thirty in the morning.

He found his cell phone by the fourth ring.

"Where are you?"

"At home. You owe me payment," Weido said.

"Stay put. I'll have it delivered to you by eleven."

"Good," Weido said, and then he went for another beer.

Johnson had asked Lopez to contact Officer Cutler and have Davey meet him at the office of Sound Sleep Security.

Cutler was waiting when he arrived. They were directed to Bill Cataneo, Operations Manager.

"It's about one of your employees," Johnson said.

"It's Justin, right? Did he turn himself in?"

"Justin Walker was murdered sometime last night," the sergeant said.

"My God, it's my fault," Cataneo said, visibly distraught. "What I am going to tell my wife."

"Slow down," Johnson said. "Tell me about Walker."

"On Wednesday I discovered an electronic chip key had been generated without authorization. I traced it to Justin."

"A key to Roberto Sandoval's apartment."

"Yes. I told him I would have to report it to the police. He talked me out of it."

"How?"

"He asked for a chance to see Sandoval, confess his action and plead for lenience. He hoped his voluntary confession and information as to who paid him to obtain the key might help his case. I was standing right beside him when he called to make an appointment with Sandoval. He was told he would have to wait until Thursday morning."

"So you let it wait," Johnson asked.

"He was my wife's brother; I believed he would follow through. When I heard about Sandoval's death, I didn't know what to do. I've been trying to reach Justin since Thursday morning."

"Did Walker tell you who paid him for the key?"

"No. He said he didn't want to get me involved."

"You are very involved," Johnson said. "Cutler, call for the nearest unit to come to take Mr. Cataneo into custody and read him his rights. He is complicit in the death of Roberto Sandoval."

"My God," Cataneo repeated. "What will I tell my wife?"

"I suggest you tell her to call a lawyer. Stay with him, Davey. I need to check a few phone messages."

"Yes, sir," Cutler said.

Johnson retreated to a neutral corner.

The first message was from Yeatman. The gun sent over from Oakland, used by Blake Sanchez in the attempted liquor store robbery, was the weapon that had killed Sal DiMarco.

Unbelievable, Johnson muttered to himself.

He might have considered it incredible luck if not for the fact that Blake Sanchez had died in the hospital before being able to talk.

The second message was from Desk Sergeant Yardley, asking him to call Officer Perry as soon as possible. Johnson decided to delay the call to Perry until after the uniforms arrived to take Cataneo into custody.

. . .

Carmine Cicero was polishing off a hearty room service breakfast when his cell phone rang.

"Yes."

"Where are you?"

"I'm still at my hotel," Cicero said. "I can be on my way in thirty minutes or so."

"He's expecting you before eleven."

"No problem. I'll stop on my way out to the Oakland airport. I have a flight back to Los Angeles at twelve-thirty."

"Good. Call me as soon as you touch ground."

Sergeant Johnson was standing on the sidewalk outside the Sound Sleep Security office when the squad car pulled up. Two uniformed officers exited the car and approached Johnson.

"Take Mr. Cataneo down to Vallejo Street, ask Yardley to find an interrogation room, and let Lieutenant Lopez know you have arrived," Johnson said. "And ask Officer Cutler to come out."

The uniforms entered the building just as Johnson's phone rang.

"Rocky, it's Yardley. Officer Perry phoned a third time, he insists it's urgent."

"Give me the number again."

Johnson punched in the cell number. It was answered in the middle of the first ring.

"Sergeant Johnson?"

"Perry, what's the emergency?"

"My name is Ralph Morrison, Sergeant. I'm sorry for the deception, but I needed to talk with you personally."

"I am extremely busy, Mr. Morrison," Johnson barked, "and impersonating a police officer is against the law."

"It's about the gun that killed Sal DiMarco."

"What about the gun that killed Sal DiMarco?"

"I think I discovered where it came from."

"Tell me," Johnson said, hardly believing his ears.

"Not on the phone."

"Don't play games with me."

"I'm not. Trust me. You need to meet the source of the information. Can you be at Highland Hospital by ten?"

"Where?"

"Fourteenth Avenue and Thirty-First Street in Oakland. The Beaumont exit off the MacArthur Freeway. In front of the hospital entrance. I'll be with a teenage Hispanic boy. I'm wearing a green Army jacket. I have a ruined left hand."

"If this is bullshit I will be insanely angry, Ralph," Johnson warned.

"It's on the level, Sergeant. Please be there by ten."

The line went dead. Cutler came out to the street.

"Do you think Cataneo knows more than he told us," Cutler asked.

"I doubt it, but he held back information that ultimately led to four deaths. He will have to answer for that. It looks as if you and I are going to Oakland."

"Why Oakland?"

Before Johnson could answer his phone rang again.

"Yes?"

It was Joe Beggs with the forensics team at the Walker murder scene.

"We found something here in the motel room that may interest you."

"Go ahead."

"A key to a pay locker at SFO," Beggs said.

"I'll send Officer Cutler over to pick it up."

"Roger that."

"Change of plans?" Cutler asked.

"I need you to pick up an airport locker key from Beggs back at the Travelodge, and go to SFO to check the contents," Johnson said, moving to his car. "I need to get to Oakland. Call me as soon as you open the locker."

Johnson climbed behind the wheel and headed out for the Bay Bridge.

Marco Weido was watching the clock, pacing the living room and feeling like shit.

He went to the bedroom, took his service revolver from the bedside table, and he tucked it into the back of his belt.

The oversized sweat shirt would conceal it nicely.

Weido understood you could never be too careful when dealing with fellow felons.

Johnson spotted Ralph Morrison and the boy as soon as he pulled up in front of the hospital.

"Okay, Ralph," Johnson said. "Let's hear it."

"The boy is Raul Sanchez," Morrison began. "His older brother Blake attempted to rob a liquor store Thursday night and Raul can tell you where Blake found the gun."

"Where is my money?" the boy said.

Ralph gave Johnson a look of embarrassment, and then he took two twenties from his pocket and handed them to the boy.

"Now, tell Sergeant Johnson what you told me," Morrison said.

"Under the porch," Raul said. "The cop's house."

"What cop?" Johnson asked.

"Weido," the boy answered.

"Marco Weido?"

"Yes," Ralph said.

"Do you know where he lives, Ralph?"

"Yes."

"Come with me," Johnson said to Morrison.

They left the boy there, the cash held tightly in both hands.

"Stop here," Morrison said, ten minutes later.

Johnson pulled the car over to the curb and killed the engine.

"Which house?"

"Across the next street, fourth house from the corner, the green wood porch."

"Stay in the vehicle, Ralph."

When Johnson stepped out of the car he spotted a man fifty yards further up the street who appeared to be watching Marco Weido's residence.

Johnson recognized the man immediately.

He instinctively moved his hand to his weapon and picked up his pace.

TWENTY SIX

I slept late Saturday morning, but I logged little sleep.

The events of the previous day had been overly stimulating to put it mildly. I kept waking up through the night to escape disturbing dreams. I had not witnessed so much violence in one day since Sally was killed.

I had missed three phone calls. All from Darlene.

Her messages were all the same, *Jake, please call me at the office.*

I called her at the office.

"Diamond Investigations, always in season."

"Nice," I said.

"I thought you'd never call, Jake. Are you all right?"

"I'm fine. What are you doing at the job?"

"I needed to take care of a few financial snags—and I was hoping you could do me a favor."

"Shoot."

"I was hoping you could give me a ride to Stinson Beach," Darlene said. "I am seriously pining for Tug McGraw."

"He is one lucky mutt. Give me a little time. I should be there by ten."

I drove down Columbus Avenue toward Vallejo Street, the Trans-America Building poking through the clouds straight ahead.

I knew most of the doormen at the Columbus Hotel, across Vallejo, just past Molinari's Deli. I also knew that a five-spot pressed into the right hands would allow me to leave the car parked in front of the hotel until I collected Darlene.

I pulled into the passenger loading area. A parking valet was stepping out of the vehicle in front of me. He handed the keys to a very large man who proceeded to climb in.

It was Carmine Cicero.

Cicero rolled out into Columbus Avenue traffic.

Against all better judgment, I followed.

Carmine turned right onto Pacific Avenue. I could see the Bay Bridge up ahead. When I was sure we were headed across the bay, I called Ray Boyle.

"Try to stay with him, Jake," Boyle said. "Call me as soon as he gets to wherever he is going."

"I'll try," I said.

I followed Cicero to a quiet, tree-lined street near downtown Oakland. He parked in front of a house with a green wood porch. I pulled over to the curb, on the opposite side of the street, fifty yards away.

Cicero left the vehicle and moved to the front door of the house. A few moments later he was let in.

I was reaching for my cell to call Boyle when I thought I heard someone coming up behind me. Then a familiar voice. He didn't sound very happy to see me.

"Diamond, what the hell are you doing out here?" Johnson said.

"I followed someone here," I said.

"What for?"

"For Ray Boyle. A favor. I owe him a few."

"Who is it?"

"A mug named Cicero. Boyle has questions for the ape."

"Where did he go?" Johnson asked.

"The house with the green porch. Opposite side of the street."

"Jesus."

"What?"

"I'm here to question Marco Weido."

"Who is Marco Weido?"

"Former Oakland police detective, presently investigating for the San Francisco District Attorney's Office. He may have been party to Roberto Sandoval's murder," Johnson said. "That's his house."

"Terrific. A pair of ruthless killers," I said. "What's the connection?"

"I have no idea."

"Is he with you?" I asked, looking past Johnson at a man coming up from behind.

Johnson turned on his heels. His service weapon magically appeared in his hand.

"Ralph," he said, lowering the gun. "I asked you to stay in the car. Do I need to handcuff you to the steering wheel?"

"But..."

"Go."

Ralph, whoever the hell he was, put his head down, did an about face and walked away.

"I need to call Boyle," I said. "Calling Oakland PD for back-up might not be a bad idea."

We were both reaching for our cell phones when the gunfire in the house began.

Johnson called for back-up.

"Do you have a gun?" Johnson asked.

I was tempted to say I had left it in my other pants.

"No."

The sergeant pulled a .38 from an ankle holster.

Pretty cool, if you're into that sort of thing.

I tend to be more impressed by a good book.

"Coming or watching?" Johnson said, offering the weapon.

I took the gun and I followed him.

Johnson went in first.

Thankfully.

His weapon gripped in both hands, arms fully extended, sweeping the front room like Jack Bauer badly sketched.

Both men were down. Cicero was closer to the front door. He looked finished. Johnson kept his weapon trained on Weido, who was convulsing on the floor. Johnson kicked the gun that rested near Cicero's hand clear across the room and checked the gorilla for pulse.

"Dead," he reported, and swiftly moved to Weido.

"The fuck sent him to kill me," Weido whispered. "London."

London.

It was the last word Marco Weido ever said.

. . .

I told Johnson why Boyle was after Cicero.

The runaway Russian girl, the murdered nightclub owner, and Bobo Bigelow.

Johnson told me why he had come for Weido.

The gun that killed Sal DiMarco.

And he told me about Cicero's visit to the D.A.'s office and Justin Walker.

Weido and Cicero had taken us down the same road.

Beyond that, all we could be sure about was their shooting match had led us to a dead end.

I called Ray Boyle, to fill him in on the gunfight at Weido Corral and the outcome.

"Weido said, *The fuck sent him to kill me?*" Boyle asked.

"Johnson and I are guessing Weido and Carmine Cicero were working for the same man and Weido was double-crossed."

"I won't be saying a novena for Cicero. He was a menace," Boyle said. "But he was my only lead."

"Weido may have been involved in the murder of Assistant D.A. Sandoval up here, and Cicero was identified visiting the D.A.'s office inquiring about a man named Justin Walker."

"And?"

"Walker supplied the key that allowed Sandoval's killer to enter his apartment."

"Damn it. There's a connection. Have they questioned Walker?"

"Walker was killed, Ray."

"Weido?"

"Maybe. Maybe Cicero," I suggested. "Could have been either one of them. Or both."

"Damn it. And Weido said nothing else?"

"London."

"London? What does that mean?"

"No clue, Lieutenant. But it sounds like something way out of your jurisdiction."

"Will you let me know if anything else turns up?"

"I will."

"And follow up on it for me?"

"If I can, Ray."

Two Oakland PD uniformed officers, Bruce Perry and a rookie sidekick, had arrived to secure the scene. Oakland would be taking over.

I walked outside and saw Johnson's buddy Ralph standing across the street trying to figure out what went down.

Johnson joined me on the porch and waved Ralph off when Ralph started to cross over.

"I just got a call from Lopez. Justin Walker was planning to run. He left a bag in an airport locker. Forensics found a key and I had an officer check it out. Twenty thousand dollars, in neat bundles, in a small travel bag. His passport was also in the bag, and a slip of paper with a phone number inside the passport book."

"Okay."

"When Cutler couldn't reach me he called Lopez. She tried the number. It connected to the office of Daniel Gibson at the Bureau of Immigration at the Appraiser's Building on Washington Street in San Francisco. The office is closed, but Lopez found a residential address for Gibson. She said she would meet me there in forty-five minutes."

"There's the connection. A straight line between Gibson, Walker, Cicero and Weido. And Roberto Sandoval."

"Straight lines can be deceiving and often lead nowhere," Johnson said. "I need to meet the lieutenant."

"Can I come along?"

"Lopez won't like it."

"I promised Boyle I would stay on this if I could."

"Okay. Meet us there. But don't be surprised if Lopez chases you off."

"Thanks. And thanks for the loan," I said, offering to return the gun Johnson had handed to me earlier.

"Maybe you should hold on to it," Johnson said. "Two-seventy-two Seventh Avenue, Inner Richmond."

"I'll be there," I said, and we both headed for our cars.

I called Ray Boyle as I was crossing the Bay Bridge, to bring him up to speed.

And then I remembered Darlene was still waiting.

I decided to go straight to Darlene at the office. Try to make amends.

Not only had I made her wait for more than an hour, now I would need to renege on my offer to transport her to a reunion with the pooch. On top of that, I had little time for excuses or explanations.

"Thanks, Jake," she said when I walked into the office.

Darlene was being facetious.

"I'm really sorry, Darlene. I can explain, but not right now. And I can't take you to Marin."

"You could have said all of that on the phone. You didn't have to come down here if you are so busy."

"I said I'm sorry, Darlene, really." I felt like a heel. "But if I didn't come down here I couldn't give you the Impala to drive to Stinson. I know how much McGraw loves to ride with the top down."

"Can I keep the car overnight?"

"Sure."

"I forgive you. And I want a total account tomorrow or your name is mud."

"Wow. I haven't heard that one for awhile."

"Like it?"

"I've always liked it. Can you give me a lift to Seventh and Clement on your way out?"

"Let me think about that," Darlene said, finally unable to conceal a smile.

"Think fast. I'm already late."

Darlene dropped me at the small house on 7th, just up from Clement near the Green Apple Bookstore. I had spent many hours at the Green Apple, trying to decide between Dickens and Dumas. I saw Johnson's unmarked parked out front. I walked up to the front door and rang the doorbell.

Johnson opened the door and ushered me in.

"What did I miss?" I asked.

"Not a thing. We just arrived."

I followed him back to the kitchen. Lieutenant Lopez was standing over a man seated at the kitchen table. Lopez looked up at me and then she glared at Johnson.

"What is he doing here?"

"He backed me up in Oakland, and he's trying to pay off a debt to Ray Boyle," Johnson said.

They were talking about me as if I was not there.

Johnson and Lopez had always been very good at it.

"Try to remain silent, Diamond," Lopez said.

Then she focused her attention entirely on Daniel Gibson.

It was soon evident Daniel Gibson was not going to be very cooperative in the comfort of his own home. He was already demanding a lawyer.

Lopez instructed Sergeant Johnson to take the suspect into custody.

Johnson handcuffed Gibson and we walked out to the street.

Lopez went to her car and drove off.

Johnson placed Gibson in the back seat of his car for the trip to Vallejo Street Station.

I got to ride in front.

Gibson, handcuffed in the back seat, continued to complain about a violation of his rights until Johnson threatened to gag him.

Then Sergeant Johnson told me what I could expect when we reached the station.

I almost felt relieved until Boyle called.

"Where are you?" he asked.

"I'm with Johnson and Gibson. They're bringing Gibson in for questioning."

"Will you be there?"

"Johnson is sure Lopez will stick me in a corner like a dunce. I agree. Johnson is going to drop me off at my office and keep me informed."

"We spoke to three of the girls who were forced to work at The Volga, including the girl Katya. They told the same story.

They all entered the country through San Francisco. They were all taken to the Bureau of Immigration on Washington Street."

"Okay."

"At Washington Street, someone arranged accommodations for the young women at the Powell Hotel. They were told to remain at the hotel until transportation to their domestic positions here in Los Angeles was arranged. All three identified Cicero as the man who brought them down to L.A."

"What do you need, Ray?"

"I need Lopez to keep Daniel Gibson at the station as long as possible, ask Johnson to do everything he can to facilitate, and ask him to send me a photograph of Gibson."

"I'll talk to Johnson. I think you may get more cooperation from Lopez if she hears it from you."

"I'll call her," Ray said. "I'll be back in touch."

When Johnson pulled up in front of my office I asked him for a word in private. We both left the vehicle and we moved out of Gibson's hearing range. I filled the sergeant in on my conversation with Boyle. He returned to his car, climbed in, and drove off with his suspect.

I walked into Molinari's Deli.

Angelo Verdi looked up from behind the counter.

"Jake," he said. "I feel like you have been avoiding me."

"Don't be silly, Angelo," I said. "What's for lunch?"

TWENTY SEVEN

When Johnson brought Gibson into Vallejo Street Station, Lopez and Yardley were waiting.

"Did you succeed in losing Diamond?" Lopez asked.

"Yes," Johnson said. "You might think about cutting him some slack occasionally."

"I'll think about it when the next occasion comes up. Sergeant Yardley, please escort Mr. Gibson to Interview Room Two."

"You can't do this," Daniel Gibson insisted. "I haven't been charged with anything. I want to call my lawyer."

"Calm down, Mr. Gibson," Lopez said. "You will get your phone call. I just have a few simple questions. If you help me, you could be gone before your lawyer can even get here."

"I don't like being handcuffed like a common criminal."

"Will you behave?"

"Yes."

"Yardley, please escort Mr. Gibson to the interview room. Sergeant Johnson, please remove the gentleman's handcuffs. I will be with you shortly, Mr. Gibson. Sergeant Yardley, please make sure Mr. Gibson is made comfortable while he waits."

"Yes, Lieutenant," Yardley said, and pointed the way for Gibson.

"Rocky, let's talk in my office," Lopez said, once Yardley and Gibson had walked off.

"It may have been a mistake bringing Gibson in," Lopez said when they were settled in the lieutenant's office. "A phone number in an airport locker is not enough to hold him. We're working on getting land line phone records for Walker and Weido, but it will take a while."

"How about Gibson's home phone?" Johnson asked.

"We would need a warrant for that, since Gibson is alive

to cry foul. We're trying to get a judge to sign off on one, but I'm pessimistic."

"How about cell phone calls?"

"We didn't find a cell for Walker. I spoke to Folgueras. Oakland is going through both Weido and Cicero's cell phones and will let us know if something helpful jumps out."

"Did Ray Boyle call you?" Johnson asked.

"Yes. He asked that we hold Gibson as long as possible. I don't know how long we can keep him. Sergeant Yardley will routinely photograph Gibson and rush the photo down to Ray."

"Gibson could be stubborn."

"How should we deal with him?"

"You are much better at this than I am, Lieutenant."

"That is very flattering, Rocky," Lopez said. "But I would really like your input."

"I'd start with Walker, it's our strongest connection."

"And if Gibson denies knowing Justin Walker?"

"Ask him why he thinks we found his telephone number in Walker's possession."

"He could still play dumb," Lopez suggested.

"If all else fails, you will need to put a serious scare into Gibson."

"I agree. Let's hope we get something to scare him with before we have to cut him loose. For now, we can let him stew for a while."

"In that case, how about ordering out for a large sausage, mushroom and black olive pizza?"

"Works for me," Lopez said.

The pizza could not have been better, unless it had given Lopez and Johnson some ammunition to use against Daniel Gibson.

As they walked over to the interview room, they were both feeling inadequately armed.

"He has been pacing the room since I put him in there. Must have walked two miles," Yardley reported. "And he's been yelling for a lawyer the entire time. The man is not happy."

"I'm not very concerned about his happiness," Lopez said.

"Noted," Yardley said. "If and when you have to let him go, his wallet, keys and such are in that top desk drawer."

"Thanks, Yardley. You can go back to your post," Lopez said. "We are hoping for a phone call or two."

"I'll let you know, Lieutenant," he said, and he moved off. "Well, here goes."

"Good luck," Johnson said.

Lieutenant Lopez walked into the interview room.

Sergeant Johnson settled in front of a video monitor in the adjoining room.

"Mr. Gibson, I am truly sorry for the delay."

"You are going to be a lot sorrier if I have anything to say about it."

Lopez let it slide.

"Tell me about your relationship with Justin Walker."

"I have no such relationship. I do not know the man."

"We found your office phone number in his possession."

"Anyone can get that number and have called it or not. It is easy to find, it is listed in the Blue Pages of every phone directory. We receive countless calls, inquiries concerning a number of issues related to international travel, customs, and citizenship. We often receive misdirected inquiries, many are redirected to more appropriate agencies. I have never known a man named Justin Walker, or talked with him to my knowledge. I have no clue as to why he possessed my office phone number or, for that matter, if he ever used it. I would like to get out of here. I cannot help you, and I can only wonder what this Mr. Walker has to say about any of this."

Lopez turned her back to Gibson.

"Justin Walker has nothing to say about it," Lopez said. "He was murdered last night, by a man named Carmine Cicero."

Johnson caught Gibson's reaction on the video monitor. He quickly rose and rapped on the interview room door.

Lopez excused herself and walked out.

"I have to hand it to Gibson," Johnson said. "It was an impressive monologue. But the mention of Justin Walker's death and Carmine Cicero definitely messed with his blood pressure."

The telephone rang.

Johnson took it.

Yardley with word that Beggs from forensics was on the line for the lieutenant.

"Joe Beggs," Johnson said, offering the phone to Lopez.

"Anything?" Lopez asked.

"It's almost too much. Here is what we have from Justin Walker's home phone and what Lieutenant Folgueras sent over to us from Oakland. There was a call from Carmine Cicero's cell to Walker's land line. There were calls made on Weido's cell, Cicero's cell, and Walker's land line to the same number. It's an L.A. number with an extension. It is an answering service, they do not connect to the client, instead they take a message and a callback number. And they will not say who the extension belongs to without a court order," Beggs said, stopping to take a breath. "Are you with me so far?"

"Yes," Lopez said. "There's more?"

"There were phone calls to Weido, Walker and Cicero from Los Angeles in the past several days, all soon after they had called the answering service, and all from public pay phones."

"Is that it?"

"There was one more number called from Cicero's phone that we can't identify, at least not quickly, without calling it."

"You haven't called it?"

"I thought you might want to try that one yourself."

"Give me that number," Lopez said, "and let me have the answering service number as well."

Lopez scribbled down the first number, then the answering service number, and she thanked Beggs.

Lopez called the first number.

"What's that sound?" she said, when it started ringing.

Johnson opened the top desk drawer, the sound got louder.

"That sound," Johnson said, pointing to the open drawer, "it's Daniel Gibson's cell phone."

"Wow," Lopez said. "Is that cool or what?"

"It's still not enough to hold him," Johnson said.

"It's something to work with in Round Two," Lopez said. "I need to go back in there. Beggs gave me a second phone number, I wrote it down. See if you can locate it in Gibson's outgoing call log. Let me know if you do."

"Okay."

Lopez walked back into the interview room.

"Mr. Gibson, I appreciate your patience."

"I ran out of patience an hour ago," Gibson said.

"Tell me about Carmine Cicero," Lopez said.

"I cannot tell you anything about someone I do not know."

"Let me tell you a little about him. Cicero caused the deaths of at least four men in the past week—in Los Angeles, Oakland, and here in San Francisco."

"Then you should be looking for him, and not wasting your time, and mine, asking me about people I know nothing about."

"We have confirmed Cicero called your cell phone, Mr. Gibson," Lopez tried. "Do you believe he found it listed in the Government Blue Pages of his phone directory?"

"You have been holding me here for more than an hour, and I have not been charged with any crime," Gibson said. "I will not answer any more questions until I call my lawyer."

There was a tapping on the door.

Lopez excused herself again.

"Damn it. We are going to lose him," Lopez said. "Tell me you found that answering service number in his phone."

"Nothing," Johnson said. "And I mean absolutely nothing. There were no records, at all, of incoming or outgoing calls. Gibson must have deleted everything before we got him here to the station."

"Son-of-a-bitch."

"However, Ray Boyle just called to save the day."

"What?"

"The three girls who identified Cicero as the man who

took them to L.A. and then handed them over to a man named Rimsky at The Volga nightclub, where they were coerced into giving sexual favors to patrons, fingered Gibson from the photograph we sent down to Boyle. They all identified Gibson as the man they met at the immigration office on Washington Street, the man who set them up at the Powell Hotel on Cyril Magnin Street, and the man who was present when Cicero collected them from the hotel. Ray assured me he would have collaboration from as many as ten more girls by the end of the day."

"What are we missing here, Rocky?"

"Missing?"

"Walker supplies a key to Roberto Sandoval's apartment, and then he is killed to keep him quiet. DiMarco comes into possession of the key, kills Sandoval, and Weido takes care of DiMarco. Weido and Cicero battle it out to the end in Oakland. They were all working for the same someone in Los Angeles who is very, very serious about covering up involvement in human trafficking."

"Nicely summarized," Johnson said.

"Where is the motive for Sandoval's death?"

"Good question," Johnson conceded.

Lopez returned to the interview room.

"Mr. Gibson," Lopez said. "I understand your concern, being detained without charges, and not being granted the opportunity to phone an attorney. I have good news. I am ready to address both complaints."

"Finally," Gibson said.

"Daniel Gibson you are under arrest for kidnapping. You have the right to remain silent. You have a right to legal counsel, you may call an attorney. You and I can chat further when your attorney arrives."

"I want to make a deal," Gibson said. "I can tell you why Roberto Sandoval was murdered."

TWENTY EIGHT

The most comfortable piece of furniture in the two-room headquarters of Diamond Investigations above Molinari's Deli on Columbus in North Beach is also the *only* truly comfortable piece of furniture.

It is a short length upholstered couch, sofa if you like, often referred to as a love seat, although it has never been used for that particular purpose.

It was a gift from my mentor Jimmy Pigeon to celebrate the opening of the office, my own private investigation enterprise, after I left Jimmy's employ in Santa Monica.

Jimmy insisted it was essential to have at least one such office fixture. He claimed it was an important tool, with the ability to land a potential client who might be having second thoughts about hiring a total stranger to spy on his or her wayward spouse or unruly child.

Jimmy's generosity was legendary, but I suspected the gift was in part motivated by the desire to have a place to sit during his visits that wouldn't leave him crippled.

As much as anyone can love an inanimate object, I love the thing. It sits up against the wall that divides the two rooms, facing my desk. It is complimented by a side table and a pole lamp.

I had been relishing its pleasures for more than an hour, catching up with Esmeralda's dilemmas, and Quasimodo's valiant efforts to aid her in her plight, while I waited for word from Johnson or Boyle which I honestly hoped would never come.

I finally concluded I was off the hook and, since the phone wasn't ringing-in other business, I felt free to consider options for enjoying a Saturday afternoon of mindless play.

Then Lopez called.

"Jake, could you come over to my office?" she asked.

Her use of my first name was always a red flag.

"I don't see why not," I said, although I could think of a few reasons. "I'm on foot, give me ten minutes."

I set the Hugo novel on the end table, I picked up the .38 I had failed to return to Sergeant Johnson, and I strolled down to Vallejo Street Station.

When Roberto Sandoval received his law degree from Yale he was offered positions at high-powered east coast law firms from Washington to Boston. The future looked very bright.

Sandoval chose instead to return to his native home in San Francisco and accept a job with the District Attorney's office, a job considered by partners in the firms that had courted him as no more than a glorified civil service position.

The decision surprised many people, including Sandoval's new bride and his new father-in-law. Theresa Ward was the daughter of John Ward of Ward and Barnum, one of the most prestigious firms in New Haven. John was determined to employ Sandoval for two reasons. Ward recognized Sandoval's unique talents and he also wanted to keep his daughter close to home and hearth.

Roberto got a lot of heat, but refused to be dissuaded. Sandoval carried his law degree and his new wife across the continent, abandoning the Atlantic for the Pacific.

He was not warmly received at the San Francisco D.A.'s office. Roberto's colleagues, many of whom would have given their right arm for the opportunities he had been offered in the east, chose to remain distant. One of the few who chose to befriend Sandoval early on was Alexi Kutzen, a janitor at the Hall of Justice. Sandoval often sought out the Russian immigrant when he could find no one else to talk with.

When Kutzen accepted a higher paying position as the Assistant Director of Janitorial Services at the Powell Hotel at Union Square, Roberto was sorry to see him leave.

Alexi Kutzen's primary responsibility at the Powell Hotel was to make certain the janitorial staff were doing their jobs satisfactorily.

To that end, Alexi conducted a daily midday inspection of the common areas of the hotel. He began in the lobby and then walked the hallways from end to end and from floor to floor to verify the shared areas of the hotel looked their best.

During one such midday inspection, Kutzen ran into a young woman who was having difficulty persuading a soft drink vending machine to accept a well-worn dollar bill. Alexi took over the challenge and after a few attempts he accomplished the task, and handed the young woman a can of Diet Coke.

Her difficulty in pronouncing the two simple words *Thank, you* was all Alexi needed to determine the woman was from his part of the world.

"*Pozhaluysta,*" he replied.

The woman could not hide her pleasure, the excitement of meeting a fellow Russian.

Before long they were conversing like long lost friends.

Her name was Katya Ivanov. She came from Lobnya, a town seventeen miles north of Moscow, an area Alexi knew well. She reminded Alexi of one of his sister's girls. He reminded Katya of one of her mother's brothers.

She had come into the country, sponsored by a placement agency in Moscow, to take a domestic position in Los Angeles. She was excited about the possibility of earning enough money, in time, to bring her widowed mother and her younger sister over to the United States.

Katya expressed some concern about not having any family or friends for support, Alexi assured her she could call him at the hotel anytime she needed someone to talk with.

The following morning, Alexi saw Katya and two other young women in front of the hotel. Two men were talking nearby. Alexi had seen one of the men before. He had learned from the hotel concierge that the man worked at immigration services and had delivered Katya and the other girls to the hotel.

The three girls climbed into a waiting van, and the second man drove them off.

Alexi hoped Katya and the other girls would find good fortune waiting for them in Los Angeles.

A few days later, Alexi received a phone call at the hotel from Katya. She said she was confused. Instead of working as a housekeeper for a family down in L.A., she found herself serving drinks at a night club and would be required to do so until she worked off relocation expenses.

Alexi Kutzen did not like the sound of it, and promised he would look into it.

He called Roberto Sandoval.

Sandoval was suspicious also. He acquired personnel photos from the immigration agency and had Alexi go through them.

Alexi identified Daniel Gibson.

Sandoval called Gibson and asked Gibson to report to the D.A.'s office on the following Thursday to talk about a young woman named Katya Ivanov.

Gibson called the answering service in Los Angeles.

"When he called back, I told him about Sandoval," Gibson said. "He told me he would take care of it."

"Did he say *how* he would take care of it?" Lopez asked.

"No."

"Who is he?"

"I don't know. I have never met him or learned his name, I only spoke with him on the telephone—and he did most of the talking."

"How were you enlisted?"

"Carmine Cicero. I was offered a great deal of money," Gibson said. "All I had to do was flag the girls that were brought over and have them sent to me at my office."

"And you took them to the Powell Hotel."

"Yes. Then Cicero would pick them up at the hotel and he would transport them to Los Angeles. I was to receive five thousand dollars, in cash, for each girl. I still have fifty thousand dollars coming."

"Don't hold your breath," Lopez said. "How could you sell young girls like that, for any amount of money?"

"As far as I knew, they were being offered legitimate jobs in Los Angeles. All I did was cut through a lot of red tape to facilitate work visas."

"I find your alleged ignorance hard to believe," Lopez said.

"Believe what you will."

"When was the last time you spoke to the man in Los Angeles?"

"He called just before you arrived at my house. He said he was having trouble reaching Carmine. Asked if I had heard anything from Cicero. I told him I had not."

"What about Justin Walker?"

"I was asked to deliver twenty thousand to Walker but I had no idea what for," Gibson said. "If you want to find the man behind this you need to find Cicero. I can't help you."

"Cicero is dead," Lopez said. "And I think you *can* help."

"How?"

"Call the answering service. When he calls back tell him you need to talk with him, face-to-face. Say you will go down to Los Angeles to meet him, tell him it concerns the D.A.'s office up here and Carmine Cicero. Insist you won't discuss it over the telephone."

"I won't do that. I am sure he would never agree to such a meeting, except as a means to shut me up the way he has silenced everyone else who could lead to him. I am not willing to die in order to help you."

"Is that your final answer?"

"Yes."

"Then you are looking at a very dismal future, Mr. Gibson. And, for the record," Lopez said, "I think you are a creep, and being in the same room with you has been repulsive. I hope you spend the rest of your sorry life behind bars."

Lopez walked out of the interview room, slamming the door behind her.

"Why not tell him how you feel?" Johnson said.

"It's not funny," Lopez said, though she had to suppress a smile. "What now?"

"We call Boyle to fill him in, find out if he has any clever ideas."

Lopez spoke to Ray Boyle.

Then she called me with the invitation to her office.

. . .

When I arrived at Vallejo Street Station, Sergeant Johnson and Lieutenant Lopez walked me through the epic tale of Roberto Sandoval, Alexi Kutzen, Katya Ivanov, Carmine Cicero, Weido and Walker and Gibson and the man with no name.

It was a narrative that would have impressed Hugo.

Finally, they told me what Ray Boyle had suggested.

I was as enthusiastic about the prospect as Daniel Gibson had been when he was offered the very same opportunity and had turned it down emphatically.

But, how could I say no?

Actually, I could think of a hundred ways to say no.

"What the hell," I said instead.

My ability to stay out of trouble lately convinced me I was destined for a trip to Los Angeles.

Lopez had me use Gibson's cell phone to make the call to the answering service in L.A.

The conversation with the operator who answered was short and sweet. I identified myself as Daniel Gibson. She assured me the message would be promptly forwarded.

While we waited at the station for a return call, all of my travel itineraries were arranged.

Roundtrip airfare and ground transportation in L.A. would be provided courtesy of the Los Angeles Police Department.

Transportation to and from SFO would be provided free of charge by the San Francisco Police Department.

I was being treated like a V.I.P.

I was feeling like a sucker.

Twenty minutes after leaving the message, Daniel Gibson's cell phone rang. Judging from his articulate speech, the man was no Russian or Italian mafia thug. He spoke intelligently and clearly. He agreed to the meeting in Los Angeles without any argument, which, if Daniel Gibson knew anything about it, was not necessarily a good sign.

I told him when my flight was scheduled to arrive in Los Angeles. He told me to call him as soon as the plane landed, at which time he would let me know exactly where the meeting would take place.

And that was that.

Sergeant Johnson would drive me out to SFO and Lieutenant Ray Boyle would pick me up at LAX.

I would be discreetly followed to the rendezvous, I would be well protected from any possible harm, and then the bad guy would be apprehended and brought to justice.

A piece of cake.

One far less appealing than Zeppole di San Giuseppe.

Johnson and yours truly were on our way to San Francisco International Airport.

"So, a chance encounter between a young Russian woman and a hotel janitor brought Roberto Sandoval into the picture."

"And got him killed," Johnson added.

"Do you have enough to nail this guy?"

"Once we get the records from the answering service, and with Gibson's testimony, the short answer is yes."

"Why not just wait for the phone records?"

"It would take some time," Johnson said. "And Ray Boyle is not one to wait when it comes to taking a murderer off the street. Are you beginning to feel uneasy about this?"

"I never felt easy about it."

"We just need the man to expose himself, once he has been identified, you are finished."

Johnson's choice of words was not very comforting.

I was putting myself in the position Daniel Gibson was willing to do anything to avoid. The man who I was going to meet would consider Gibson the last loose end unless I, in the acting role of a lifetime, could convince him it was Carmine Cicero he needed to worry about.

I suddenly remembered I was still carrying Johnson's back-up weapon. I reached into my jacket pocket, pulled it out and handed it over.

"Would have made it interesting on the security check-in line at the airport," I said.

I also remembered I had left the Hunchback sitting on the table in my office and *that* realization was more disarming.

An airplane ride without a good book is like a day without sunshine, or without a cigarette.

Johnson dropped me off in front of the terminal and wished me luck.

I hoped luck would not be necessary.

The terminal was jammed. It took nearly thirty minutes to check-in, make it through the security check point, and find my way to the departure gate. Sergeant Johnson had insisted we allow at least ninety minutes. I had a little more than an hour to kill. I picked up a copy of *The New Yorker* at a newsstand. I liked the cartoons.

After leaving Diamond at the airport terminal, Johnson called Desk Sergeant Yardley.

"Vallejo Street Station."

"It's Johnson. What's the word?"

"Ready to go when you are," Yardley said. "You have less than ten minutes."

"Tell him I'm on my way."

"Copy that," Yardley said. "What if Lieutenant Lopez begins asking where you are?"

"Tell her anything except where I am."

Once in the air, I wondered what might happen if the man in L.A. did not believe I was Daniel Gibson.

Or what would transpire if he did believe I was Gibson.

Or if it would make any difference if Ray Boyle couldn't stay close enough to watch my back.

And what Quasimodo would do if it was Esmeralda instead of Jake Diamond confronting a man who made Archdeacon Frollo look like a boy scout.

I decided I was thinking too much.

I ordered bourbon over ice from a flight attendant and I went back to the magazine cartoons.

TWENTY NINE

Ray Boyle's instructions had been explicit.

Diamond was not to call the answering service until Ray met Jake at the airport. Ray needed to know the location of the meeting before Diamond left LAX.

Jake exited the plane and began walking from the gate to the arrivals area in Terminal 7. Daniel Gibson's cell phone rang before Jake reached the terminal atrium.

"Yes?"

"Welcome to Los Angeles, Mr. Gibson."

"Thank you."

"I arranged for a driver. Look for a man holding a sign bearing your name. He will take you to me."

"I was just about to call *you*," Jake said. "I expected I would be waiting a while to hear back. I was planning to have a drink at the airport and find my way to you on my own."

"Well, that won't be necessary now, will it?"

"You didn't need to go to the trouble."

"No trouble at all. If you need a drink, I can take care of that as well. Locate my driver. I look forward to meeting you very soon."

And the line went dead.

Jake saw the man with the sign first. Then he spotted Ray Boyle. Boyle was moving to meet him. Diamond turned away from Boyle, making a big deal of waving his arm at the driver while he signaled with his other arm that Ray should back off.

Boyle saw Jake greet the driver and watched as they both walked toward the terminal exit. Boyle was unprepared. All he could do was follow at a distance.

Once outside the terminal, the driver opened the back door of a limousine parked a few feet away. Jake climbed in and his chauffeur moved around the car to the driver's door.

A man entered a taxicab standing a hundred feet behind the limo.

"Follow that car," the man said.

"Are you joking?" the cabbie asked.

"I couldn't be more serious."

The limousine began to pull away.

The taxi followed.

When Ray Boyle exited the terminal, Jake was gone.

"Fuck," Boyle said, loud enough to turn the heads of a group of Japanese waiting to board an airport shuttle van.

Ten minutes later, the limousine pulled into the parking area in front of the Sheraton Gateway Hotel less than a mile from the airport.

The driver escorted me to a room on the third floor and he tapped lightly on the door.

The man who opened the door was very well dressed, and he looked about as threatening as Regis Philbin.

He flashed a perfect talk-show host smile.

"Wait out front," he said to the driver. "Keep your eyes open. Make sure you weren't followed."

The driver walked off.

"Please come in, Mr. Gibson," my host said.

He moved aside to let me pass and closed the door behind us.

"Daniel," he said, "my name is Derek London. May I offer you a drink, the room is well stocked."

London.

Marco Weido's famous last word.

I had learned what I had been sent to learn.

Mission accomplished in record time.

And an ideal time to get the hell out of there.

Victor Hugo said, *During a wise man's whole life, his destiny holds his philosophy in a state of siege.*

I said, "Bourbon, rocks."

. . .

London poured two tiny bottles of Booker's over ice. He handed the drink to me and invited me to take a seat.

The choice was between an upholstered chair and a matching upholstered chair.

Eeny meeny miney mo.

I sat.

London poured a drink for himself. Glenlivet and soda, also known as a senseless waste of fine Scotch. He settled into the other chair, facing me.

"So, Daniel," London began. "What is it we could not discuss over the telephone?"

I employed all the skills I had developed in a remedial English class at City College of New York and my acting classes in California to sound like someone who was not born and raised in Brooklyn.

And all I had picked up from Travis Duncan about sounding more confident and tougher than I really was.

"I thought I could get what I need more expediently if I talked with you face-to-face," I said.

"And what is it you need?" London asked.

"I need the balance of the payment you owe me, and I need to get out."

"Get out."

It sounded like a question. I would have been much happier if it was a request.

"Get out of our arrangement, and get out of the country."

"Out of the country?"

"Yes. And quickly. And I recommend you consider doing the same."

"May I ask what brought this on, Mr. Gibson?"

I had liked it better when he was calling me Daniel.

"Carmine Cicero was picked up by the police."

"How do you know that?"

"They granted him a phone call, he called me."

"Why would he call you?"

"I suppose it was simply a matter of convenience. I would guess he was looking for someone who might come to his rescue in a timely manner. I sent a lawyer over to try to help smooth out the bumps, but it isn't going to stall the cops for very long. They have Cicero cold on two murders in Oakland—a small timer named Bobo Bigelow and a police investigator named Marco Weido. It's just a matter of time before Carmine gives us both up."

"Cicero has no idea who I am, only what I look like."

"They will subpoena the answering service and have Cicero identify your photo."

"The answering service cannot identify me either," London said. "In fact, the only person who can truly identify me is you, Daniel. Would you care for another drink?"

The taxi that had followed the limousine to the hotel sat tucked away in a parking spot a good distance from the hotel entrance.

Meter running.

The passenger in the back seat of the cab had watched the limo driver escort Diamond into the hotel and come out alone a few minutes later.

The limousine driver moved his car to a parking space across from the entrance and remained in the vehicle.

"Are we going to sit here all day?" the cab driver asked ten minutes later.

They watched as the limo driver climbed out of his car, leaned up against the driver's door, and lit a cigarette.

"Do you smoke?" the passenger asked the taxi driver.

"Yes."

"You can drop me off at the front entrance now. Let me have a cigarette, put it on my tab."

He climbed out of the taxicab, he paid the cab driver, and he watched the taxi pull away.

Then he casually moved toward the limousine.

The limo driver had been looking away. The taxi passenger was only a few feet from London's driver when he spoke.

"Do you have a light?" he said.

The limo driver turned quickly, but not quickly enough.

The man who had suddenly materialized was pointing a .38.

"Do you have a weapon?" the man asked.

"Glove box."

"You are going to get into the front seat and place both hands on the steering wheel. I am going to get into the seat behind you. I will not hesitate to shoot you if you deviate, understood?"

"Understood."

"What can I call you?"

"Frank."

"Now, Frank, you will slowly pass me the car key," the man said, once they were in the vehicle.

Derek London's driver complied.

"Will your employer do anything final before calling you?"

"Not likely. So, what now?"

"Now you place your hands back on the wheel. You will keep your mouth shut. And we will wait."

While Derek London was refreshing my drink, I was afforded a minute or so to review my situation.

I was in a hotel room with a man who had orchestrated at least five murders in less than a week.

And I didn't have him reaching for his checkbook.

I was convinced London's chauffeur was more than just a driver, in the tradition of Carmine Cicero. I felt confident he was stationed just outside the door, waiting to be summoned in or waiting for me to try getting out.

I used the remaining moments of idle thought wondering if Ray Boyle had managed to follow us from the airport.

I was not very optimistic.

London handed me the drink and sat again, facing me on the matching upholstered chair.

"Would you like to know how this whole business began?" Derek London asked.

I was mildly curious.

I was guessing the authentic Daniel Gibson couldn't care less.

And in this evening's performance the role of Daniel Gibson, a.k.a. the last loose end, will be played by Jake Diamond.

"I came down here to end this business," I answered. "Why would I want to know how it began?"

"I don't know. Either you do or you don't."

"I don't"

"I am going to tell you anyway, Daniel."

That settled it. I had nothing smart to say, so I took a healthy swallow of bourbon and I waited.

"Do you know what a talent agent does?" he asked.

I knew what a talent agent was *supposed* to do, but in my personal experience they didn't do much. I let him continue.

"I ran a small but successful agency. Did well enough to live in this unlivable city, put my wife and kids into a nice house in the Hills, employ a few domestics including a driver, gardener—and a young woman who did some cleaning, shopping, a little cooking and kept an eye on the kids.

"The girl was from Moscow. My wife found her through an employment agency that sponsored the relocation of foreign men and woman for domestic work here in the states. Marina was an exceptionally good worker, bright and likable. My wife and the children loved her. Then, after more than a year with us, she suddenly disappeared.

"We couldn't understand, we paid her well, gave her a safe place to live, room and board, and treated her like a member of family, so we naturally assumed she had come to some harm. I was ready to report her missing to the police, but my driver assured me we would have better results finding her if I let him look into it. That driver was Carmine Cicero.

"A week later, Cicero took me to a nightclub. The place was jammed. We sat at a table, many young girls glided across the floor serving the patrons and being very friendly. Cicero pointed to the bar, and I saw Marina, dressed up like a street walker, working her charms on an older man. As I watched from across the room, Cicero told me how profitable it was, how the girls were luring big spenders into nightclubs up and down the coast. And how these clubs couldn't find girls quickly enough to meet the demand.

"I confronted Marina. She was surprised and embarrassed to find me there. I simply asked her *why*. Marina simply answered she needed more money than she could make cleaning windows and needed it sooner to help her family back in Russia. I was not in a position to offer her an alternative. My business was floundering. Most of my clients weren't landing any roles, and those who were doing well began moving over to larger agencies. I wished Marina good fortune. Carmine and I left the club.

"I had a lot of questions for Cicero as he drove me home. I was formulating an idea, and Carmine was quickly on the same page. I was thinking I might be in the wrong business. I was thinking perhaps I was representing the wrong kind of talent. What if I sponsored the placement of young women from Eastern Europe for jobs in the states, walking the floors of a nightclub, instead of walking the family dog. The stipulation was in the contract they signed, whether they fully understood or not, requiring the girls to work off their relocation costs. And we offered them a way to expedite the obligation working in the clubs. A majority of the girls voluntarily decided to stay on, the money was that good. Those who were very serious about getting out were let go after four months and referred to other employment agencies. There were no formal complaints.

"I made more in a year than I had in all my years as a talent agent, but I wanted more. I couldn't meet the demand for these girls fast enough. By then I had learned Cicero possessed talents that went far beyond driving a limousine. We talked about the possibility of cutting through red tape in the immigration process by throwing cash around and Cicero said he could handle it. And as *you* well know, Daniel, he succeeded.

"And everything was peaches and cream, and fists full of cash, until a janitor at a hotel in San Francisco rang a bell and got Roberto Sandoval involved.

"Three years ago, my hottest actor was filming in Oakland. One night he was discovered in a hotel bed with a male prostitute. The detective who busted him called me from the hotel room. I knew immediately he was fishing. I asked him what it might take to make the incident go away. We settled on ten thousand dollars. The little fag rewarded me for saving his career by signing with another agency, but that's another story. In any event, the detective was Marco Weido. So, when the problem of Roberto Sandoval came up, I felt Weido could take care of it. Cicero agreed, and we reached out to him."

"So you put out a contract on Roberto Sandoval."

"And Bigelow. And Justin Walker. And then Weido himself."

London paused. He rose, walked across the room, and fixed another watered-down Scotch. During this short intermission in his epic tale I tried finding a more comfortable position in my chair, but I couldn't locate one.

I had no idea why he was telling me all of this. Or I had an idea and didn't care for it much.

I was wondering when Ray Boyle was going to burst into the hotel room with a gun in one hand and my return airline ticket to San Francisco in the other.

As it turned out, it was London who held a weapon in *his* hand as he walked back toward me with his fresh drink.

"I know Carmine Cicero is dead, Daniel," he said.

I did the math. The two men who actually knew who they were working for were DOA, and he knew it. No one else could identify Derek London as the man behind the curtain. Except, now, I could. And I doubted it would make any difference to London that I was only pretending to be Daniel Gibson.

"Look," I said. "This is not necessary. Just pay me what you owe me and I will disappear. Forever."

"That is not going to happen, Daniel," London said. "At least not as you describe it."

"So, you are going to kill me?" I asked lamely.

"I will if I have to, but I prefer leaving it to someone more at ease with that sort of thing."

"Like Cicero or Weido."

"Or like the driver who brought you here."

"Frank?"

"I see you got acquainted on the ride over."

"What do you do about Frank? Frank is another loose end. Sooner or later you'll have to do your own dirty work."

It was as tough a delivery as I could muster. Travis Duncan

would have been proud of me, if only for a moment.

London flashed an ugly smile.

"I will deal with that in my own time," London said. "Does it matter that much to you who pulls your plug?"

Nice idiom.

"I'll go with Frank," I said.

London set his drink down, reached into his jacket pocket, and pulled out his cell phone.

Derek London's driver had been sitting perfectly still in the front seat of the limousine, with both hands motionless on the steering wheel. He felt the barrel of the gun softly kiss the back of his head before his cell phone rang a second time.

"Okay, Frank," the man sitting behind him said. "Answer it, put it on speaker, and don't be stupid."

Frank took the call.

"Yes, sir?"

"It's time we took our guest for that ride we talked about."

"I'll be right there."

"Are you certain you weren't followed?"

"Positive, sir. It's clear out here."

"Excellent, use the knock," London said, and ended the call.

"The knock," asked the man in the back seat.

"Two hard raps, three soft."

"Very original. Was he talking about the *long ride*?"

"Yes."

"Have you killed for him before?"

"No. I never killed anyone. I heard about the job, had a good idea about what he was looking for, and bluffed my way in. The money was great, and with Carmine Cicero on his payroll, I never thought it would come to this."

"Cicero is dead."

"Thanks for sharing."

"I kind of like you, Frank. I really don't wish for you to get hurt. So we are both going in there, and I will explain what I need you to do while we are on our way up."

. . .

There was a rapping at the door of the hotel room. Two hard and three soft knocks. Very original. Not to mention I was already familiar with the secret code, having heard it used when I arrived. It was good old Frank.

"Don't move," London said.

I didn't move.

He walked around me, his eyes and his gun trained on me all the way to the door. He opened the door with his back to it.

Frank walked in.

London handed Frank the gun.

"Keep him covered, I'll get my things. If he moves, put one in his brain."

Nice talk.

London started moving away and then Frank shocked the hell out of me. He took the gun off me and turned it on London.

"Hold on a minute, sir," he said. "I think I hear something in the hall."

"I thought you said it was all clear," London said, turning to Frank.

And that's when London noticed the tables had turned, so to speak. And that's when Frank opened the door and I was truly astounded.

In walked Sergeant Roxton Johnson.

"Hit the road, Frank," Johnson said, taking the gun.

Frank disappeared.

"Derek London, you are under arrest for conspiracy to murder."

London didn't know whether to shit or go blind.

"How did you get here," I asked, finally coming out of my stupor.

"Private jet, I followed you in a cab from LAX. Good luck for you, Ray Boyle lost your scent."

"Where is Boyle?"

"I don't know, I'm guessing he's out looking for you."

"Why didn't you call him?"

"I was afraid if the troops stormed in, I would lose the element of surprise."

"How did you know Frank would cooperate?" I asked.

"I told him he could walk," Johnson answered. He had not taken his eyes off London for a second. Had not even blinked. "When I gave him my handkerchief and told him to wipe down the limo, he decided to trust me, and trusting *him* was my best bet. I'll call Ray as soon as I get handcuffs on this piece of crap. Boyle is going to eat this creep up alive."

"Can you do me a favor first?" I asked.

"I've already done you a favor, Diamond."

"Will you put one more on my tab?"

"Sure. You deserve it. You really went out on a limb."

I quickly crossed the short distance to London and hit him in the face with all I had. He went down like a bowling pin.

"Feel better now," the sergeant asked, while he snapped the cuffs on.

"I will, as soon as my hand stops hurting," I said.

An hour later, Johnson and I were in a taxi on our way to LAX for the return trip to San Francisco.

Derek London had been turned over to the LAPD. He was safe in Ray Boyle's hands. Though, knowing how Lieutenant Boyle felt about the way London had exploited those girls, *safe* may not have been the most precise word for it. If there was a bright spot to any of it, it was that Boyle believed a very high profile trial would result in more public awareness of the problem, and increased diligence by authorities.

"Do you think London will be convicted?" I asked, sitting beside Johnson in the back seat of the cab.

"Slam dunk. With London in custody, Daniel Gibson will testify. And Gibson knows enough to make the case, especially now that he can swear to London's confession."

"Gibson didn't hear London's confession," I said. "I know I can be fairly convincing at times, but let's not forget it was me in that hotel room with London."

"We made a deal with Daniel Gibson. *He* was in that hotel room with London."

"I see."

"Thanks for helping us wrap this up, Diamond. And for offering to help clear Lieutenant Lopez."

"You're welcome, but it's not exactly all wrapped up."

"What do you mean?"

"London knew Carmine Cicero was killed."

"How could he have known?"

"He must have heard it from someone, and it wasn't me."

"That's not possible. We kept it quiet. Only a handful of people knew about Cicero's death. And all of those people were police."

"I know."

"That is really bad news, Diamond."

"Sorry."

THIRTY

I woke up on Sunday morning feeling pretty good although the time projected on the ceiling above my bed in bright green numbers still really annoyed me. But I had boldly faced danger, for the public good, and come away unscathed, if you didn't count the bruised knuckles.

I dragged myself out of bed, threw on a robe, unplugged the table alarm clock and headed downstairs to whip up breakfast. Sergeant Johnson called, to thank me again for my help and bring me up to speed.

Johnson had wasted no time hooking up with Lieutenant Folgueras in an attempt to swiftly discover who had tipped London about Cicero's demise. Aside from Folgueras, Lopez and Johnson, who were quickly cleared of suspicion, no one was told the identity of the other victim in the fatal shootout at Marco Weido's house in Oakland. Even the Oakland crime scene investigators and medical examiner had been kept in the dark as to Cicero's identity. Of the two Oakland uniformed officers who first arrived at the scene, only one had known Weido, had worked with Weido in the past.

The question arose, did Bruce Perry know Carmine Cicero as well.

Folgueras brought Officer Perry into his office and unceremoniously delineated the consequences of holding back. Perry folded like an accordion. Weido had enlisted Perry, offering a substantial reward, to keep an eye on the progress of Blake Sanchez who was fighting for his life in a hospital after using Weido's weapon in a liquor store robbery attempt. He also gave Perry the phone number of an answering service in Los Angeles to call if he had news and couldn't reach Weido. Perry did in fact recognize Carmine Cicero, and Weido was out of the picture, so Perry called Los Angeles hoping to earn a bonus with the news of both their deaths.

"How is Lieutenant Lopez?" I asked Johnson, once he completed the update.

"I'm on my way to breakfast with Lopez now," Johnson said. "I'm sure she will chew me out for going down to L.A. yesterday without her blessings."

"Won't Lopez be glad you saved my bacon, once again?"

"I'm not certain," Johnson said, and he ended the call.

Good old Johnson, always the charmer.

I started a pot of coffee and then I crossed to the refrigerator hoping to *find* bacon.

Lieutenant Laura Lopez and Sergeant Rocky Johnson sat together in a window booth at Café DeLucchi on Columbus Avenue in North Beach.

"So," Lopez said.

"So," Johnson said.

"So, your wife is coming home today."

"Yes. I pick her up at SFO this afternoon."

"I'll bet you are anxious to see her."

"Even more anxious than I am to see the waitress bringing my sausage and swiss cheese omelet out of the kitchen."

"Can I ask you a serious question, Rocky?"

"Shoot."

"Did you think, at any time, I had something to do with Roberto Sandoval's death?"

"I told you before, Laura, I didn't know what to think. I was concerned, and the concern was about your well-being. Removing evidence from a crime scene is not characteristic behavior."

"It certainly got you juiced up. Maybe I should behave out of character more often."

"Don't do me any favors," Johnson said.

"Speaking of favors, it would have been good of you to tell me about your plan to visit Los Angeles."

At last, thought Johnson.

"It was a spur-of-the-moment decision. I didn't have much time to consult with anyone."

"You found time to ask Yardley to hush it up."

"Guilty," Johnson admitted.

"I have to say I was hot about it, but it did pan out. In the future, however, drop me a little hint. That being said, you did a commendable job down there, Rocky."

"Thank you. Jake Diamond had a lot to do with our success. I'm beginning to rethink my opinion of him."

"Good luck with that," Lopez said, as the waitress finally arrived with their food, "and, Johnson."

"Yes."

"Please tell me you didn't reach out to Diamond when you were all jerked up about the envelope."

"Could you pass the pepper?" was all Johnson would say.

Reporters from print and broadcast media had been trying for days to obtain a statement from Theresa Sandoval regarding the murder of her husband, with no success. Until a rookie reporter from the *Examiner*, with all of the ambition associated with youth, and working off information he acquired from a doorman named Kenny Gerard with the help of a fifty-dollar bill, discovered where the Assistant District Attorney's widow was residing while the Sandoval apartment was being readied for her return. The reporter staked-out Mrs. Sandoval's sanctuary, and he followed her to a Santa Rosa restaurant on Saturday evening. And suddenly the story became not what the woman felt about her husband's death, but about how she was dealing with her loss.

Carmella Carlucci called upstairs to her husband.

"Tony, breakfast is almost ready."

Carlucci came down, collected the *Sunday Examiner* from outside the front door, carried it into the kitchen and sat at the table. He unwrapped the newspaper and looked at the front page.

"Would you like toast with the frittata?" his wife asked.

"Is this fucking beautiful or what?"

"Anthony, please, your language," Carmella said, bringing food to the kitchen table.

"I can't think of a better way to describe it," Tony said, showing her the headline.

GRIEVING WIFE, SECRET LIFE

There was a half-page photo below the headline, above the fold. A man and a woman sitting together at a restaurant.

"What is it?" Carmella asked.

"Get this," Tony Carlucci said, reading. "Theresa Sandoval, wife of the recently slain Assistant District Attorney, was followed to a Santa Rosa bistro where she was met by District Attorney Liam Duffey. Following dinner, the two were followed to the Good Nite Inn off Redwood Highway where they shared a room for the evening."

"That's horrible."

"It's fucking beautiful. Liam Duffey's career just went down the toilet. I love it. My brother John will love it. There is not enough cheerful news at the prison."

"Why are you always so cynical, Tony?"

"Read the newspaper. The number of idiots out there on the streets makes it very easy."

"Eat you breakfast, before it gets cold."

"Hold your horses, Carmella, it says there are more pictures on page three," Carlucci said. "Do you have any grated parmesan for these eggs?"

I had left a voice message for Travis Duncan on Saturday evening. Duncan called me Sunday morning.

"What can I do for you, Jake?"

"I just wanted to thank you again for helping with the Manny Sandoval problem. Vinnie will be relieved to hear the heat is off."

"How is the kid doing?"

"I'm headed over to the hospital later to check it out."

"Want me to come along?"

"Thanks, Travis, but I should go alone. No offense, but I think Vinnie finds you frightening."

"No offense taken, it's what I do. Get him my regards."

"I will."

. . .

After speaking with Duncan, I called Joey Vongoli.

"I'm going over to visit Vinnie in a while, do you want join me?"

"Sure, I can pick you up."

"Give me an hour."

"You got it. Did you see the *Examiner* this morning?" Joey asked.

"It's still sitting out front."

"Check it out. It's a kick."

While I waited for Joey to arrive, I used the time to call Darlene at her friend's place on Stinson Beach.

"When are you coming home?" I asked.

"Are you in a yank to get the Impala back?"

"I thought I would take you out to dinner."

"What's the occasion?"

"Do I need a reason?"

"I don't know. I'm a suspicious girl," Darlene said. "I should be back late afternoon. I'll drop Tug McGraw at my place, get the sand out of my hair and ears, and pick you up."

"Six?"

"Six it is," Darlene said. "Thanks again for letting me use the Chevy."

"My pleasure. I'm looking forward to dinner."

"You may change your tune when I start grilling you about what went down in Los Angeles."

"I'll take my chances."

"How *is* Vinnie?"

"I'm off to see him now, news at six."

"Speaking of news, did you see the *Examiner* this morning?"

"As a matter of fact I did."

"How about that creep Liam Duffey?"

"Lieutenant Lopez must be doing an Irish jig."

. . .

Ralph Morrison was very nervous about the meeting with Lieutenant Folgueras. Folgueras had called earlier that Sunday morning and asked if Ralph would come down to the police station.

Ralph had been beating himself up since Saturday. Disillusioned and disappointed in himself for being so horribly wrong about Marco Weido. He was planning to apologize and promise to keep his nose forever out of police business the moment he walked into the lieutenant's office.

Folgueras beat Ralph to the punch.

"I will get directly to the point, Mr. Morrison," the lieutenant began. "Your activities have not gone unnoticed."

Here it comes, Ralph thought.

"Activities, sir?"

"We are instituting a new program here in Oakland, a beefed-up, more structured civilian crime watch effort. We are hoping to make the public more aware of the challenges we face every day, as members of law enforcement, combating crime. And at the same time, we want to educate civilians with regard to the many ways they can assist in the battle."

"That's good," Ralph said, a little tongue tied, not sure where Folgueras was headed with it.

"I was asked to be in charge of our end, in the police department, and I gladly accepted."

"Congratulations."

"We need someone to head the civilian side of the program, act as a liaison between the department and the public. I recommended you for the position, and the request was granted."

"Me?"

"You would be working for the City of Oakland. The salary is modest, but then again so is mine."

"Salary?"

Ralph was afraid he might be hallucinating.

"And full benefits—medical, dental, paid vacations and holidays, and tuition if you choose to take classes in police work."

"I don't know what to say, Lieutenant."

"Say yes, Ralph."

"Yes."

"Shall we shake on it?"

"Absolutely," Ralph Morrison said, extending his good arm.

Joey and I walked into the hospital room. Vinnie looked much better, at least physically. Emotionally he was a wreck.

"Jake, Joey, thank God," Vinnie said, visibly shaken.

"Calm down, Strings," I said. "You're going to blow the heart monitor."

"I lied to you, Jake."

"About what?"

"About how I got hurt. It was Manny Sandoval. He had two of his goons work me over. I owe Manny on some luckless wagers."

"I know, Vinnie. Darlene let the cat out of the bag. You can stop worrying about it."

"Stop worrying? Look at *that*. I'm freaking out."

Vinnie pointed his finger at something behind us, Joey and I turned to find a vase sitting on a small table against the wall.

"Flowers?" I asked. "The flowers are freaking you out?"

"Sandoval sent them, with a get-well note."

"That was sweet of Manny."

"Don't you get it, Jake? It's a message. It's like the kiss of death."

Vinnie Strings was an imaginative young man.

Next he would be alluding to a horse's head under the bed sheets.

"I told you, Vinnie, you can stop worrying about Manny. We got him off your back."

"You and Joey?"

"Jake and Travis Duncan," Joey said, not one to take undue credit.

"Travis Duncan, he's even scarier than Sandoval."

"That's exactly what I was counting on," I said. "You don't owe Manny a penny, and he promised to stay away from you. And I recommend you stay clear of him and find a new bookie."

"After this mess, I might never make another bet," Vinnie said. "I've really been thinking I should try to give up gambling entirely."

"That's an interesting thought, Vinnie, but be careful not to set unrealistic goals. I'd hate to see you beating yourself up on top of the beating you already took. That being said, we're very happy to see you looking so much better, and it might please you to know the two apes who roughed you up are doing a lot worse than you are."

"A lot worse?"

"A *whole* lot worse," I said.

"Okay, I'll admit it doesn't break my heart. You really came through for me, Jake. I don't know what to say."

"Say you'll be well enough to join us in box seats at the Giants' home opener," Joey suggested.

Carrying a badge had its advantages. Police identification could often open doors that were otherwise restricted, and garner unauthorized perks and favors.

Sergeant Johnson was not in the habit of exploiting these benefits. He paid for his coffee while on duty, he paid the bridge and road tolls when off-duty. He even paid the occasional parking ticket, if the transgression was committed when not on official police business.

But that Sunday afternoon he took full advantage of his status.

Arriving at the airport, he flashed his detective's shield at the security check point. It served as effectively as a boarding pass in allowing him admission to the concourse where his wife's flight from Philadelphia was about to arrive. When Amy came off the plane, her husband was waiting at the gate.

"Miss me?" she asked, giving him a peck on the cheek.

"That's an understatement," Johnson said, taking her carry-on bag.

"If it's any consolation, with the exception of an hour alone with my mother and sister, it was a senseless waste of time."

Johnson resisted the urge to admit he was glad to hear it.

"That's too bad," he said.

"Have you been staying out of trouble?" Amy asked.

"You know me, *staying out of trouble* is my middle name."

He would wait until they were safe at home before concerning Amy with details about the wild ride he had been on since her departure.

"Let's blow this pop stand," Amy said.

"I did learn some things about myself while you were gone," Johnson said, when they reached the car. He had difficulty holding anything back from his wife.

"For example?"

"I learned I am smarter and maybe a bit braver than I thought I was. And a better man—for the most part, because of you."

"That is very sweet, Rocky," Amy said, eating it up and wanting to hear more. "What else?"

"I learned I can't even grill a cheese sandwich."

I filled Darlene in on my daring adventures down in Los Angeles, and on Vinnie's greatly improved physical and psychological situation, over linguini with red clam sauce at Carlucci's Ristorante in North Beach.

True to form, Darlene had opted for the ziti with garlic, olive oil and broccoli rabe.

I had called ahead, to ask if Tony Carlucci would be at the restaurant. I was told he rarely made an appearance on Sunday evenings.

I faked disappointment.

Once I felt the coast was clear, I had made reservations for two.

I had ordered a carafe of Pinot Grigio, for Darlene's sake. It was not my drink of choice, but I was afraid that pairing bourbon on the rocks with a seafood dish might be considered unsophisticated.

Darlene was an excellent interrogator. Her ability to dig up every last detail of my past twenty-four hours was as effective as sodium pentothal. Once she was satisfied she had got it all, she moved on to new business.

"What do you think of Megan Nicolace?" she asked.

"Detective Nicolace?"

"Yes."

"I wasn't thrilled about the way she used you as bait for Norman Hall."

"She was doing her job, and we caught the creep. Megan asked about you."

"Asked what about me? My shoe size?"

"She asked if you were taken."

"Taken where?"

"Taken, spoken for, married, engaged or seeing someone. God you're impossible," Darlene said. "Megan seems interested in seeing you again. Socially. She's a sharp woman, Jake, and not hard to look at."

"I'm flattered, but a vice cop is not exactly the girl of my dreams. I would be more inclined to get sociable with Lieutenant Lopez."

"Okay, fine, then *how about* Lopez?"

"Get serious, Darlene. I'd have as much chance with Laura Lopez as I would have with Rachel Weisz. Besides, I'd hate to jeopardize the dynamic of the special relationship Lopez and I have so effectively developed."

"Special relationship?"

"Smart-mouthed public servant and nuisance private dick."

"You are worse than my father," Darlene sighed.

"And you, my dear friend, are as bad as my mother."

"It wouldn't hurt you to spend time with a bright, attractive female once in a while."

"I'm doing that right now."

When she had a mind to, Darlene Roman could exhibit a truly dazzling smile.

Sunday night.

I was alone and protected inside the walls of my house in the Presidio.

I should have been tired, but I couldn't sleep.

So instead, nestled in the bosom of a well-worn armchair, I kept company with a tall glass of George Dickel sour mash whisky over ice and a dog-eared paperback.

And in a few hours, I had followed Quasimodo's journey to its end.

Esmeralda had taken the rap for killing Captain Phoebus. She was innocent of the crime, but confessed to avoid further torture. The gypsy girl was sentenced to be hung.

Frollo, who actually did murder the captain, kept that inconvenient truth under his archdeacon's hat.

The hunchback took the gypsy girl into Notre Dame, to protect her within the sanctuary of the cathedral. He had fallen in love with Esmeralda, for her kindness.

Pierre Gringoire, the poet, rescues the girl from the cathedral, but she eventually falls into the hands of Claude Frollo, arch villain.

Frollo, who was attracted to the beautiful gypsy girl for what could be called un-Christian like reasons, offers her a choice—Esmeralda can either declare her love for the archdeacon, or face the hangman.

Esmeralda chooses what she feels is the lesser of two evils and ends up on the scaffold.

Quasimodo discovers the girl missing, and frantically searches for her.

Finally, from the north tower of Notre Dame, he spots Esmeralda, in a white dress, hanging from the gallows.

Realizing this was the work of the archdeacon, Quasimodo's quasi-father, the hunchback throws Frollo from the tower.

Seeing Esmeralda and Frollo below, both dead, Quasimodo cries out.

There is all I ever loved!

Quasimodo's story saddened me.

But for me, the true tragedy was voiced in the hunchback's ultimate lament, Quasimodo's sense of loss.

It defied the suggestion, *If you ain't got nothing, you got nothing to lose.*

Even the wretched, tormented bell ringer, disfigured and abandoned at birth, shunned by his peers, had something to lose.

My personal feelings of loss and sadness, which visit me occasionally, were intensified when Hugo's epic finale brought to mind those I had loved and who were now gone. Forever.

Jimmy Pigeon. Sally French. My father.

But then, the little voice in my head that thankfully reminds me at times I am luckier and more fortunate than a good number of tragic figures from classic literature did just that.

And I considered those I cared about, and who seemed to feel the same about me, who were still among the living.

Darlene. Joey. Vinnie. My mother.

Maybe even the good Sergeant Johnson, a little bit.

With these thoughts in mind, and as much as I had regretted doing so in the past, I fell asleep in the chair.

ACKNOWLEDGMENTS

Although he made a guest appearance in *Chasing Charlie Chan* (2013), this is the first new Jake Diamond novel since *Counting to Infinity* (2004). There are many to thank for the support and inspiration necessary to continue the crazy business of writing books. I would like to recognize those most guilty.

All of the readers who thought enough of the series, and *Gravesend*, to spread the word privately and publically—and kept pressing me for word about when Jake Diamond would be back.

Down & Out Books and Eric Campbell, who gave Diamond a new lease on life.

Sonny Wasinger and Daniella Ba'Rashees—for always being there to welcome me when I finally hit the tarmac.

Linda Abramo, my remarkable sister and friend, for her endless encouragement and tireless promotion.

And to whatever it is that *drives* me to write—thanks for the lift.

—*J. L. Abramo, Denver, Colorado*

ABOUT THE AUTHOR

J. L. ABRAMO was born in the seaside paradise of Brooklyn, New York on Raymond Chandler's fifty-ninth birthday. A long-time educator, journalist, theatre and film actor and director, he received a BA in Sociology at the City College of New York and an MA in Social Psychology at the University of Cincinnati.

Abramo is the author of the Jake Diamond mystery series including *Catching Water in a Net* (recipient of the MWA/PWA Award for Best First Private Eye Novel), *Clutching at Straws, Counting to Infinity,* and the prequel *Chasing Charlie Chan*—as well as the stand-alone crime thriller, *Gravesend.*

Abramo is a member of the Mystery Writers of America, International Thriller Writers, Private Eye Writers of America and Screen Actors Guild.

The author lives in Denver, Colorado.

For more information please visit:

www.jlabramo.com

www.facebook.com/jlabramo

OTHER TITLES FROM DOWN AND OUT BOOKS

See www.DownAndOutBooks.com for complete list

By Anonymous-9
Bite Hard

By J.L. Abramo
Catching Water in a Net
Clutching at Straws
Counting to Infinity
Gravesend
Chasing Charlie Chan
Circling the Runway

By Trey R. Barker
2,000 Miles to Open Road
Road Gig: A Novella
Exit Blood
Death is Not Forever

By Richard Barre
The Innocents
Bearing Secrets
Christmas Stories
The Ghosts of Morning
Blackheart Highway
Burning Moon
Echo Bay
Lost

By Eric Beetner and
JB Kohl
Over Their Heads (*)

By Eric Beetner and
Frank Scalise
The Backlist (*)

By Rob Brunet
Stinking Rich

By Dana Cameron (editor)
Murder at the Beach: Bouchercon Anthology 2014

By Stacey Cochran
Eddie & Sunny

By Mark Coggins
No Hard Feelings (*)

By Tom Crowley
Vipers Tail
Murder in the Slaughterhouse

By Frank De Blase
Pine Box for a Pin-Up
Busted Valentines and Other Dark Delights
A Cougar's Kiss (*)

By Les Edgerton
The Genuine, Imitation, Plastic Kidnapping

By A.C. Frieden
Tranquility Denied
The Serpent's Game
The Pyongyang Option (*)

By Jack Getze
Big Numbers
Big Money
Big Mojo
Big Shoes (*)

By Keith Gilman
Bad Habits

(*)—Coming Soon

OTHER TITLES FROM DOWN AND OUT BOOKS

See www.DownAndOutBooks.com for complete list

By Richard Godwin
Wrong Crowd (*)

By William Hastings (editor)
*Stray Dogs: Writing from the
Other America*

By Matt Hilton
No Going Back
Rules of Honor (*)
The Lawless Kind (*)

By Terry Holland
An Ice Cold Paradise
Chicago Shiver

By Darrel James,
Linda O. Johnston &
Tammy Kaehler (editors)
Last Exit to Murder

By David Housewright &
Renée Valois
The Devil and the Diva

By David Housewright
Finders Keepers
Full House

By Jon & Ruth Jordan (editors)
Murder and Mayhem in Muskego
Cooking with Crimespree

By Andrew McAleer & Paul D. Marks
(editors)
Coast to Coast (*)

By Bill Moody
Czechmate
The Man in Red Square
Solo Hand
The Death of a Tenor Man
The Sound of the Trumpet
Bird Lives!

By Gary Phillips
The Perpetrators
Scoundrels (Editor)
Treacherous

By Robert J. Randisi
Upon My Soul
Souls of the Dead
Envy the Dead (*)

By Ryan Sayles
The Subtle Art of Brutality (*)
Warpath (*)

By Anthony Neil Smith
Worm

By Liam Sweeny
Welcome Back, Jack (*)

By Lono Waiwaiole
Wiley's Lament
Wiley's Shuffle
Wiley's Refrain
Dark Paradise

By Vincent Zandri
Moonlight Weeps

(*)—Coming Soon